CROSSROADS

Acclaim for Radclyffe's Fiction

In **2012 RWA/FTHRW Lories award winner** *Firestorm* "Radclyffe brings another hot lesbian romance for her readers."—*The Lesbrary*

2010 RWA/FF&P Prism award winner *Secrets in the Stone* "is a strong, must read novel that will linger in the minds of readers long after the last page is turned."—*Just About Write*

Foreword Review Book of the Year finalist and IPPY silver medalist *Trauma Alert* "is hard to put down and it will sizzle in the reader's hands. The characters are hot, the sex scenes explicit and explosive, and the book is moved along by an interesting plot with well drawn secondary characters. The real star of this show is the attraction between the two characters, both of whom resist and then fall head over heels."—*Lambda Literary Reviews*

Lambda Literary Finalist *Best Lesbian Romance 2010* features "stories [that] are diverse in tone, style, and subject, making for more variety than in many, similar anthologies...well written, each containing a satisfying, surprising twist. Best Lesbian Romance series editor Radclyffe has assembled a respectable crop of 17 authors for this year's offering."—*Curve Magazine*

In **Benjamin Franklin Award finalist** *Desire by Starlight* "Radclyffe writes romance with such heart and her down-to-earth characters not only come to life but leap off the page until you feel like you know them. What Jenna and Gard feel for each other is not only a spark but an inferno and, as a reader, you will be washed away in this tumultuous romance until you can do nothing but succumb to it."—*Queer Magazine Online*

2010 Prism award winner and ForeWord Review Book of the Year Award finalist *Secrets in the Stone* is "so powerfully [written] that the worlds of these three women shimmer between reality and dreams...A strong, must read novel that will linger in the minds of readers long after the last page is turned."—*Just About Write*

Lambda Literary Award winner *Stolen Moments* "is a collection of steamy stories about women who just couldn't wait. It's sex when desire overrides reason, and it's incredibly hot!"—*On Our Backs*

Lambda Literary Award winner *Distant Shores, Silent Thunder* "weaves an intricate tapestry about passion and commitment between lovers. The story explores the fragile nature of trust and the sanctuary provided by loving relationships."—*Sapphic Reader*

Lambda Literary Award Finalist *Justice Served* delivers a "crisply written, fast-paced story with twists and turns and keeps us guessing until the final explosive ending."—*Independent Gay Writer*

Lambda Literary Award finalist *Turn Back Time* "is filled with wonderful love scenes, which are both tender and hot."—*MegaScene*

Applause for L.L. Raand's Midnight Hunters Series

"Raand has built a complex world inhabited by werewolves, vampires, and other paranormal beings…Raand has given her readers a complex plot filled with wonderful characters as well as insight into the hierarchy of Sylvan's pack and vampire clans. There are many plot twists and turns, as well as erotic sex scenes in this riveting novel that keep the pages flying until its satisfying conclusion."—*Just About Write*

"Once again, I am amazed at the storytelling ability of L.L. Raand aka Radclyffe. In *Blood Hunt*, she mixes high levels of sheer eroticism that will leave you squirming in your seat with an impeccable multi-character storyline all streaming together to form one great read." —*Queer Magazine Online*

"*The Midnight Hunt* has a gripping story to tell, and while there are also some truly erotic sex scenes, the story always takes precedence. This is a great read which is not easily put down nor easily forgotten."—*Just About Write*

"Are you sick of the same old hetero vampire/werewolf story plastered in every bookstore and at every movie theater? Well, I've got the cure to your werewolf fever. *The Midnight Hunt* is first in, what I hope is, a long-running series of fantasy erotica for L.L. Raand (aka Radclyffe)."—*Queer Magazine Online*

"Any reader familiar with Radclyffe's writing will recognize the author's style within *The Midnight Hunt*, yet at the same time it is most definitely a new direction. The author delivers an excellent story here, one that is engrossing from the very beginning. Raand has pieced together an intricate world, and provided just enough details for the reader to become enmeshed in the new world. The action moves quickly throughout the book and it's hard to put down."—*Three Dollar Bill Reviews*

By Radclyffe

Romances

Innocent Hearts

Promising Hearts

Love's Melody Lost

Love's Tender Warriors

Tomorrow's Promise

Love's Masquerade

shadowland

Passion's Bright Fury

Fated Love

Turn Back Time

When Dreams Tremble

The Lonely Hearts Club

Night Call

Secrets in the Stone

Desire by Starlight

Crossroads

Honor Series

Above All, Honor

Honor Bound

Love & Honor

Honor Guards

Honor Reclaimed

Honor Under Siege

Word of Honor

Justice Series

A Matter of Trust (prequel)

Shield of Justice

In Pursuit of Justice

Justice in the Shadows

Justice Served

Justice for All

The Provincetown Tales

Safe Harbor

Beyond the Breakwater

Distant Shores, Silent Thunder

Storms of Change

Winds of Fortune

Returning Tides

Sheltering Dunes

Visit us at www.boldstrokesbooks.com

CROSSROADS

by

RADCLYFFE

2012

CROSSROADS

ISBN 13: 978-1-60282-756-1

This Trade Paperback Original Is Published By
Bold Strokes Books, Inc.
P.O. Box 249
Valley Falls, NY 12185

First Edition: November 2012

CREDITS
EDITORS: RUTH STERNGLANTZ AND STACIA SEAMAN
PRODUCTION DESIGN: STACIA SEAMAN
COVER DESIGN BY SHERI (GRAPHICARTIST2020@HOTMAIL.COM)

Acknowledgments

Medical romances are a niche within a niche, but for me each is a little piece of my history, and as I have written them, a part of a community of books featuring continuing and overlapping characters. I have written two lines of medical romances, one set in the fictional Philadelphia Medical College (*Fated Love* and *Night Call*) and the other in the University Hospital system (*Turn Back Time, The Lonely Hearts Club*, and the First Responders book *Trauma Alert*). My first medical romance, *Passion's Bright Fury*, is the prequel to *Fated Love* and takes place in NYC. Each novel explores a new set of characters, but like the hospital where I spent twelve years training, the community at the center of each feels like home. Everyone knows everyone else, often better than friends and family. Any of the books can be read in any order, and familiar faces will show up as they often do in real life, around the next corner. I hope you find coming home as enjoyable as I.

Thanks go to Sandy Lowe for perseverance, patience, and unflagging support; to author Nell Stark for taking the time from her ever-busier schedule to comment and encourage; to Ruth Sternglantz for expert editing; to Stacia Seaman, for never missing a step; and to my first readers Connie, Eva, Jenny, and Paula for never growing tired of me.

Special thanks to Sheri for a great cover that captures the essence of the story.

And to Lee, for the fun of it all—*Amo te.*

Radclyffe, 2012

For Lee, for sharing the road

CHAPTER ONE

The on-call phone rang, waking Hollis from an uneasy sleep. She rolled over on the narrow bed, groped in the darkness for the cell, and swiped *accept* without looking. "Monroe."

"It's Honor Blake in the ER, Dr. Monroe. We need you down here STAT."

"What is it?" Hollis sat up, the last vestiges of sleep driven from her mind by the familiar tightening in her belly and surge in her blood. Adrenaline rush—as potent as sex and twice as satisfying. She glanced at the battered plastic digital clock on the equally battered metal bedside stand. 3:32 a.m. Why did the complications always come in the middle of the night? For that matter, why did most babies choose to show up after midnight? Questions obstetricians had been asking without answer for centuries, probably.

"A twenty-four-year-old in the range of thirty-five weeks, and she's hemorrhaging."

"On my way. Can you call Labor and Delivery and tell them we're coming?"

"Already done," the ER chief answered.

"And page the on-call neonatal—"

"Already done."

"Yeah, sorry. Guess this isn't your first rodeo."

"Not by a long shot. Are you awake?"

"And moving. Be right there." Hollis disconnected, stuck the phone in the back pocket of her scrubs, and grabbed her lab coat off the back of the door on her way out. She'd only been at Philadelphia Medical Center a week after finishing her fellowship at a friendly rival hospital across town, but she knew all the shortcuts to the ER already. She took the stairs three at a time down two levels and pushed through the fire door to the ground floor. The wide, tan-tiled halls were nearly empty in the middle of the night. Empty stretchers covered with plain white sheets were lined up head to toe along one wall like sentries, awaiting six a.m. when the transport teams would begin ferrying patients from the ER and hospital rooms to X-ray, the OR, and all the many other destinations in the hospital. By the time the walk-in clinics opened at nine, the halls would be congested with foot traffic. Now the only people around were men and women from housekeeping—pushing floor polishers, rolling supersized trash bins, and steering canvas carts piled high with soiled linens.

Hollis cut around all of them as if she were still running track and dodging runners ahead of her. She held her stethoscope to her chest with one hand to keep it from banging her in the face and mentally ran the list of what she'd need to check on a third-trimester patient bleeding out. She hit the button for the automatic doors to the ER on the run and barely slowed as they lumbered open, squeezing through the narrow gap without breaking stride. A blonde in her mid-thirties wearing a Scooby-Doo smock looked up from the centrally located nurses' station with a startled expression. Hollis called, "OB emergency?"

"End of the hall—cubicle ten," the blonde said, pointing to the left-hand corridor in the T-shaped ER.

"Thanks…Linda." Hollis hoped she'd gotten the name right and swerved around a couple of wheelchairs angled together, as if their invisible occupants were having a late-night conversation, and sprinted the short distance to room ten. A crash cart surrounded by resuscitation litter stood in front of the brightly lit space. Plastic IV bag wrappers, multicolored intravenous catheter caps, the tail end of a spool of EKG paper, and a deflated BP cuff marked the site of the action. A cacophony of voices reached her as she drew near.

Hang another unit…

Fetal heart tones are dropping…

BP's crashing…

Where is OB?

"Right here." Hollis skidded to a halt at the foot of the stretcher. She'd known what to expect—she was a brand-new attending, but this wasn't *her* first rodeo either. Still, the chaos rocked her for a millisecond. The adrenaline surge made her vision swim, and then her focus kicked in. The analytical part of her brain took the wheel and she settled into the zone. One quick scan told her all she needed to know. The blue plastic-backed chucks under the woman's hips, designed to keep her and the mattress dry, had long since reached their capacity. The white sheets under her parted legs were crimson. Blood dripped in fat red splatters onto the floor, making delicate snowflake patterns as it congealed.

Honor Blake said, "The ultrasound shows—"

"It's an abruption," Hollis said, pressing through the nurses and techs congregated around the stretcher to get up to the patient. Couldn't be anything else, not with that much blood, but she grabbed the ultrasound printout just to confirm. Yeah, there it was—the placenta had torn away from the uterine wall, leaving a latticework of enlarged vessels wide open to pour out blood. "How much blood has she had?"

Honor wasn't fazed by the obstetrician's overbearing manner. Her spouse was a surgeon, and trauma or ortho or obstetrics, it didn't matter—surgeons were all gunslingers with a touch of God complex. Maybe you had to be to cut into a living being with absolute confidence. This one was new, but by all reports, Monroe had a quick mind and quicker hands. Not much on sociability. Typical surgeon. "We're on our third unit. The blood bank is sending another four upstairs to L and D."

"Good." Hollis assessed the mound of pale belly ribboned with delicate blue veins exposed where the white cotton sheet had been pulled aside. Above, the full breasts were capped with swollen chocolate nipples. She ran her hand over the distended abdomen. The uterus was a rock. A rock filled with blood and a baby who was going to be in trouble soon. "What do we know?"

"She's in and out. History is scant. Twenty-four years old, prime ip, not much else."

First pregnancy—always a bit unpredictable. Thirty-four weeks looked about right for her size—not dangerously premature if she delivered the baby now, but still, the baby would be at risk for pulmonary insufficiency and neuro complications. Couldn't be helped, though—the mother was gushing blood faster than the nurses could pump it into her. "Any prenatal issues?"

"We don't have records," Honor said.

"Coags?" Women with *abruptio placenta* often developed bleeding disorders, and that spelled major trouble in the OR.

"Not back yet. But she's clotting."

"For now." Hollis moved to the head of the stretcher. The dazed young woman looked younger than twenty-four, and pale to the point of translucency, her golden brown hair framing a finely etched face with luminous green eyes and lips that were still full and sensuous despite being nearly drained of color. "I'm Dr. Monroe. What's your name?"

"Annie." Lids tinged with gray shuttered closed. "Colfax."

"Annie," Hollis said gently, "when did you start bleeding?"

"An...hour...not sure. Can I have some water?"

"I'm sorry, no."

"What about my baby?"

"You're having quite a bit of bleeding and we're going to need to operate. The baby needs to come out and we need to get the bleeding stopped."

Eyes the color of spring grass—now surprisingly clear, considering her blood pressure was only sixty and she had to be scared out of her mind—opened wide and fixed on her face. "It's too soon for the baby. I want to wait."

Hollis bit off a retort. She didn't have time to argue, but the young woman's voice was strong. She was competent to decide. "I don't think you can wait. You're losing blood and the baby will suffer for it."

"Just a little more time."

"Look, is there someone with you or someone I can call? Spouse? A boyfriend?"

"No."

"How about a family member we can—"

"No," Annie said quite distinctly. "There is no one."

No one. No friend? No lover? No family at all? The patient didn't look like a street person or some paranoid dropout likely to be living off the grid, but Hollis didn't have time to speculate on why Annie Colfax was alone during one of the critical moments of her life. "Okay, Annie—we don't have time for much discussion. The baby's at risk. So are you. You need a C-sectio—"

"No. No surgery."

Hollis clamped down on a flare of temper. "We don't have any choice, you—"

"No. Don't believe…" Annie's voice faded and her chin sagged.

"Pressure's fifty palp," a nurse announced. "Fetal heart tones are slowing."

"We need to move here," Honor said from next to Hollis. "I can try for a court order, but it'll take time."

"Goddamn it." Hollis gripped Annie's shoulder. "Annie. Annie! Look at me."

Annie blinked, focused.

"If you don't let me operate, your baby is going to die. You might too. Do you understand? You have to trust me on this, Annie."

Annie was silent, searching Hollis's face.

"Trust me," Hollis said fiercely.

"No choice," Annie murmured, a flat, dead patina stealing over her eyes. "Go ahead."

Hollis turned to Honor, a flash of triumph and anticipation energizing her. Now she could take care of things. "Let's go."

Hollis grabbed one side of the stretcher and Honor took the other. Honor called, "Coming through. Get the elevator."

Together they maneuvered the stretcher out of the cubicle and into the hall. One of the nurses raced ahead to get the doors. The elevator was waiting.

Two minutes later Hollis guided the stretcher into the delivery area where anesthesia and the labor and delivery nurses took over. Hollis went to scrub. *Trust me*, she'd said, and she knew what she was asking. *Place your life and the life of your baby in my hands. Trust that I'll know what to do to keep you both safe.* The responsibility was enormous and everything she wanted. All she wanted.

The swinging door to the delivery room banged open and one of the nurses leaned out. "She's crashing, Dr. Monroe. We need you in here now."

"Prep the belly for an emergency section." Hollis rinsed fast and, water dripping from her elbows like a trail of tears, followed the nurse into the OR. Another nurse waited with an open gown, and Hollis pushed her arms down the sleeves and snapped on her gloves. Fixing on the square of pale skin hastily draped with green cotton towels, she stepped up to the table and held out her left hand. "Scalpel."

The steel handle slapped sharply into her palm, and with her free hand she tensed the skin on the Betadine-coated belly above the top of the uterus. She opened a twelve-inch incision just above the pubic bone, cutting down in one long, deep slice through fat and muscle and peritoneum until the uterus appeared. "Get the suction ready." The uterus extended up out of the pelvis, pushing aside the internal organs, claiming its place of primacy. She palpated it quickly and found the baby's head, mentally positioning the rest of the body as it curled up in the muscular sac, thinking about small fingers and limbs just beneath the last layer of muscle. With the blade she made a small incision low in the uterus, handed off the knife, and said, "Scissors."

The large instrument snapped into her hand, and she inserted the lower blade into the uterus, sliding it close to the underside of the muscle and away from the baby's appendages. She cut, and amniotic fluid and blood gushed out onto the table, running over the sides and onto the booties covering her shoes. She slid her hand in, found the head, and delivered the infant on a sea of blood. The little girl was blue and flaccid.

"Suction," Hollis said sharply. The nurse passed her a soft plastic tube, and she gently cleared the baby's airway.

Time halted for those heart-stopping few seconds before the first breath. Hollis's gut writhed. The baby shuddered, the small chest contracted...expanded, and then she cried. Loudly. Tiny fists closed, arms flailed, and she struck out at a universe that had so rudely claimed her. The red face below a surprisingly thick shock of golden hair was indignant. Hollis grinned behind her mask. A fighter, this one.

"Welcome to the world, baby girl." Hollis clamped the cord, divided, and she handed the baby to the scrub nurse. "Pass the baby to the neonatologist. We've got bleeding here."

Her job wasn't done. The uterus was atonic—soft and spent, unable to contract and close off the multitude of gushing vessels within its walls. Blood welled up, filling the pelvis.

"Push the Pitocin." While anesthesia administered drugs to help the uterus contract, Hollis packed the cavity, applied pressure, and evacuated the remains of the placenta. But the bleeding continued.

"I'm having a hard time maintaining her blood pressure," the anesthesiologist reported, his voice strained with tension. "I'm hanging unit five. She's tachycardic and starting to show some aberrant beats. I'm not liking this."

Hollis checked the clock. She wasn't liking it either. The bleeding should've slowed by now, but it kept on.

"Got a run of V-tach here, starting lidocaine," the anesthesiologist called.

Hollis felt the uterus again. Still soft, blood pouring out and no sign of stopping.

"We need to take this out," Hollis said and held out her hand. "Clamp."

❖

Annie awakened to an ocean of pain. She didn't know where she was, only that she hurt. She reached for her belly, the automatic motion she'd made thousands of times in the last eight months. And then the memories of the last few hours came rushing back. She'd been studying when the pain started, waves of cramping, agonizing pain. Relentless pain, unending. And then the bleeding. So much bleeding, and the dizziness and the weakness, and the fear. All of that without warning. She'd been helpless, and alone. But she was used to being alone.

She forced her eyes open, forced herself to think beyond the panic and the pain. She was alone in a dimly lit room, nothing on the walls, plastic vertical blinds partially blocking a gray, overcast sky. A faint odor of drugs and death. Hospital.

She tried to sit up, and the pain rose from her belly and consumed her. She dropped back, whimpering softly. With her right hand she followed the plastic cord wrapped around the handrail, found the call button, and pushed it. A minute later a youngish woman in a blue and red floral smock and pale blue scrub pants came into the room.

"Hi," the woman said softly. "You're awake. Are you hurting, honey?"

"My baby. Where's my baby?"

The woman leaned over, her face coming into view. A kind face. Dark eyes, a wide, smiling mouth. "Your daughter is in the neonatal intensive care unit. She's doing fine, but she's a preemie, and considering how she chose to get here, the neonatologist wants to keep her in there awhile."

"She's all right?"

The nurse nodded and readjusted Annie's covers. "Someone will be in to talk to you about how she's doing and to check you over soon. But the last I heard, she was stable and sleeping."

"When can I see her?"

"In the morning. Do you need something for pain?"

"No. I don't want any drugs—"

"Honey, you've had a big operation. You're going to need—"

"I'm fine. I don't want any. Thank you."

"All right. If you change your mind, just ring the bell."

"Yes, thank you." Annie closed her eyes, too tired to protest. The baby, her daughter, was going to be all right. Nothing else mattered.

She drifted until the sound of the door opening and closing roused her. With awareness came pain, a pattern she'd grown used to.

"Are you awake?" a deep, gentle voice inquired.

Annie opened her eyes. A black-haired woman in green scrubs leaned over her, both hands braced on the side rail. Her deep blue eyes were steady, piercing, unnerving in their focus. She looked tired—smudges of fatigue darkened the lids above sharp cheekbones. But even fatigued, she radiated strength.

"I...I...remember you. You were in the emergency room," Annie said.

"Yes. I'm Dr. Monroe, the obstetrician. I delivered your baby. She's beautiful. Green eyes like yours."

Annie smiled. "The nurses said she's all right. Is that true?"

"Yes. No one here will lie to you."

"Everyone lies," Annie said softly.

The doctor's dark eyes flashed, but she said nothing. Annie was too weary and in too much pain to care that she might have offended her.

"There's something you need to know, Ms. Colfax," the doctor said. "You had what we call an abruption—the placenta separated from the wall of the uterus, causing you to hemorrhage and endangering the baby."

Annie's pulse tripped, stuttered, and started again. "I thought you said the baby was all right."

"She is. She isn't as close to term as we'd like, so she's being monitored for any signs of immaturity."

"I wanted to wait. To be sure she would be safe." Annie's chest tightened. Why wouldn't anyone listen? Why must she always fight to be heard?

"I understand, but that wasn't possible." Hollis stifled her impatience. She understood women wanting to deliver vaginally, to be alert and aware so they could remember the birth, but sometimes safety—the mother's and the child's—was more important.

"But you said she's all right…"

"She is. And you will be too." Hollis looked into Annie's eyes— the green verged on black, her irises almost eclipsed by her pupils. "How much pain are you having? I ordered morphine, but—"

"I'm all right. Tell me."

"I had to do more surgery in order to stop the bleeding."

A chill settled in Annie's depths. "More surgery?"

"Yes. After the C-section, the bleeding didn't stop. Usually it will once the rest of the placenta is removed. You were bleeding very heavily."

"But that's stopped now, isn't it?"

"Yes, it is." Hollis knew she'd made the right decision, but still, it was hard to admit she hadn't been able to alter the outcome. "I had to remove your uterus, Ms. Colfax. It was the only way to stop the bleeding and save your life."

Annie's mind went blank. She was so cold. So cold.

Warm fingers clasped her hand. "I'm sorry, I know it's a shock. I had no choice. You're going to be fine now."

Annie withdrew her fingers from between the surgeon's. "You don't know that. You have no way of knowing that."

"You're going to recover, you have a beautiful baby, and you're going to go on with your life."

"I never would have agreed," Annie said, looking deep into Hollis's eyes. "And I never should have trusted you."

CHAPTER TWO

Four and a half years later

Linda propped her feet on the coffee table in the flight lounge and sipped her unsweetened iced tea. She had thirty minutes left on her shift and then she could head home for a breakfast of pancakes and eggs prepared by her loving wife, who had miraculously managed to go through this three times herself while making it look easy. If only her ankles weren't the size of cantaloupes at seven o'clock in the morning, her pregnancy would be perfectly easy too. She still had four months to go. This was going to be the longest summer of her life. When the door opened, she held her breath and prayed it wasn't McNally coming to tell her they had a call-out. She loved to fly, but she'd had enough for one night. "Oh, thank God it's you."

"As opposed to—?" Honor eyed the coffeepot warily. "How old is that?"

"Last night's. And McNally."

Honor frowned, as if searching for a connection as she poured coffee and doused it with cream. "Oh—you're glad I'm not Jett coming to tell you there's a call. Why don't you just go home? Eddie's in the locker room already. If something comes up in the next twenty minutes, he can start his shift early."

"Nah. I don't have all that much longer to fly." She patted the mound of her belly. "One more month and I'm grounded."

"Oh gosh, Ms. Flight Nurse, then you'll have to work in the boring old ER like the rest of us for a while."

"You know I won't mind working with you again," Linda said. Honor's tone had been teasing, and her deep brown eyes were filled with affection, but Linda couldn't help think Honor was still a little hurt she'd left the ER to fly with the medevac team. "I miss you."

"Ditto." Honor flopped on the nearby sofa and pushed her honey-brown hair back from her face with an idle motion that always managed to look sexy. Not that Honor probably ever intended to look sexy—she just was one of those women who naturally looked hot.

"I think I hate you," Linda said.

"Why is that?" Honor said.

"You look great and I'm a blimp."

"You're pregnant and beautiful."

"Okay—I don't hate you quite so much."

Honor laughed. "So, you and Robin still set on going the natural route?"

"Yep. Got the birthing room all ready." Linda studied Honor's pensive expression. "It's just because you work in the ER—you see the worst of everything. That's why you think it's a bad idea."

Honor shook her head. "I never said I thought it was a bad idea."

"You didn't have to." Linda stared at her elephant feet. "You didn't have to say anything. You've got that little frowny thing between your eyebrows, just like the first time I told you."

"What frowny thing? I don't have any frowny thing."

"Yes, you do. You get it when you disagree with something, but you're being too polite to say so."

"Linda—you're my best friend. If I thought you were doing something crazy, I'd tell you. All I said was to make sure you researched everything and that you had a Plan B if Plan A doesn't work out."

"I know, I know. Robin wants to do it as much as I do, or I wouldn't even think of it. My mother and my sisters all think I've got bats in the belfry." Linda sighed. "It's the last one, Honor. I want it to be special, for all of us."

"I don't know how you do it with three, let alone four. The two I've got seem like an army sometimes."

"Robin and I come from big families—four won't be a stretch."

"As to you being crazy," Honor said, "I know the stats. Home delivery is becoming more common all the time, and let's face it… women have been having babies at home, out in the fields, and every other place far from modern medical care for centuries with no problem. All the same, I want you and the baby to be safe."

"Believe me, so do I." Linda shivered, too many images of what could go wrong indelibly etched in her mind. "I'm a nurse, I've seen what can happen. But I've done my time on Labor and Delivery too, and I've seen hundreds of births with no complications. I don't want to deliver in the hospital when I'm half out of it and the baby gets whisked away somewhere for me to see every couple of hours. I want to deliver at home with Robin and the kids there, so they can share in it."

"I understand. I would've given anything for Arly to have been able to see Jack right after he was born. To see me and know that I was all right." Honor turned her coffee cup between her hands, remembering. She'd hated being away from her family at one of the most important times in their lives, seeing the fear in her daughter's eyes while she was recovering from surgery, seeing the fear in Quinn's eyes when all there should have been was joy. "But I have Jack, and I'll always be grateful for the surgeon who kept us both safe."

"Amen." Linda squeezed Honor's hand. "I don't think I could go ahead with this if you weren't behind me on it. After all, you're Robin's backup."

"I'm behind it as long as you agree that at the first sign of trouble— and I get to make the call—we whisk you over to the hospital and get one of the OB people involved."

"Not *one* of the OB people—I want Hollis Monroe," Linda said. "I'm forty, and I know there could be problems, and Hollis is the best with high-risk pregnancies. If it makes you feel any better, I'll even see her for a prenatal visit so we can be clear that I'm okay for home delivery."

"Fine. Hollis is the best. And you're all set with the midwife?"

"Absolutely. Robin and I both love her."

"All right, then. I'm on board."

❖

"I'm not entirely on board with this," Hollis said at the eight a.m. staff meeting. "Integrating certified nurse anesthetists or nurse practitioners into established medical teams is one thing. Having a group wholly devoted to natural birthing methods functioning as independent copractitioners is totally different."

"That's pretty much what midwifery is all about," David Elliott, the chairman of the obstetrics and gynecology department, said dryly. "Although maybe your definition is a little narrow for today's reality."

"I know what today's reality is about," Hollis said, and she doubted much had changed in the years since her brother's widow had decided she'd flee the unsafe city after 9/11 and go back to her roots in the hills of West Virginia. Nothing Hollis or any of the rest of the family had said could stop Nancy from leaving with Rob's unborn child. And nothing they had said could stop her from choosing to give birth far from traditional medical care. Hollis pushed the memories and the unabating pain aside. Her personal feelings weren't the issue. "I've seen some pretty hairy situations arise during these home births, even with low-complication pregnancies, and you're talking about giving primary responsibility for high-risk pregnancies to nonmedical professionals."

"Not sole responsibility," Dave said. "*Co*-responsibility. And, Hollis, these are professionals."

Hollis considered that a matter of debate, but that wasn't her fight. Turning the care of her patients over to someone she didn't choose, might not even trust, was. "All the same, we're dependent on the midwife to make the call about transferring for appropriate care in an emergency."

Dave cocked a brow. "That's the point, isn't it? You don't consider anything short of hospital-based obstetrical care to be appropriate."

"I didn't say that."

"Look, Hollis," Dave said with the patience that had won him the dubious honor of heading the department, "it stands to reason that someone who specializes in high-risk pregnancies, who sees only the worst complications under the worst possible circumstances, would be leery about practices that seem completely counter to your own. I understand your position, but we're not going to be able to ignore the groundswell in natural birthing methods."

"Nor are we going to want to," noted Bonnie Cramer, a fertility specialist. "More and more of my patients are asking about home deliveries, and I've been referring them to midwifes. It's what the patients want, and if we don't address their needs, they're just going to go somewhere else."

"And that's why," Dave said with a gleam of triumph, "the hospital board wants this combined high-risk care program. We're going to have to deal with this marriage of methods, and the board wants us to initiate the alliance."

"I'm not going to refer to anyone, anywhere, if I don't believe it's in the best interest of the patient," Hollis said.

"And we wouldn't want you to," Dave said reasonably. He leaned forward, his calm blue eyes set on Hollis. "I know you're far too professional to let your personal opinions affect your judgment. If this combined clinic gets off the ground, just keep an open mind."

"I'm not going to have any choice, am I?" Hollis hated being railroaded, but she was a team player at heart. If she wasn't, she wouldn't have joined the department.

"Actually…no."

Hollis's colleagues laughed quietly. Dave was the ultimate diplomat, but he wasn't one to be swayed once he made a decision. If the joint high-risk OB-midwifery clinic went through and forced her to work with alternative-birth midwifes, she was just going to have to live with that.

"I'll do my best," Hollis said.

"I have no doubt." Dave smiled. "That's why I'm putting you in charge of the exploratory committee that will evaluate this group and propose the best way to integrate the midwifes into our management program."

"Me?" Hollis looked around the table. There were at least three people she could think of who were better qualified—or at least whose practices weren't as busy as hers. From the look on Dave's face, arguing wasn't going to make a difference. She was stuck with this job. The most she could hope for was to get it done quickly, and if she was lucky, she'd find some reason to sink the whole crazy idea.

❖

Annie spread a thin layer of mustard—*not mayo, we don't like mayo*—on wheat bread, closed the cheese sandwich, and cut it into neat quarters—*not triangles, squares are nicer*. She slid it into the Batman lunchbox and added an apple, a small bag of animal crackers, and boxes of milk and juice. She zipped Batman closed and set the lunchbox next to a bright pink hoodie. *The one just like your black one, only prettier.*

"Callie, time to go." She listened for the rush of footsteps while mentally running through her get-ready-for-preschool list. Silence. "Cal? You can finish the drawing later. Let's go."

"Have you ever seen a blue elephant?"

Annie turned, lunchbox in hand. Today Callie had chosen a bright green T-shirt with multicolored stars and a pair of lemon-yellow shorts. The T-shirt made the deeper green of her eyes even richer, accented the fiery highlights in her copper curls, and induced the smattering of freckles on her milk-and-honey skin to dance. Her daughter was beautiful, and Annie allowed she was only a tad biased. "I've only seen the elephants in the zoo—remember them? And they're gray."

"They were muddy." Callie took the lunchbox, her eyes serious behind the lenses of her round, pinkish-brown eyeglasses. "My elephant is blue."

"When you get home you can show me all the animals you drew, okay?" Annie took Callie's hand and scooped up the hoodie on the way out the back door for their two-block walk to the Friends school on Green Street.

"Are you going to be home tonight or is it a baby night?"

"Mmm, I think tonight is a watch *Cars* night."

Callie grinned. "You always want to watch *Cars*."

"Okay," Annie said, swinging Callie's hand. "You choose."

"*Cars*."

Annie laughed. "Smartie. If I can't pick you up after school, Suzanne will, okay?"

"'Kay."

Moving into the Germantown section of Philadelphia had been the right decision. The Fairmont area had been more convenient when she'd been in school and juggling daycare and classes, but now she had a little more freedom in her schedule and Germantown had a great community atmosphere. Many of her patients lived in the area, the schools were affordable and known for their diversity, and three of her associates, all with children about Callie's age, lived nearby, so they could share childcare when one of them was on call or had an emergency. Plus, the Philadelphia Medical Center was a five-minute ride from just about anywhere in the area if she needed to send a patient in, which thankfully had been rare so far. She disliked everything about the place, but hospital backup was still a necessity.

"Mommy, there's Mike. Can I go see him?"

"Hmm? Oh, hi, Robin. Hi, Mike." Annie waved to the mother of one of the other children in Callie's preschool class. Robin was a muscular, dark-eyed, dark-haired forty-year-old and the partner of one of Annie's patients. A towheaded four-year-old jumped by her side, grinning wildly at Callie. Annie bent down, kissed Callie, and handed her the hoodie. "Go on. Have fun today."

"I will." Callie raced to Mike.

"I'll take the cubs the rest of the way," Robin said as she met Annie on the sidewalk.

"Thanks. I've been meaning to ask you—Callie isn't five yet, but she really wants to play T-ball this summer, and I was wondering if I could sign her up? Her coordination is pretty good already."

"Sure—it's mostly a social thing anyhow."

"Great."

"We could use an assistant coach," Robin said with a devilish grin.

Annie laughed, betting that Robin got a lot of mileage out of that grin. "Linda has my e-mail. Send me a schedule and I'll let you know if I can help out."

"Will do. Oh—Memorial Day barbecue at our place Sunday. Bring Callie. You can meet the rest of the neighborhood."

"Thanks—we'll be there." Annie watched Robin and the kids head down the block to the big red brick building on the corner, waited to wave to Callie one last time, and headed for home. She had a half hour to get ready and drive over to the Germantown Women's Wellness Clinic where she had a full morning of patient visits scheduled. She picked up her pace. Maybe she'd have time for a quick bagel and another cup of coffee. Being a single mom with a full-time job that frequently took her out at all hours of the day and night left her no time for herself, but at least she was never bored. Or lonely. *Almost* never lonely, and those times when the stillness caught up to her in the dark and her bed seemed as big and empty as an ocean, she thought about how lucky she was. She could support herself, she loved her job, and she had Callie. She was her own woman at last and no one would ever take that from her. She had everything she needed.

Just as she'd passed through the gate in the white picket fence and started up the walk to the pale yellow gingerbread Victorian she had been lucky to rent, her cell chimed. She paused to check the readout, mentally preparing to rearrange her day if she had a delivery. At least a dozen patients were due in the next month, and with babies—well, they kept their own schedules.

Her heart sank. It wasn't the switchboard. It was her boss.

"Hi, Barb," Annie said.

"Are you on your way to GWWC?"

"Not yet—I just took Callie to school."

"Oh good." Barb Williams sounded brisk and efficient, as always. She had to be that and a whole lot more to oversee seventy-five midwifes in Pennsylvania alone, and another three hundred in the Northeast.

Annie waited, pretty sure she knew what the call was about. Her stomach tightened.

"The board met on a conference link this morning. They voted six to one in favor of the resolution."

Annie sat down on her front steps. A fat sparrow plucked at the grass in the small square of front yard inside the meandering fence, searching for worms. At not yet nine the sun cut through the leaves of the huge maple by the corner of the house with enough heat to warm her skin. Summer weather and it wasn't quite June. She loved spring, but nothing lasted forever. She drew a breath and chose her words carefully. Barb would have been one of the yes votes.

"I'm still not sure I see the reason for this. We already have well-established protocols for urgent situations requiring hospital care. Why formalize anything further? The more we ally ourselves with medical practitioners, the more likely we are to be subjected to outside regulation."

"I know you're not sold on this, but our insurance premiums will go down if we're handling high-risk pregnancies in association with an obstetrician. That alone was incentive enough to sway the board."

"If we become hospital based, we lose our main purpose for existing," Annie said, hearing the heat in her voice but helpless to stop it. Their whole specialty was geared toward providing women with a safe alternative to hospital birth—why weaken their mission by allying with hospital-based practitioners?

"They're not the enemy," Barb said as if reading her thoughts. "From a professional point of view, this will allow us to take care of even more women outside the hospital setting."

Annie closed her eyes. None of her colleagues knew her history—only that Callie's father wasn't in her life and Annie wasn't interested in dating anyone. They didn't know about the nightmare of Callie's delivery or the agony of recovering, when the psychic pain of knowing she'd never have the opportunity to share the birth of another child with someone she loved was even worse than the physical. Her choice had been taken from her in a flurry of technology and medical imperative. All perfectly justifiable, but in her heart, she would never be sure of the necessity. And she'd never forgive herself for believing so many lies. Jeff had only been the beginning.

"Annie, you there? Damn cell pho—"

"I'm here. Sorry. Bad battery."

"We need a regional director of the new program to work with the hospital on training schedules, supervisory details, triage protocols, that sort of thing."

"Chris Ames was an OR nurse before he got his CNM, he could—"

"Chris is terrific, no question. But we want a Philadelphia U graduate, since that's where the program will be based."

Annie's chest hurt. Barb's jovial, already-been-decided tone confirmed her fears.

"We want you for this, Annie. You'll meet with your OB counterpart at ten o'clock this morning at PMC."

CHAPTER THREE

Hollis pulled off her surgical cap and snapped the paper tie on her mask, balled them up, and tossed them toward the trash can across the small anteroom adjoining the delivery room. She'd gotten a few hours' sleep the night before, but her eyes felt gritty and her shoulders ached. She washed her hands and splashed her face with cold water. With luck she'd be able to put some time in on her bike before the end of the day—twenty miles cycling along the Schuylkill ought to work out the kinks.

"I thought you were off today," Ned Williams said, stopping in the hall that ran the length of Labor and Delivery.

"I am—was." Hollis pulled a few paper towels from the dispenser and mopped the water off her neck. Ned was a few years her senior in the department, a good-looking redhead with playful blue eyes, a smile that put patients immediately at ease, and an ex-wife and four kids. She gestured to the delivery room behind her. "One of my patients is a week early. I got the call just as the staff meeting finished. I'm waiting on her now."

Three other rooms like the one where her patient was being monitored were reserved for women in labor. A fifth room was reserved for scheduled C-sections during the week and for emergency surgeries, day or night. Hollis spent a lot of time in that room. High-risk pregnancies usually went well, but when they went bad they went bad fast, and she often had to operate emergently to save the baby and mother.

"Anything problematic? I don't mind giving an assist," Ned said, a hopeful note in his voice.

Ned was double-boarded in adolescent medicine and did a lot of teen pregnancies along with routine OB, and he regularly referred his surgical cases to Hollis. He frequently hung around when he was off call, and Hollis often wondered if the excitement of the hospital was more satisfying for him than his personal life. Her father had loved his job, but he was home at five p.m. every day for supper unless he had a fire call-out. Then no one cared how late he was as long as he came home. Hollis dismissed the unfair comparison—her family wasn't like most families she knew. She and her five brothers never fought, her mother and father were affectionate and still in love after thirty-nine years, and there was an unspoken rule that no matter how bad things got, together they could handle anything. That's how it had been until one Tuesday in September when the Towers came down and Rob never came home. Everything changed after that. The world had changed, *her* world had fractured, and she'd vowed she'd never be that vulnerable again.

Ned was waiting, a faint smile on his face. He was just being friendly. He couldn't know she didn't want friends.

"Hopefully this will go smoothly," she said. "She's thirty-eight and had preeclampsia with her last delivery, but she's been on bed rest for the past six weeks and her pressure's looking good. She's already fully effaced and moving right along."

"Good enough." He started to turn away, then paused. "What do you think about this whole thing with the midwifes? One of the OB practices I did a rotation with when I was a resident worked with midwifes. It was great, actually. I don't know why, but for some reason, mothers seemed more comfortable with them, especially around all the prenatal stuff."

"I think there's plenty of room for other caregivers to get involved with prenatal and aftercare," Hollis said. "But delivering high-risk mothers in an outpatient setting? Seems like a recipe for disaster to me."

"Well, I guess you'll get the chance to find out. Glad Dave volunteered you and not me." He grinned. "Kind of feel sorry for the poor midwife, though."

"Thanks," Hollis said dryly. "I'll try not to bite."

"You off the weekend?" Ned asked.

"Yes," Hollis said, although she'd told Bonnie McCann, who had the call on Monday, she'd back her up if she got busy. She wasn't doing anything and Bonnie had three kids and a birthday party scheduled.

"I've got the kids on Sunday and I promised them a barbecue. If you're free—"

"Uh…thanks, really. But I've got some stuff around the house I've been meaning to do for months. I think it's home-repair weekend." She didn't spend a lot of time socializing with her colleagues—fortunately her schedule gave her an easy excuse to pass on dinners and department get-togethers. Friendships didn't come without a price, and she was just as happy not to have even casual ties. She'd rather invest her energy and time in her patients. Those relationships were short but intimate and intense, and then everyone moved on with their lives. If she never made a long-term investment, she'd never be disappointed or, worse, devastated by loss.

Ned nodded as if anticipating her answer. "Okay, but if you change your mind, we're only ten minutes from you."

"Appreciate it, but I think I'll be knee-deep in sawdust for the foreseeable future." She wasn't lying. Her second year on staff, she'd purchased a once-stately old Victorian opposite the small park a few blocks from the hospital. She could walk to work, and if she had an emergency in the middle of the night, she could be on-site in less than fifteen minutes. Somewhere in the last hundred and eighty years, the second and third floors had been divided up into apartments and then later reconverted, leaving many false walls and odd corridors that divided rooms in haphazard fashion. She'd been slowly working to restore all the original architectural details. She enjoyed returning the place to its lost grandeur. This spring she'd started exterior work and still had half the wraparound porch to go.

"Have a good weekend," Ned said over his shoulder as he went off down the hall.

Hollis checked her watch. Mary Anderson was likely to deliver in the next two or three hours. She ought to be home by one and could get in a few hours' work on the back porch, a bike ride before dinner, and maybe even get out on her Harley for a quick run after that. She was planning to pull up the pressure-treated wood someone had put down on the porch and replace it with stained oak planks. Some of the posts on the banister also needed replacing, and she had to find a carpenter who could cut her new ones to match.

Happily reviewing her plans for the day, she pushed open the door bearing her name in plain black letters and stepped into the anteroom adjoining her office. Her secretary allowed no one through without an appointment, and the single chair in front of her desk didn't do much to encourage drop-in visitors. When she was at work, she wanted to work, not kill time with meaningless gossip.

"Hi, Sybil. Anything doing?" Hollis kept walking toward her office, not expecting Sybil to have much in the way of news. If there'd been anything important, she would have paged her. Sybil Baker, forty-five and looking thirty, twice divorced and "done with men," had been with her since she'd taken the position at the hospital. She had been the executive assistant to the chairman for five years before Hollis arrived but didn't like juggling all the departmental meetings that went along with the job. She preferred taking patient calls and scheduling office hours. She was also very good at settling down anxious patients and their families, leaving Hollis to concentrate on her clinic and delivery schedules. Hollis was the envy of every doc in the department.

"Actually," Sybil said, and Hollis slowed, "your ten o'clock appointment is here."

Hollis frowned. "I'm not scheduled to see anyone."

Sybil gave her an odd look. "I thought you knew. You have a meeting about the midwife clinic?"

Hollis clenched her jaws, biting off a retort. God damn Dave. He could have warned her. "I didn't know it was today."

"Oh," Sybil said, looking relieved. "That's why I didn't know about it. I was afraid you'd told me and I forgot to put it in your book. She seemed certain, so I thought it was best to have her wait in your office."

Hollis glanced at her watch. Ten fifteen. Great. She disliked keeping anyone waiting—she ran her office hours as close to on schedule as she possibly could, and her patients often remarked how unusual that was for an obstetrician. There were times she was late or missed office hours altogether, but only when she had an unexpected delivery. Otherwise, she wanted her patients to know that she would be there when she said she would be there, for any reason. And that extended to other appointments she made. She'd missed a critical appointment once in her life, and she'd be paying for it until the day she died. She'd vowed then it would never happen again.

"Hold my calls," Hollis said. "What's her name?"

"Colfax. I won't bother you unless it's L and D."

"Thanks." Hollis pushed on through into her office. "I'm so sorry for keeping you waiting, Ms. Colfax."

The woman in the chair rose and turned to face her. Hollis looked into the deep green eyes she remembered so very clearly. She could remember, too, the last words Annie Colfax had said to her before requesting another doctor. *I never should have trusted you.*

❖

Annie had started out with reservations about this politically mandated project, and when she'd seen Hollis Monroe's name on the office door, she'd known it wouldn't work. She'd spent the last twenty minutes while she was kept waiting formulating her reasons why. Only now she couldn't think of a single rational argument—anger blanketed her mind with a thick red haze.

Hollis Monroe was just as Annie remembered—arresting blue eyes, thick, tousled black hair, toned body. Her slightly rumpled scrubs gave her a faintly renegade air. She could see Monroe on the quarterdeck of a pirate ship, sword in hand and a victorious smile lighting her handsome face. At the moment, the surgeon appeared supremely focused, her intense gaze fixed unwaveringly on Annie as if nothing else mattered except this moment and what was happening between them. A rare skill that probably endeared her to patients, but Annie wasn't endeared.

She'd always known she'd run into Hollis someday. Fortunately, hospital trips for her were rare. Her whole focus as a midwife was to provide safe, individualized, supportive birthing care at home or in an equally natural setting. On those rare occasions when a patient developed perinatal complications, she arranged their transfer to the nearest hospital if they had no pre-arranged obstetrician, but beyond the phone calls to exchange medical data and her report to the paramedics, her involvement with the hospital establishment ended then. She had hoped this new assignment wouldn't require her to spend much time at PMC, and she'd hoped even more that she wouldn't have to deal with Hollis Monroe for a long time to come. So much for hopes, as if she hadn't learned that a long time ago.

"I'm afraid this won't work." Annie grabbed her briefcase. She wanted out of this room and away from the woman who reminded her of one of the worst days of her life. "I'll find a replacement and have the clinic contact you."

"That might be a little premature," Hollis said, suddenly wanting to prove Annie Colfax wrong—despite the fact she'd been of the same mind not ten minutes before. Annie's abrupt assessment and thinly veiled animosity bothered her more than they should. If the hostility had been purely professional, she might have dismissed it, but she knew it wasn't and she didn't know how to redress the past. She'd never had a chance to establish a relationship with Annie. At the first opportunity, Annie had requested another physician, as was her right. Hollis had accepted the decision and stepped aside. She'd understood the decision at the time—Annie was devastated by her unexpected surgery and terrified for the safety of her child. Annie needed to have control of her life, and if firing Hollis and blaming her for the outcome of her precipitous delivery would give her that control, Hollis couldn't argue. Now so much time had passed she didn't know this woman, and any explanation she might have offered would have to remain unspoken. "Why don't we take a few minutes to discuss things. I just found out—"

"I'm sure you're busy," Annie said, striding quickly toward the door. "I was just leaving."

"Ms. Colfax—" Hollis reached out without thinking and Annie shrugged away. Hollis held up her hands and took a step back, giving Annie space. "I'm sorry. Look, I know there were some difficulties between us—"

Annie snorted softly. "That's a mild way of putting it."

"Okay." Hollis sighed. "This is unexpected and…awkward in the extreme, but we're both professionals—"

"Are we? Tell me, Dr. Monroe, do you see me as your professional equal?"

Hollis had been hoping for détente, but if this was the way Annie wanted to play it, she wasn't going to sugarcoat anything. "I'm not sure the comparison is fair, but it would be disingenuous of me to say I consider our *training* equivalent. Our expertise lies in different areas. I will grant that you are probably much better at counseling patients and their families prenatally and in the postpartum care of the mother and baby." She shrugged. "My specialty is labor and delivery. The other aspects matter, sure, but that's what I'm trained for."

"Well, I'm not surprised." Annie shook her head. "You're not a whole lot different than many of the OBs I've met who somehow think the birthing part of bearing a child can be neatly carved out of the whole experience. Plus, considering your proclivities—"

"Excuse me? My proclivities?"

"You're a surgeon at heart—and surgeons want to operate. That's your raison d'être, isn't it? If you didn't operate, you'd be just like every other ordinary physician, or in this case, a lot like a midwife." Annie smiled wryly. "God forbid."

"So you're saying I fabricate reasons to operate, that's where this is going, isn't it?" Heat flared in Hollis's chest. She'd expected she and the midwife would have philosophical differences, but she hadn't expected accusations about her ethics. "You don't know me well enough to make that kind of assumption."

Annie stared. "Really? I think I know you just about as well as anyone can, from personal experience. Tell me—what would have happened if you'd waited another ten minutes after Callie—that's my daughter, in case you're interested—was delivered? What if you'd continued uterine massage and given the drugs a chance to work? Do you think you might not have needed to take out my uterus?"

"I made a judgment call," Hollis said. They were going to revisit the past after all. Four years might have passed, but she remembered those last few moments in the OR with absolute clarity. She hadn't changed her mind. "In my opinion—in my professional, *expert* opinion—in another ten minutes, as you say, you would have suffered significant organ failure due to protracted blood loss, kidney failure, adult respiratory distress syndrome, and possibly death from hypovolemic shock. My goal was to get you out of that delivery room in the best possible shape so that you could take care of your daughter—"

Annie's eyes sparked fire. "Don't use my daughter as an excuse."

"An excuse?" Hollis resisted the urge to strike back in her own defense, but Annie Colfax had been her patient, and she was angry and still grieving. "I'm sorry you feel that way. I can only tell you,

you're wrong. I did think about her when I made the decision to do the C-section, and I thought about both of you when I made the decision to take out your uterus. And I don't regret either one."

"No," Annie said softly, "of course you don't. Are you always so certain, Dr. Monroe?"

"When I pick up a scalpel, always."

Annie's anger drained away, leaving only an unanticipated melancholy. "That's the point, isn't it? You're always sure it's time to operate, but my expertise is in knowing when *not* to operate. In knowing what's natural and tolerable and ultimately safe before, during, and after delivery. There's a reason that the United States has one of the highest incidences of cesarean births in the world—because surgeons are making the decisions."

"It's pretty clear we're at an impasse here," Hollis said.

"For once, we agree." Annie walked to the door and looked back over her shoulder. She'd thought she'd feel better if she ever had the chance to vent her anger and frustration to the one person who deserved to hear it, but she didn't. The hint of pain in Hollis's eyes made for a hollow victory. "Good-bye, Dr. Monroe."

CHAPTER FOUR

Hollis stared at the closed door while she warred with herself about going after Annie. She didn't like to admit defeat, and even though she had been the one to suggest they were at loggerheads, she wasn't ready to just walk away without a fight. And that made no sense at all. She didn't like this whole idea of a combined OB-midwife service—never mind the potential for a medical disaster, just the coordination of appointments, communication between patient, doctor, and midwife, and extra paperwork would be a nightmare. After this morning she had the perfect opportunity to call Dave, report that the concept might be a good one but the execution was impossible, and get on with her work.

The whole mess would disappear, sure, but Annie Colfax would go on believing she was a blade-happy surgeon with a limited vision of the birthing experience, too arrogant to even investigate other possibilities. Not that anything she was likely to do or say would change Annie's opinion of her. How was she supposed to convince a woman whose mind was made up that she wasn't who she had appeared to be four years ago, seen through a veil of pain and anger and sorrow?

Annoyed, frustrated, confused by how much Annie's harsh judgment of her care, Annie's cold assessment of *her*, personally, stung, Hollis went back to her desk and pushed files around. She dictated a few follow-up notes and practically cheered when her cell rang and L and D's number popped up.

"Monroe."

"She's ready for you, Hollis," Patty Richards, the delivery room nurse, said.

"On my way." Hollis waved to Sybil on the way out. "I'll be

leaving once Mary delivers, as long as everything is okay. If you need me for anything, call me."

Sybil gave Hollis an appraising look. "That was a pretty short meeting."

Hollis paused, leaning on the partially open door. Sybil was more than her secretary, she was a trusted confidant who had steered Hollis through the minefield of departmental politics early on in her career. She relied on Sybil's judgment and thought of her as a friend. "I knew this was going to be touchy. We ran into a few roadblocks."

"Hmm. She did look a little overheated on the way out."

"Unfortunately, I think we have a personality conflict."

"Really?" Sybil frowned. "That's not like you. I thought I taught you better than that."

Hollis grinned. "You did, and I've managed to keep out of trouble this long." The brief flicker of humor died when she remembered the pain and anger in Annie Colfax's eyes. "But this one's a little different."

"Anything you want to tell me about?"

"It's complicated." Annie wasn't her patient anymore, but she had been, and what had transpired between them was confidential. She couldn't really talk to Sybil about it, even though Sybil knew most everything about all of her patients. All the same, what was going on between her and Annie was more than just medical. It was personal in a way that was unusual for her. She cared about all her patients and cared about doing what was right for them. She had complications sometimes, and outcomes less than she desired—if you didn't, you weren't operating enough—but she couldn't remember a time when her judgment or her actions had created such antipathy. She didn't know how she felt about that, and for the first time the personal and the professional were all tangled up in her head. "Thanks. It'll sort itself out."

"I'm sure you'll handle it," Sybil said. "You know, Hollis, you're really, really good at what you do."

"Thanks. That means a lot."

"So go get Mary's baby started in the world."

Smiling at the prospect of doing what she did best, the one thing that gave her uncomplicated pleasure, Hollis tipped a finger to her forehead in salute. "Yes ma'am. I'll tell Mary you said hi."

By the time she got to the delivery room, the nurses had Mary on the table in position. "What's the status?" Hollis said, holding out her hands for her gown and gloves.

"She's moving through stage two pretty fast."

"Pressure?" Mary had had serious hypertension during her last pregnancy, and now was the time when they were likely to see a recurrence.

"Holding nice and steady," the anesthesiologist said.

Hollis moved to the head of the table and looked down at Mary, who was awake. She'd opted for an epidural to help relieve the pain, but she hadn't been given any other drugs that might sedate her or the baby. "How are you doing?"

"I'm ready for this to be over." Mary's brown hair was black with sweat at the temples and her cheeks flushed from exertion. Her deep green eyes were bright with anticipation.

Hollis's mood lifted, buoyed by Mary's excitement. "I'll just bet you are. Sounds like it won't be too long. Everything's going fine."

Mary searched her face and must have seen the certainty in Hollis's eyes because she nodded and smiled. "I feel fine. If it weren't for the God-blessed contractions I'd be perfect. Thank you for this—I can hardly remember the first time." She caught her breath and her face tightened with a wave of pain.

"No need to thank me," Hollis said when the contraction passed, noting the time on the big clock on the wall. "You're the one doing all the work." She glanced across the table to Mary's husband, who sat on a high stool holding Mary's hand. His face was pale above his mask, but his eyes were calm. "You doing okay, Cliff?"

"Just fine," he said hoarsely. "Mary's a champ."

"That she is. So I guess I better get to work or you two won't think I'm necessary."

Cliff brushed Mary's hair, his hand trembling. "Okay, baby, just a little bit longer."

"Easy for you to say," Mary grunted.

"Don't I know it. I love you."

Hollis eased back down the table and motioned for the circulating nurse to slide over a stool for her to sit between Mary's legs. When she performed an internal exam, she found the baby's head ready to emerge. Her pulse jumped. She'd been in this exact position hundreds of times, and every time was still a thrill. In this moment, all that mattered were

Mary and this baby. "All systems go. Next contraction, Mary, I want you to push."

❖

Annie left her car in the parking lot at PMC and walked, no particular destination in mind. She'd already canceled her clinic appointments for the morning, expecting to be tied up at least part of the day in the meeting. Now she was at loose ends and too agitated to work. She'd thought she was prepared to see Hollis Monroe again, knowing it was inevitable. She'd thought she'd put the anger and frustration and fear behind her a long time ago. Callie was the best thing in her life, and she didn't regret having her for one single second. She wished with all her heart the delivery had been different—that she could have experienced what so many of her patients experienced—a joyous, miraculous birth surrounded by loved ones in a safe environment, with only wonderful memories to cherish for a lifetime when it was all over. She wished she could have watched the face of the person she loved when Callie emerged and felt her child's first tentative movements on her breast. But instead of holding Callie in her arms and taking her daughter to her breast seconds after she drew her first breath, she had no memories at all—only of awakening to confusion and pain and a terrifying emptiness where Callie had once been. She would never have the chance to experience the complete cycle of birth, and part of her wept at the loss.

But she had Callie, and Callie was all the miracle she'd ever need. She hadn't realized how much anger she had buried. She sighed and turned into the park a few blocks from her house. She hadn't had much time to explore the neighborhood, but she and Callie often came here after school to talk about Callie's day and enjoy the spring weather. Late morning, the park was nearly deserted, and she found a bench under a big maple. She so rarely had any time to just be. Between her busy practice and her busy little girl, she didn't have much time to be quiet.

As soon as she sat, she was back in Hollis Monroe's office, railing at her. She replayed the conversation in Hollis's office and heard herself saying things out loud she hadn't even allowed herself to think. She'd taken Callie home from the hospital alone and raised her alone while finishing school with distance courses, and then she'd gone to work helping other women experience what she hadn't. She'd thought she'd put the past behind her, but today she'd totally lost control. Seeing Hollis had triggered all the memories of that terrifying day, and thinking about it now, a lot of her anger had been toward Jeff. She'd never had any place to put that either. Maybe she hadn't been entirely fair this morning. She'd unloaded on Hollis, and Hollis had let her.

She was still too close to her feelings to even know if she regretted what she'd said. No, that wasn't right. She'd said what she truly felt, but maybe if she hadn't been taken by surprise, she might have kept some of it to herself. Hollis had been a lot more rational—and sensitive—than she had been, and that embarrassed her. She didn't let her emotions run away with her, and with this particular person, she really didn't want to appear as if she were unable to handle her emotions. Not that she was going to see her again.

Personal things aside, she'd been right about one thing. Professionally, she and Hollis were at opposite ends of the universe, and there was no possible way they could work together.

❖

Hollis changed into jeans and a dark blue button-down collar shirt, shed her OR clogs for an old pair of plain brown loafers she couldn't part with, and signed out for the day. She'd underestimated the speed of Mary's labor—it wasn't quite noon and Mary was securely tucked away on Maternity with baby Thomas in her arms and her husband giddily taking videos. She should have felt completely satisfied, but the meeting with Annie still haunted her. She didn't second-guess her decisions if things didn't go as planned, but she always reviewed the facts to see what she might have done differently when a case didn't turn out well. She wasn't too proud to learn from her mistakes—if she ever discovered otherwise, she'd have to seriously rethink what she was doing. She remembered Annie's angry question—*What would have happened if you'd waited another ten minutes?* Maybe there was a way to give Annie an answer she'd believe. Hollis paused in the hall outside Labor and Delivery and called her office.

"Obstetrics and Gynecology, Dr. Monroe's office, how may I help you?" Sybil said.

"Do me a favor, would you—pull a patient chart from four years ago. The name is Colfax, Annie."

"I certainly will," Sybil said without hesitation and without questions. She'd be curious, but she was too professional to pry. She'd wait for Hollis to fill her in, when and if the need arose. "I take it everything went well?"

"Seven pounds, six ounces, Apgar 9 and 10. Mother doing great. Father too."

Sybil laughed. "Then that's an A-plus job. Now you go on home and get some rest. I'll see you tomorrow."

"Thanks. I'm off call, but if something comes up—"

"Then you're still off call. Go. Do something fun."

Hollis thought about her plans for the day. For some reason, the solitary pursuits didn't seem as appealing any longer. "Working on it. See you tomorrow."

"Have a good one."

Hollis pocketed her phone and took the stairs down to the ground floor. She always walked out through the ER, stopping to check the whiteboard just to be sure nothing was coming in for her. She was as superstitious as any surgeon, but this wasn't superstition. She *knew* for sure if she didn't check, she'd be ten minutes away when she got the page telling her one of her patients had shown up and she was needed back in the ER. The board looked clear. No OB cases at all.

"Trolling for business now, Dr. Monroe?" Linda called.

"Not so you'd notice. Got any for me?"

Linda laughed and patted her belly. "Not just yet, and I have to say—hopefully not at all."

"Are you working down here now?"

"Just visiting this morning, but I'll probably be here before too long."

Hollis tried to think who was doing Linda's prenatal care, but drew a blank. Usually, the hospital staff opted for an in-house OB, but sometimes for privacy reasons they went elsewhere. "Well, I'm sure you won't see me until I stop by to see the new baby."

"You've got an open invitation. You know where I live."

Hollis paused. "Sorry?"

"Oh," Linda said softly, coloring faintly. "No reason you should know. I'm having this one at home."

"Are you?" Hollis's chest tightened. Linda looked to be in her late thirties—not unusual any longer, but still, complications were more likely. "This your first?"

"Yes, lucky me, my partner took care of the first three."

Hollis laughed. "I hope you both have a great time with this one."

"Me too. Our midwife is terrific."

Of course they'd have a midwife. She just couldn't get away from it today. Hollis injected enthusiasm into her voice. "Home birth is really taking off."

"Well, I know it's not for everyone, and to each her own for sure. But I hope it works out because we're really looking forward to this."

"I can imagine."

"You look like you're on your way out. Better get going before something comes through the door."

"You're right about that." Laughing, Hollis headed for the exit.

She cut through the ER parking lot, planning to cross through the park that stretched for four square blocks between the hospital and her house. As she skirted around parked ambulances and fire rescue vans, she saw Annie Colfax headed toward her. She stopped when Annie's eyes widened in surprise. "Good morning again."

"Oh," Annie said, almost not recognizing Hollis in street clothes. Hollis looked even younger with the sun gleaming on her dark hair, lanky and lean in worn denim jeans and a shirt with the sleeves rolled up. Incongruously, her forearms were deeply tanned, as if she spent a lot of time outside in the sun. Running, she bet. Maybe not, though. Hollis had a lot more upper-body development than most runners she knew. And she was staring, wasn't she. Could she get any more off balance around this woman? "I was just coming back to pick up my car. It's around the corner. Visitors' lot."

Hollis frowned. "You left it here?"

"I wanted to walk."

"Huh." Hollis slid her hands into her pockets. "When I'm out of sorts, I like to pound on something." Annie looked wary and Hollis added quickly, "Wood. Hammer and nails?"

Annie laughed. "Odd pastime for a surgeon. Aren't you worried about your hands?"

"Not really. I'm careful. I've jammed my thumb a time or two, but you can't sit around doing nothing because something might go wrong, right?"

"Are you saying that caution isn't in your vocabulary?" Annie asked, an unexpected teasing note in her voice.

Hollis shook her head. "I'm not saying anything. I don't want to get in any deeper."

Annie flushed. "About this morning...I—"

"Why don't we start this morning over again," Hollis said. Something about Annie had changed. She was still cautious, still reserved and a little edgy, but there was warmth in her eyes and it wasn't the hot hard fire of anger she'd had earlier. Not exactly welcoming, but maybe an olive branch. Her plans to pull up the porch suddenly lost all appeal, but something told her she'd have to move fast before Annie's guard went up again. "Look, I don't live very far away. I haven't had breakfast..." She glanced at her watch. "Well, it's lunchtime now, but I can rustle up something and we can start our meeting over again."

"That seems like a lot of trouble," Annie said, desperately trying to work through her surprise. She didn't know how to handle a friendly Hollis, not on a personal level. She couldn't really have lunch with her, could she? Well, she could, but certainly not at her house. "Maybe we can find a diner or something? Or there's always the hospital cafeteria."

Hollis shook her head. "No way. I just spent thirty-six hours in there. And hospital food isn't great even in the best of circumstances. Omelets...mushrooms, a little broccoli, cheese? It's safe, I promise."

Laughing, Annie nodded, taken by the unexpected charm. Lunch was lunch, right? A business lunch should be safe enough. "All right, Dr. Monroe. Omelets it is."

CHAPTER FIVE

I'm parked right over there," Annie said. "Do you want me to drive?"

"My place is only a few blocks away, if you don't mind walking," Hollis said. "I could stand a little fresh air and the weather's perfect."

"Sure." Annie fell in beside Hollis as they walked back to the street. Every time she started questioning her decision to join Hollis for lunch, she firmly pushed the doubts from her mind. After all, Barb expected her to work with Hollis on the clinic project, and they hadn't gotten off to a very good start, mostly because of her. She was a professional and she could keep her personal feelings at home. That didn't mean they *would* come to any kind of professional agreement, but they hadn't even taken the first step. And she wasn't doing a very good job meeting Hollis halfway. She was usually good at small talk—she had to meet new people all day long, women and families equally ecstatic and terrified by the prospect of a new baby. Why was she practically tongue-tied around Hollis?

"So," Hollis said, "where did you train?"

Almost sighing with relief, Annie said, "Right here in the city…at Philadelphia College."

"Nursing school?"

Annie shook her head. "I was at Temple for my BSN, but I never actually practiced nursing. I lost some time with Callie…well, anyhow, I transferred my senior year into the midwife program and they advanced me credit toward my bachelor's so I could get my degree and accelerate my midwife training."

"Explains why you're so young."

Annie laughed, ridiculously pleased. She thought of herself in two ways—as a mother and a midwife. She rarely thought of herself as a woman others might see as attractive. Of course, Hollis hadn't said *that.* She quickly covered her embarrassment with a wave of her hand. "I'm not young. I'm probably your age, and…Oh God, I didn't mean to suggest you're old—"

"Thirty-three in a few weeks," Hollis offered, laughing. Annie hadn't actually asked her age, but for some reason, she liked getting to know her, even if it did mean sharing things she ordinarily wouldn't. She liked learning about Annie, and that was as good an explanation as any she could come up with for why she wasn't behaving at all like herself. "So?"

"What? Oh! Twenty-eight." Why she wasn't able to carry on a simple conversation escaped her. Even Callie was better at it.

"See? I told you you were young."

"Hardly." Annie snorted. "A four-year-old will age you decades. I feel like I'm fifty sometimes."

"Yeah, I don't know how my mother did it with six."

"A lot of patience or a really big bark."

Hollis grinned. "She has both."

"No kids yourself?" Annie asked lightly, hoping she didn't sound too curious. She was, infinitely curious. Outside the hospital, in this strangely personal sphere they'd somehow fallen into, Hollis was a very interesting woman. And a very attractive one. Bright, good-looking, and surprisingly easy to talk with.

"Who, me?" Hollis shook her head. "No. I'm single, no kids."

"But kids aren't necessarily *not* in your future?"

"Geez, I never really thought about it." An uneasy prickle skittered between Hollis's shoulder blades. How did they get around to her and what she wanted in her personal life—she didn't even go there in private if she could help it. She sure didn't discuss it with anyone, although her mother kept trying. *When are you going to bring a girl home to meet the family, Hollis? Your brothers can't do all the work of making me grandchildren.* God, the family was big on kids, and after losing Rob's—

"Hey," Annie said gently, "I didn't mean to pry."

"That's okay. Fair question." Hollis flushed, her chest tightening. Annie's eyes shimmered with a combination of tenderness and concern, and Hollis wondered what was showing in her face. She cleared her throat. "I suppose a bunch of kids would feel natural. But with my job—I'm hardly ever home and I'd hate being an absentee parent. I'm probably not cut out for it."

"You might be selling yourself short," Annie said quietly.

"Maybe." Embarrassed, Hollis looked away. "Anyhow, the point is moot."

"True. Besides, you're not required to predict the future as one of your many talents."

The pressure in Hollis's chest eased as Annie subtly redirected the conversation. Annie was very perceptive, and that was both intriguing and worrisome. "Thanks for letting me off the hook."

Annie laughed. "I think I owe you a couple of free passes."

Again, Annie surprised her. She hadn't been sure Annie was willing to put the past aside, at least for now, and the small bit of humor felt like a victory. She raised a brow. "Well, now that you mention it. Maybe a few free passes."

Annie sighed. "I suppose we have to talk about the clinic situation sooner or later."

"Yes, but fortunately, later." Annie's expression had shuttered at the first mention of the clinic, and Hollis wanted to put the laughter back in her eyes. She pointed to the sweeping three-story Victorian with a turret at one corner and a huge wraparound porch that sat on the corner of two quiet streets bordering the park. "This is my place."

"Oh my God. That's gorgeous."

Hollis smiled, pleased that Annie saw the tarnished beauty of the old place. "Well, it was once, and I hope it will be again one day."

"Are you having it renovated?"

"Nope—I'm doing it myself."

Annie laughed. "You *are* a woman of many talents."

"Not going there."

"Wise."

Hollis's fatigue drifted off on the soft waves of Annie's laughter. The lightness in her chest was strange, and a little addicting. And Annie was the cause. "I don't have a lot of time to work on it, so it keeps me pretty busy."

Annie cocked her head and studied the house. "It looks like you've already restored the detailing on the roofline and the front porch." She narrowed her gaze. "And if I'm not mistaken, that's original glass in the first-floor windows. You don't see those a lot anymore."

"I had to drive around to every estate sale in three states before I found those windows," Hollis said, "but it was worth it."

"They really set off the porch. The hardware on the door is Eastlake, isn't it?" Annie said as they walked up.

"Good call." Hollis swung open the scrolled wrought-iron gate leading to the random flagstone walkway she'd placed to the front porch, surprised by Annie's comments. Most people were more drawn to superficial glitz and modern elements, buying historic homes and modernizing them in ways that destroyed the integrity of the original style and design. The average person would never notice that. They might just sense that the house seemed devoid of character, and that, in her opinion, was almost always because all the subtle details that defined a particular era were missing. She'd spent an entire weekend hunting for a doorknob that suited the size and design of her heavy oak front door. "You seem to know quite a lot about that sort of thing."

"My father is a cabinetmaker. I used to watch him work and he'd tell me the stories he saw in the wood."

"Did he teach you to work the wood too?"

"No," Annie said abruptly. "That was for the boys to do."

"Ah. I wanted to be a firefighter like everyone else in my family, but my dad wasn't so keen on the idea." Hollis sensed there was more to Annie's story than just the gender divide, but she didn't want to make her uncomfortable. What she wanted was to hear her laugh again.

"I've always loved architecture," Annie went on in the sudden silence. "I think I was drawn to the intimate connection between form and function—a well-designed building should allow for smooth flow and seamless function without ever making it noticeable."

"I agree with you." Hollis unlocked the door and held it open. "Me, I just like to look at them, though. I like how all the parts make a beautiful whole. A lot like babies."

"How whimsical." Annie smiled. "And how sweet."

Hollis flushed. "Well, let's keep it our little secret, if you wouldn't mind."

"My lips are sealed." Annie laughed and shook her head. Hollis made her behave very foolishly, and the oddest thing was, she was enjoying herself. "I can't believe I actually said that."

"You did, and now we each have a secret to hold. I won't tell if you don't."

"It's a deal." Annie followed Hollis down the wide central hall, trying to catch glimpses into all the rooms they passed. As she took in the gleaming woodwork and antique light fixtures, she wondered how she had gone from untamable anger to this easy camaraderie.

"Well, let's see if I can win more favors with breakfast." Hollis smiled, a lock of dark hair falling in her eyes. "Hungry?"

"Yes," Annie said slowly, realization dawning. Hollis Monroe was charming. Charming and intriguing and unexpectedly sweet, a combination of traits Annie found hard to resist. The understanding came to her with a sudden memory of herself a decade ago, caught in the spell of another handsome charmer. She hurried to catch up to Hollis, feeling her control settle firmly into place. Now that she recognized what drew her to Hollis, she could be more careful.

❖

Hollis pointed to a high wooden stool next to the counter. The large kitchen faced the back porch and yard beyond. "Have a seat. This won't take more than a few minutes." As she spoke, she extracted ingredients from the large refrigerator tucked into an alcove next to the breakfast nook. From there, she passed ingredients onto the small table in front of the bay windows.

"You must have taken out a wall in here to get a kitchen this size," Annie said.

"I did. There was a butler's pantry where this alcove was, and I had to sacrifice something in order to get enough counter space. Since I didn't have a butler, I figured it wasn't a big loss. You think it works all right?"

"I do. I think the size of the room still fits with the interior layout, but there's plenty of work space and that window overlooking the yard is especially nice."

"Good." Hollis hadn't entertained before and only her family had seen the house. Annie's remarks made all the hard work worth it.

"Can I do anything?"

Hollis shook her head as she assembled ingredients. "No, but I forgot to ask if you wanted coffee."

"I've already had more than my quota for the day. Would you happen to have sparkling water?"

"In the fridge." Hollis inclined her head. "If you don't mind, you'll find a few bottles of Saratoga water. You can open one for each of us."

Annie jumped off the stool and retrieved the water from the fridge. She twisted off the tops and set one of the bright blue bottles next to Hollis. Sipping the effervescent water, she watched Hollis, relaxing despite her vow to remain on guard. Hollis worked quickly and efficiently, no surprise. She sliced mushrooms and broccoli with precise, swift movements, grated cheese with a few long, even strokes, and mixed it all together with eggs she whipped in a crockery bowl.

"Do you operate like you cook?"

"Hmm?" Hollis shot her a questioning look.

"Fast and efficient?"

Hollis grinned. "I don't do any general GYN surgery, so when I do operate it's almost always an emergency. So I guess the answer is yes. Speed and efficiency on my part means a better outcome for mother and baby."

"I can't help thinking it must be a little bit of a letdown to have to deliver the baby surgically. I mean, I love that moment when the baby emerges and I can lift her up and pass her onto the mother's breast."

Hollis stopped chopping and regarded Annie contemplatively. "What do you think is the most exciting moment in a delivery?"

"That's a very difficult question. I think mothers really remember—"

"I meant for you."

Annie drew a breath and took her time. She didn't feel as if she was being tested, but the question tested her nevertheless. How much of every birth was for her? How much of what she did was about her personal pleasure, and not the patient's? Questions she wasn't sure she wanted to answer. But, in the interest of their fragile truce, she tried. "For me, the greatest joy is when the baby takes his first breath. Then I know my part is over and the rest of his life is about to begin." Hollis was watching her intently, and she wondered what her answer revealed about her. "I don't imagine you have an opportunity to savor the birth, do you? When you're operating?"

"Most mothers come to me because they have complications or are at risk to develop complications, so a large percentage of my births are surgical. You're right about that." Hollis fired up the gas flame under the cast-iron skillet. "But, believe it or not, I do more vaginal deliveries than C-sections."

That wasn't a topic Annie wanted to reopen just now. She was enjoying their unexpected connection too much to spoil it. "So? What do you like best?"

"I guess when it's all over, and I know I've done the best I can do and both of them are okay." Hollis shrugged. "Guess we're not so very different after all."

"Maybe not." Annie rose to take one of the plates with the perfectly turned omelet and half a toasted bagel. "But then, we haven't even begun to find out, have we?"

CHAPTER SIX

A t the sound of a familiar voice just outside her cubicle, Honor paused in the middle of giving discharge instructions. The deep, throaty timbre was unmistakable and never failed to stir her. Refocusing on her young patient and his mother, she said, "And no swimming while that cast is on, all right?"

"What will happen?" the six-year-old asked, his eyes alight with some inner vision Honor was afraid to contemplate. She sensed a wily mind at work.

"The cast will fall off and your mom or dad will have to bring you back here so I can put on a new one."

"Will it hurt?"

"Not if the cast stays on. Your wrist needs to rest so it can heal."

"Like a nap?"

"Sort of."

"I'm too big for a nap."

"I see that. Which is why we made it so just your wrist can sleep."

"I almost made it to the top of the jungle gym. Julie and I were racing. She usually wins but I'm getting faster."

Out of the corner of her eye, Honor saw the mother's resigned shake of her head and sympathized. "I imagine you'll catch her one day soon, but no climbing until you're better. You need two hands on the jungle gym, right?"

"Yeah." His bright, lively eyes scanned the room as if searching for new challenges.

"Okay, we're done." She smiled at his mother. "He should be fine tonight. If his fingers swell more than they are now or the cast starts to look tight, you should bring him back so we can adjust it."

"Does he need a sling?"

"The nurses will give him one when you leave," Honor said, "but don't rely on it. Just remind him not to dangle it, and prop his forearm up on a couple of pillows when he goes to bed."

"And if he gets it wet?" the mother whispered when her son wandered over to the enclosing curtain and stuck his head out.

"As long as he doesn't soak it, it will probably be fine, but let's make that our secret."

"Absolutely. Thanks so much."

"You're very welcome." Honor signed off on the paperwork and handed it to the mother. "Schedule an appointment in a month with an orthopedist. They'll take off the cast and x-ray his wrist. Until then, there's nothing you have to do unless for some reason you're concerned. Then by all means, make a follow-up appointment earlier." She squeezed the boy's shoulder. "You be careful, now."

"Thanksbye." The boy raced out through the curtain and the mother hastily pulled it aside to follow.

Honor listened to the thump of running footfalls, marveling at the resilience of children. The curtain twitched aside again, and she expected the mother to return, but she was mistaken. Her heart gave a little jump as Quinn stepped in and closed the curtain.

"Hi." Quinn kissed Honor a little longer than necessary for hello. "Busy?"

Honor traced the edge of the vee in Quinn's scrub shirt, letting her fingers drift over the skin of Quinn's chest. No matter how many times she touched her, she was still astounded by the miracle of loving her. "Steady, all pretty routine. What are you doing down here?" She mentally sorted through the list of patients up on the board and couldn't remember one that might need a trauma consult. "Did something come in just now? I didn't hear an alert."

"No." Quinn slid an arm around Honor's waist, rested her hips against the treatment table, and tugged Honor close. "Just wanted to steal a minute with you." She kissed her again.

Laughing, Honor rested her cheek on Quinn's shoulder. "You can steal as many minutes as you want, but you'll have to collect them at home tonight."

"Hmm," Quinn said, resting her chin on top of Honor's head. "I've got karate practice with Arly tonight, remember?"

"That's right. And Jack has a sleepover at Robin and Linda's. I promised I'd take the early shift in case he wants to come home."

"So there goes the night."

Honor kissed Quinn's throat. "There's always later-later." Quinn chuckled, the vibrations spreading through Honor's cheek and settling somewhere south of her diaphragm. Even contemplating their lack of alone time made her happy, when it was family time taking up the evening. "I love you."

Quinn stroked Honor's hair. "I love you too. I should let you get back to work."

"You should." Honor leaned back and traced the muscles in Quinn's chest. "Don't forget we have the barbecue at Linda and Robin's Sunday. You switched call, right?"

"I did. And I saw Linda leaving just now—she said to remind you to bring your macaroni salad."

"I'm on it," Honor said. "They're definitely planning on a natural birth at home, by the way."

"You sound like you don't approve."

Honor sighed. "It's not that, really. I think the idea is great and I'm sure it will be a wonderful experience. I just—" She waved her hand toward the curtain. "This I know. This I trust. Linda is so important to me, and I guess I'm just…"

"A little nervous?"

Honor nodded. "Yeah."

"Linda is too smart to take any chances. I'm sure if there's any suggestion of difficulties, she'll opt out. Besides," Quinn said, cupping Honor's cheek, "you'll be there. And this ER is only so good because you're here."

Honor smiled and kissed Quinn's throat. "How is it you always know just what to say to me?"

Quinn's eyes softened, melting into the endless blue sea that Honor always wanted to drown in. "Maybe because I've always loved you."

"I'm so crazy about you, you know." Honor tilted her forehead to Quinn's shoulder.

"Is there something else that's bothering you?"

Honor shook her head. "You always could read my mind too. I think maybe I'm a little jealous."

"Of Linda?" Quinn asked carefully.

"I would have loved to see you holding Jack when he took his first breath."

"You said after he was born you wanted another."

Honor didn't miss the cautious note in Quinn's voice and loved her all the more for it. "The two we have are amazing."

Quinn let out a breath. "I'm perfectly content. But if it's something you want—"

"Are you okay with the way things are? Because I'm sort of settling in at work now that Jack is a little bigger. And Arly will be a teenager soon—she had a rough start after Terry died, though I tried—"

"Hey," Quinn said firmly. "Arly is solid. You gave her everything she needed."

"Still, I want this time to be special for her."

"Baby," Quinn said, cradling Honor's face in both hands and kissing her forehead. "Our family is the only thing that matters to me. If we stop at two, I'm great. If you want another, I'm there too—all I ask is that we see an OB first and get clearance. Last time was scary."

"I know. I know." Honor hugged Quinn quickly. "Let's stick with the status quo for now."

"Okay, but just say the word, make the appointment, and I'll be there."

"Thanks. I love you."

"I love you too. I better let you go. I'll see you later."

"Or better yet, later-later."

Laughing, Quinn disappeared around the curtain. Even as her footsteps faded, the heat of her body lingered along Honor's. She had the perfect family—two wonderful, healthy kids and a lover who made her heart sing and her body melt. She had everything she'd ever wanted.

❖

"Let me help you with the dishes," Annie said when Hollis stood and started to clear the table.

"Thanks," Hollis said, carrying their plates to the sink. She washed while Annie put the silverware and glasses on the drain board beside her. Annie stood nearby, dish towel in hand, and Hollis contemplated how unexpectedly natural it all seemed. Lunch had been comfortable too, the conversation light and easy. She'd talked a lot about her plans for the house and Annie had seemed genuinely interested, commenting on Hollis's ideas and adding some interesting insights. She hadn't spent so much time with anyone other than family in years. Annie got her to relax without noticing it.

"That was great." Annie folded the dish towel after drying the last plate. "I can't remember the last time someone cooked for me."

"Really?" Hollis felt a surge of pleasure at the remark, and a strange kind of satisfaction. "Someone has been falling down on the job, then."

"Ah," Annie said, blushing, "I'm afraid there isn't anyone *on* the job."

"What about Callie's father?" Instantly, Hollis realized her misstep. She'd gotten *too* relaxed and dropped her guard. "I'm sorry. That was way, way out of line."

"No, it's a natural enough question." Annie's tone was crisp. "Let's just say he's never been in the picture and doesn't rate the name."

Hollis folded her arms across her chest and eased back, giving Annie space. "I am really sorry. That was thoughtless of me."

Annie registered the regret in Hollis's eyes. "Really, there's nothing to apologize for. You're certainly not responsible for my stupidity."

"That's not a word I'd associate with you."

"You didn't know me when I was an impressionable girl right off the farm."

"You mentioned your father was a cabinetmaker. Did he farm too?"

Annie turned to the open screen door and looked out over the half-finished porch. The deep yard was bordered on the street side by a row of large oaks and along the back by shrubs—while large by city standards, it was a far cry from the acres of corn and wheat that had been her backyard until she left for college at nineteen. "I grew up in western Pennsylvania on a big dairy farm. We were self-sustaining— my father built most of our furniture, my mother made our clothes, and we ate what we grew and raised. What we couldn't make or grow ourselves we traded for with neighbors."

"Amish?"

Annie turned, surprised. She usually directed conversations away from her personal history, but Hollis just kept surprising her. She had a way of moving right to the heart of the matter with a single question. Maybe it was the surgeon in her. "No, Mennonite. Similar, but not quite as rigid. We had electricity, used machinery. How did you know?"

Hollis looked uncomfortable. "I remember you didn't want surgery because of your beliefs."

"You remember that after all this time?"

"It's strange. I usually remember surgical cases in absolute detail, so that's pretty normal for me. I remember you because…"

"Why?" Annie asked, suddenly needing to know.

"You're the only patient that's ever fired me."

Heat rushed to Annie's cheeks. "A rather inauspicious honor, then. I'm surprised you fed me, let alone cooked."

Hollis wasn't ready to break their fragile truce by reliving that day. They'd have to, and when they did, she wasn't sure how their budding relationship would be changed. For now, she just wanted to know more. More of Annie. "How does all that mesh with your midwife practice?"

"I've left the congregation," Annie said, "so it's not an issue. In fact, I didn't have much choice. I was shunned."

Hollis sucked in a breath, shock and fury racing through her. "You? Why?"

"I had a child out of wedlock, and I refused to give her up. I refused to return to the fold if it meant having my child scorned. And I insisted on modern medical training, including some things the congregation outlawed."

Hollis rubbed her hands over her face. "So you had Callie and then…" Annie had been alone in the delivery room, but everything happened so quickly, she'd just assumed Annie's partner and family hadn't had time to get to the hospital. Now she realized there hadn't been anyone. Annie had been totally alone. "No wonder you were angry. Everything you've accomplished is amazing."

Any laughed mirthlessly. "Is that what you call it? I survived. I didn't have any choice. I had Callie to think of."

"I'm sorry."

"I'm sorry for bringing it all up."

"You didn't, I did."

"Well, none of that was your doing."

"I just wished I'd known."

"It wouldn't have changed anything. You still would have made the same choices."

"Yes, I would. But maybe I would have been a little more sensitive."

"The past can't be changed," Annie said abruptly. "No matter how much we wish we could do it over."

Hollis felt the doors close and the walls go up between them. The warmth in the room fell away. She was aware of being tired for the first time all day. Annie was not going to so easily forgive her, and that saddened her. "All right. We should talk about the clinic."

"Let's reschedule," Annie said. "You've been up all night and I need to pick Callie up from school in another hour or so. Tuesday?"

"I have office hours in the morning. One o'clock?"

"That sounds—"

Hollis's cell rang and she fished it out of her pocket. "I better get that."

"Of course."

"Monroe."

"Hi, Hollis, it's Patty. Mary Anderson is running a temp of a hundred and four and her blood pressure's a little on the low side. I'm kind of worried about her."

"Is she bleeding?"

"Not much more than I would expect."

"Go ahead and culture her up. Better let the neonatologist know to check the baby for signs of trans-uterine infection. Move Mary into an isolation room. I'll be in to take a look."

"Jerry Moorehouse is on call. I can have him—"

"No, don't bother him. I'll be right over."

"Thanks Hollis, I'm sorry—"

"No problem. I'll be right there." She ended the call and pushed the phone into her pocket. "I'm sorry. I have to go. My patient from this morning is febrile."

"Of course." Annie followed Hollis through the house and out the front door. Hollis's intense expression was distant. She was focused on her patient and barely aware of anything else. "Thanks again for lunch."

Hollis frowned. "Sorry, I—"

"Go, Hollis, go. It's fine."

Hollis took off at a jog. Annie followed more slowly and carefully closed the gate, making sure the latch caught. She had to go back to the hospital too, to get her car, but Hollis was gone by the time she crossed the street into the park. What a strange day she'd had. She'd started out caught up in the fear and uncertainty of that long-ago day when everything in her life exploded. She was still angry, still hurt, at having been forced to start anew, alone. First she'd lashed out at Hollis and then had somehow ended up telling her things she hadn't even told her friends. Hollis was the last person she would ever have dreamed of confiding in, but she had. And she had no idea why.

Chapter Seven

"Cal? Are you ready?" Annie rinsed the cereal bowl and stacked it with her coffee cup and plate in the sink to wash later. Yesterday she'd done the same thing with Hollis—something she hadn't done with anyone since she'd left home. Such a simple activity. Clearing away the remains of a meal. Working together, talking easily, sharing a few moments of daily life.

She'd never had times like those with anyone except her family, and then the activities had been regimented, planned, and ordered. Chores—cleaning, milking, harvesting, cooking, mending, and all the other "girl work" assigned to her—were something to be gotten out of the way because there was always more work to do. She'd wanted to ride the tractor with her brothers when she was eight, but she'd been told that was for the boys. *She* had other work to do with her sisters and her mother. She'd wanted to be outside, working in the hot sun, surrounded by the smell of animals and growing things and life. Instead, she'd spent much of her time inside, venturing out as far as the back porch to hang up the wash or to the kitchen garden to fill a basket with tomatoes and cucumbers and corn for dinner. She'd only escaped living the same life that her mother and her younger sisters led because she had excelled in school. The community valued one of their own learning a necessary skill and had expected her to come home to practice it.

Everything had changed when she'd come to the city and discovered what other women had known for decades—that she wasn't limited to women's work. The world expanded before her very eyes, filled with endless possibility and excitement. She'd been exhilarated and terrified at the same time, a little lost but still determined to see and do everything. Jeff had become her guide, her teacher both literally and figuratively, and she'd never questioned that he might not be what he claimed to be, or what she wanted. Who she wanted. He'd offered her an anchor in a rapidly changing universe, and she'd grasped it only to be cut free when she'd needed him most. Her poor judgment.

"Mommy," Callie said from behind her, "I can't find my sneakers."

Annie put a smile on, quickly dried her hands, and bent down until she was eye to eye with her daughter. "Hmm. I don't think you can go out without your sneakers. That's a long way to walk barefoot."

Callie giggled. "I can't walk anywhere except the backyard with no shoes on. The streets are dirty."

"Well, some of them are. What do you think we should do?"

"Find my sneakers."

"Good idea. When was the last time you remember having them?"

Callie frowned in concentration, the small crease between her reddish gold brows transforming her perfectly angelic face into a fleeting glimpse of what she would look like as she grew older—a gorgeous teenager and a beautiful woman. Annie resisted the urge to scoop her up and squeeze. She couldn't stop time any more than she could turn it back.

"I wore them to school," Callie said with a note of pride.

"You did. I remember that. And what did you do when you got home from school?"

"I sat on the sofa and I watched television and I took off my sneakers."

"Then I think that's where we should start our search."

Five minutes later, Callie was dressed in one of her favorite T-shirts, faded Oshkosh overalls, and her missing sneakers. "I'm ready."

"All right then. Let's take a walk."

The park, Annie had quickly learned, was a meeting ground for the neighborhood, and on Saturday mornings parents gathered there to read the newspapers and drink coffee while the kids played under the safe watch of many communal eyes. Callie already knew most of the children her age from school, and Annie was slowly getting to know everyone by sight. She looked forward to it as a chance to unwind while doing something with Callie. They stopped at a corner grocer at the midpoint of their four-block walk to the park, and Annie purchased a takeout cup of coffee, a newspaper, and a juice for Callie. She hesitated, studying the pastries in a glass cabinet on the counter next to the register. "Are those cranberry scones?"

"They certainly are," the middle-aged proprietor said, her eyes lighting up. "I get them delivered from Principato's bakery, two streets over, fresh every day. You won't find better in the whole city."

"I'll take one—and one of those powdered sugar doughnuts."

"Is that one for me?" Callie asked.

"I don't know. Do you want one?"

Callie laughed. "Sugar are my favorite."

"Then I guess that one will be for you." Smiling, Annie paid the owner, tucked her newspaper under her arm, and handed Callie the bag to carry while she opened the lid of her coffee. Memorial Day weekend had dawned bright and sunny, and the weather report promised temperatures in the low eighties for the next three days with no rain in sight. Perfect weather and she was off call. What could be better. She couldn't think of a single thing she wanted, and yet a trickle of unease shimmered between her shoulder blades, as if she'd forgotten something very important.

Shrugging off the irksome sensation, she found an unoccupied wooden bench in the center of the park halfway around the tiny pond— no bigger than a backyard swimming pool, but big enough for the kids to throw bread to the ducks and launch a boat or two. She opened the newspaper and scanned the headlines, one eye on Callie as she ran to join several children on a nearby swing set. She drank her coffee, read, and people-watched while Callie played. Usually these lazy hours were the most relaxing of her week, but today she couldn't settle. Her body hummed with restless energy and her mind kept jumping back to the disrupted meeting with Hollis and the unexpected lunch that followed. When Callie climbed up next to her on the bench, Annie welcomed the diversion from her own aimless thoughts. She offered Callie half the doughnut. "You ready for this?"

"Yes, please."

Callie leaned against her and Annie slid an arm around her slim shoulders. She folded the paper and set it aside and went back to people-gazing. Her gaze settled on one person and the others faded away.

Hollis Monroe occupied a bench across the pond, her arms spread out along the back of the bench, her head thrown back and canted at a distinctly uncomfortable-looking angle. She had to be asleep because no one would voluntarily assume that position. She was wearing scrubs and must have just come from the hospital. On impulse, Annie stood and held out her hand. "Come on, Cal, let's walk a little bit."

"Okay." Callie jumped down beside her and took her hand, the remnant of the doughnut in her other one.

Annie led the way along the rough stone path that circled the pond until she reached the bench where Hollis slept. She was pale, dark smudges beneath her eyes and fatigue creasing her cheeks. Now that she was there, Annie wasn't certain why she'd come or what she ought to do. She *should* leave Hollis to whatever rest she might be able to get, but Hollis looked so tired and uncomfortable, Annie just couldn't walk away. She gently shook Hollis's shoulder. "Hey. Hollis?"

Hollis jerked and opened her eyes, peering blearily in Annie's direction.

"Hey," Hollis whispered, her voice rusty. She looked around, her confused expression rapidly clearing. She snapped to attention and sat upright. "Annie, hey." She rubbed her face. "How are you?"

"I'm fine," Annie said, laughing softly. "How's your neck?"

Hollis winced and rubbed her neck. "Broken, I think. Thanks for waking me up before I was permanently damaged."

"I hated to do it, but I was a little worried about you."

Annie's words sent an unexpected surge of pleasure through Hollis's chest. She spent her life caring for others and rarely needed and never sought the comfort of others. Her work kept her busy enough to banish the occasional ache of loneliness, but it was nice that Annie was worried about her. She smiled at the gorgeous child by Annie's side, the green eyes that matched her mother's large and curious behind the lenses of her glasses. "Hi. I'm Hollis."

"I'm Callie," the child announced. "You have scrubs like my mommy's. Are you a midwife like her?"

Hollis laughed, the mantle of fatigue falling from her shoulders. She caught Annie's expression of horror and grinned even more. "Well, sort of. I do take care of women who are going to have babies, like your mom."

"Did you have baby call last night?"

"I did." Hollis glanced at Annie.

"Sorry," Annie muttered.

"No problem." Hollis gestured to the bench beside her. "You want to sit?"

"What do you think, Cal? You want to play some more?"

"Can I go back to the swings?"

"I don't think so, honey, it's too far and I won't be able to see you over there."

Callie looked around and her face lit up. "There's Mike. Can I play with Mike?"

"Yes, as long as you stay with Mike and his mother. All right?"

"All right." Callie dashed away and Annie watched her go until she reached Mike and Robin. Robin looked in her direction and waved. Annie waved back, calling, "Thank you."

"She's adorable," Hollis said.

Annie sat and stretched her legs into a patch of sunlight. The heat on her legs trailed up, settling in her middle, and the restless feeling slipped away. "I'm prejudiced, of course, but she is."

"She looks like you."

Annie laughed. "You know the way to a mother's heart."

"I'm being serious."

"She's the best thing in my life."

Hollis nodded. "I can certainly understand that."

"She was so small when she was—well, you know that, don't you."

"I remember. A little over four pounds."

"God," Annie said, "you really do have an amazing memory." Her gaze found Callie, followed her as she ran with Mike.

Annie's pensive expression bordered on sadness and Hollis wondered what memory she'd triggered. "What is it?"

"The first time I saw her, she was in an incubator in the NICU. She had a funny little hat to help keep her warm, a pulse ox taped to her tiny chest, and an IV in her leg. I had to ask one of the nurses if I could hold her."

"I'm sorry that you didn't get a chance to see her right after she was born," Hollis said. "It took her just a second to take her first breath. As soon as I suctioned her, she opened her eyes and took a great big breath. She was beautiful then too."

Annie turned from Callie to meet Hollis's gaze. "I'm glad you remember." She looked away again. "She had some neonatal jaundice and her lungs were a little immature. They think the prolonged oxygen may have contributed to her visual problems. A small price to pay."

Hollis's stomach tightened but she kept her voice even. Preemies often had side effects from the delivery or the supportive therapy. Not her fault, but she felt the responsibility weigh heavily on her all the same. "She's okay with the glasses, though?"

"Yes, she's nearsighted, but the eye docs don't think there'll be any long-term problems other than that."

"I'm glad."

"She never complains. Nothing stops her, and that's all that matters." Annie straightened. "Did you work all night?"

Hollis was coming to recognize the tough set to Annie's shoulders as a sign Annie was putting aside whatever bothered her. Her admiration for Annie grew—she hadn't folded when many faced with even lesser obstacles would have. She didn't imagine Annie needed her to say so, but she wanted to. Instead she said, "I was up most of the night. One of my mothers developed a postpartum infection. Rare, but we still see it. The baby's fine."

"And mom?"

"Much better this morning. I didn't want to leave until the infectious disease people had seen her and we'd gotten her squared away on an antibiotic regimen."

"That's going the extra mile."

Hollis shrugged. "Something like that, you can't take it lightly."

"Have you eaten?"

"Too much coffee to contemplate." Hollis rubbed her stomach, the acid burn reminding her she hadn't slept in almost two days.

"Can I tempt you with a cranberry scone?"

"You could tempt me with the paper bag at this point."

Laughing, Annie extracted the scone along with a napkin and handed it to Hollis. "Here. You need this more than I do."

"Thanks, want to share?"

Annie's lips parted, her quick smile soft and sensuous. "Just a little piece."

Hollis paused, the scone cradled in her palm. Annie's eyes had a faint ring of golden brown around the deep green irises. Sunlight flickered through the trees behind her head and her golden hair glowed. The sounds of children's laughter filtered into her awareness, and she was carried back to a time when the world was fresh and new and filled with possibility. She ached with the memory of long-ago innocence.

"Thanks. I really appreciate it."

Annie took the piece of scone Hollis broke off and nibbled on it. "You should eat the rest of that before I do."

"Oh." Hollis grinned and bit into the scone, instantly moaning with pleasure. "You got this from Principato's, didn't you?"

"From the grocer at the corner of Morris. They got it from Principato's."

"Good to know," Hollis said around another bite. "Fabulous."

"Mom!" Callie raced up with a blond boy right behind her. "We're going to Mike's tomorrow, right?"

"We are." Annie smiled up at Robin. "Hi. Robin, this is Hollis Monroe."

"Hi." Robin held out her hand to Hollis. "We've met, but you probably don't remember me. I'm Robin Henderson, Linda O'Malley's wife. She's a nurse at PMC."

"Of course. I know Linda," Hollis said. "Good to see you again."

Robin pointed across the park to the side opposite Hollis's house. "We're just over there on School House. We're having a neighborhood thing tomorrow about one. You're invited—just follow the noise."

"Uh." Hollis floundered. A neighborhood thing was so far out of her comfort zone, her instant response was to make up an excuse.

Robin must have read her discomfort and added, "Having an escort under three feet in height is not a requirement."

Hollis laughed and glanced at Annie and Callie, both of whom were watching her. Annie had said they were going. She'd know someone, at least. She was probably imagining that Annie seemed anxious for her answer. "Okay. Sure, that sounds great. Thanks."

"Great. See you then." Robin tugged Mike's striped T-shirt sleeve. "Let's go home and make Mommy some tea. What do you say?"

"'Kay."

"We ought to go too." Annie stood and took Callie's hand. "You should try sleeping at home and not on the bench, Hollis."

"I will. Thanks for the scone."

Annie smiled. "Anytime. See you tomorrow."

"Have a great day," Hollis said, watching Annie walk away with Robin and the kids. She couldn't believe she'd just agreed to go to a neighborhood barbecue, and knowing why didn't make it any less crazy. Annie was going to be there, and she wanted to see her again.

CHAPTER EIGHT

The phone rang and Annie checked the clock. She rarely had unexpected calls—she had no family who might suddenly decide to get in touch, no close friends who might ring with an impromptu invitation to go out, and no romantic pursuers who might call for a date. When her phone rang, it was always business. Eight thirty. Callie had been in bed a little while, and she'd just made a bowl of popcorn and picked out a book to read. Saturday night and she had big plans.

"Hello?"

"Annie," Cindy Caprood said apologetically, "I know you're off this weekend, but Donna Drake just called and she's in labor. So is Felicia Simmons."

"It's got to be the full moon. They're both a week early. I'll find a sitter and head over to Donna's."

"I'd try to get there if Felicia moves along, but I know Donna's really counting on you being there."

"That's okay. Your time will come."

Cindy laughed. "Oh, don't I know it, and it'll be three in the morning."

"Would you mind calling her back and telling her I'll be there as soon as I can? They know what to do, and if she's in early stages, she's got plenty of time."

"From the sounds of it, she's not moving that quickly. I'll make sure she calls me if anything changes before you get there."

"Thanks."

Annie rang off and sorted through her list of possibles for emergency childcare. Everyone who helped at short notice was part of her group. JoAnn and Andrea were both on call, so Suzanne was probably her best bet. Even better, she lived around the corner. She called, and Suz answered on the third ring.

"Suz? It's Annie. I've got an emergency."

"No problem. Bring her by. She can stay as long as you need."

"There's a good chance it'll be all night. It's Donna Drake, and even if she delivers before morning, I'll need to stay until I'm sure she and the baby are both settled."

"No problem."

"Listen—I don't know what you've got planned for tomorrow, but I promised Callie I'd take her to the barbecue at Linda and Robin's. If I can't get there—"

"Don't worry. Just pack clothes for her for tomorrow. Dan and I were going anyway."

"Great, thanks. She'll be so disappointed if she doesn't get to go."

"If you need anything else, just give me a call."

"You got it." Annie grabbed the overnight bag she kept packed and stashed in her bedroom closet and added extra clothes for Callie for the next day. Then she wrapped Callie in a travel blanket and scooped her up.

Callie opened her eyes. "Where we going, Mommy?"

"To Suz's."

"Okay." Callie's head drooped against Annie's shoulder and she went back to sleep. She smelled like sunshine and miracles. Annie kissed the top of her head. "I love you, baby. More than anything."

Twenty-five minutes later, Annie pulled into the drive of a single-family Victorian in East Falls, a mile from PMC and three from her apartment. The first- and second-floor lights were blazing. She parked behind the old Volvo wagon, collected her equipment bag from the trunk, and climbed the wide wooden stairs to the porch that wrapped three-quarters around the house. The front door opened before she had a chance to ring the brass doorbell.

"You're here," Donna's husband Mark said with just the barest hint of relief in his voice. Tall and broad-shouldered, he taught math at Textile and had a quiet, understated sense of humor. His dark brown hair was thinning on top, but his still unlined face and faintly rosy cheeks made him look boyish.

"Hi, Mark. The baby decided to make an early appearance, I

understand." Annie smiled and Mark smiled back, his joy warming her.

"We do everything early in our family."

"Do you have the baby kit ready?" Annie followed Mark through the house to the screened-in back porch. Donna and Mark had decided they wanted to give birth outside, or as close to outside as they could get and still have a secure and sanitary place to welcome the baby. She'd given them a list of what they'd need to have ready for the birth a month ago—supplies, clothes for the baby, towels, and linens.

"Everything you asked for is there. If you need anything else—"

"Don't worry. You go be with Donna. I'll take care of the details, that's why I'm here."

Mark and Donna were second-timers—their first child had been born in the hospital, and though they'd had no problems, Donna had found the experience impersonal and a little alienating. They'd made the choice to have this child at home. Donna had no risk factors—she was young and healthy and had normal blood pressure, no familial or personal history of diabetes, no clotting disorders, nothing that might raise a red flag. Still, Annie was always on the lookout for problems so that complications might be avoided before they happened. She'd last seen Donna just a few weeks before, and she'd been progressing perfectly.

"Hi," Annie said, walking out onto the back porch where Mark knelt by a lounger, holding Donna's hand. The night was warm, and Mark had set up a portable heater to keep the area comfortable during the night. Donna, shorter than Mark by almost a foot, had flaming red hair and a spatter of freckles across her nose. Her loose T-shirt, one of Mark's probably, said *College of Textiles* across her breasts. Her rounded belly rested on her thighs, her legs folded as she reclined on the lounger.

"Hi," Donna said slightly breathlessly. "It's good to see you. Thanks for coming."

"Of course. Wouldn't miss it." Annie sat gently on the bottom of the lounger and rested her hand on Donna's belly, lightly palpating the uterus as she talked. "How long have you been having contractions?"

"A little over an hour. My water broke right before that, but we waited to be sure before calling." Donna's face tightened and she took a long, slow deep breath. "I'm sure."

Annie took the BP cuff from her bag and checked Donna's pulse and pressure, then her temperature. "Everything looks just fine. The baby's in good position, so there's no need to hurry. Take your time and breathe through the contractions. If you want to get up and walk around, go ahead."

"I feel like I have to pee every two minutes."

Annie nodded. "That's from pressure on your bladder. Don't worry if you can't. The urgency will go away once you deliver. Are you thirsty?"

"I had some juice a little while ago. I'm okay."

"What about you, Mark? Have you eaten tonight?"

He frowned. "I was about to make supper when Donna felt the first contractions."

"Where's Lizzie?"

"My mother picked her up a while ago," he said. "We thought she was a little too young to be here for the birth."

Donna laughed. "Next time."

He grinned. "That sounds good to me."

Annie stood. "Okay. You two just relax and enjoy this. Mark, I'll hunt around the kitchen and make you something to eat. If you need me, just come and get me."

She left them to enjoy the process in private. They were both well versed in the stages of labor and knew what to expect. Her role was to monitor the labor and birth and anticipate any problems. She was also there to take care of the small things so they wouldn't be distracted during this incredibly important event. She found her supportive role every bit as satisfying as her medical one—for the midwife, it was all the same. She put together a sandwich for Mark from cold cuts she found in the refrigerator and made a cup of tea. She carried both back to the porch. "Here. Tea probably isn't your usual, but I find it relaxing."

"It looks great, thanks." Mark took the food and moved to an adjacent chair, and Annie sat beside Donna again. She rechecked her blood pressure, examined her abdomen, and after donning a sterile glove, did an vaginal exam. "The baby's coming down nicely. You're doing a great job. How do you feel?"

"Good." Donna leaned back and looked out over the yard. The moon had risen above the treetops and glittered brightly in a cloudless sky. "It's a beautiful night."

"It is. It's a beautiful time to be having a baby."

"I'm so glad you're here," Donna said.

"I'm exactly where I want to be." Annie smiled and squeezed Donna's hand. "You're going to have a beautiful baby, and I'm so happy to be part of that."

Annie knew without a single doubt she was doing exactly what she was meant to do. She glanced at Mark, who'd set his dishes aside and was watching his wife with an expression midway between wonder and pride. Annie stood and gestured to the place by Donna's side. "Go ahead and sit with her, Mark. I'll be right here. Don't worry about a thing."

❖

Zachary Allen Drake emerged into his father's waiting hands at 4:32 a.m., just as the sun came up. He had a full head of dark hair and weighed in at seven pounds. When Mark placed him on Donna's breast, he drew his first breath and began to suckle. Annie helped Mark cut the cord and did a rapid assessment of the baby. His lungs were clear, his color good, his suck reflex strong.

"He's perfect." Annie eased toward the foot of the lounger so the two of them could enjoy their new son while she waited for the placenta to be delivered. Once it had been, she put a clean sheet under Donna and cleared away the soaked linens from the birth. That was part of her job too, and she went about it quietly and efficiently so as not to disturb the bonding between the parents and their baby. When everything was squared away, she double-checked Donna's pressure, examined her to be sure there was no excessive bleeding, and packed up her equipment.

"Call me if you have any concerns at all. I'll be back later today to check you both."

"You should get some sleep," Donna said, holding Zachary.

"Don't worry about me," Annie said. "We just had the most wonderful night."

Donna laughed. "We did, didn't we."

"I'll see you later." Annie let herself out and carried her bag to her car. She packed everything away and started for home. On impulse, she detoured to the park and walked to the bench where she had sat yesterday with Hollis. She was tired but not fatigued, and she wanted to enjoy the excitement of the night a little longer.

The park was deserted except for an early-morning runner on the far side of the park. The moon had not yet set and the sun was rising. Mist rose from the tranquil surface of the pond and drifted away in lacy fingers. She loved these moments when day and night intersected, and this morning, with the wonder of birth still filling her, she couldn't help think of the timelessness of life and new beginnings. She thought of Callie, who wouldn't wake for several more hours, and all the possibilities her life would hold. She traced the worn wood along the top of the bench where Hollis had rested her head and wondered if she'd let herself rest. She'd see Hollis that afternoon, and the thought made her heart skitter in a way that was foreign and confounding. Possibility had not been something she'd had growing up, and she'd learned to distrust it as an adult. Normally Callie and her work absorbed all her energy, but Hollis had somehow opened the door to new sensations, and she found she enjoyed not knowing what the day would bring. She'd learned to be cautious, and she would be, especially since Hollis's professional philosophy was so at odds with her own. But she'd only had to spend a few hours with Hollis to see she cared deeply about her patients and took her responsibilities seriously. If they could come to terms with their professional differences, she could imagine having Hollis as a friend. After all, that was simple enough.

❖

Following the murmur of voices and the pealing laughter of children, Hollis tucked the bottle of wine she'd pulled from her pantry under her arm and walked down the driveway next to a sky-blue Victorian with cream detailing. She'd slept twelve hours, cycled around River Drive at dawn, and worked on her porch all morning. She'd considered not going to the barbecue half a dozen times but decided that would be rude. Besides being rude, she wouldn't see Annie. She should see her—they were going to have to find a way to work together, or at least to discuss issues without triggering each other's defenses. A little social interaction on neutral ground wouldn't be a bad thing.

She hadn't looked forward to spending time with a woman since her one long-term relationship had disintegrated. Sonja had left her when she was at her most vulnerable, and the breakup just reinforced her determination to remain unattached. Once in a while she acquiesced to pressure from family or friends and went on a date, but those occasions had dwindled in the last few years too. She'd finally said no to enough people that they'd stopped asking.

Not that she had any thoughts about Annie beyond the professional, but she did like talking to her. She liked seeing her smile. She liked the way she interacted with her daughter. It just felt good to be around her. That was simple enough.

CHAPTER NINE

"A rly, can you check to make sure we packed Jack's truck?" Honor tore off a strip of cling wrap and covered the large orange Fiesta bowl filled with her signature salad. She paused, the air in the room suddenly shifting, warming, carrying the scent of piney woods and spring showers. A tingle of anticipation shot through her. She waited, looking out through the window above the big cast-iron kitchen sink at the huge elm in their backyard, at her children's toys scattered over the lawn, at the small garden she'd planted with Phyllis a few weeks ago. Her life unfolded around her and solidified with the embrace that came when Quinn's arms slid around her middle. Honor settled against Quinn, her butt nestling against the front of Quinn's thighs. "Hi. I thought you were catching up on your reading."

"I was, but I missed you." Quinn kissed Honor's neck. "Jack's dump truck is in the basket with all our other supplies. Are we moving in with Robin and Linda?"

Laughing, Honor tilted her head and kissed Quinn on the side of the mouth. "If we want to have a drama-free afternoon, we have to think ahead."

"Every possible contingency is covered." Quinn tugged on the cling wrap and uncovered part of the salad bowl. Honor slapped her hand when she tried to snag a few macaronis. "Just a little."

"You have to wait."

Quinn nuzzled Honor's neck. "Story of my life."

"Poor you." Honor nipped at the edge of Quinn's jaw. "Tell me it wasn't worth waiting for."

"Oh, more than worth it." Quinn chuckled and ran her hands up and down Honor's sides, slowly turning her until they were face-to-face. "Hi, remember me?"

"You look familiar." Honor's breath hitched and the buzz of anticipation grew heavy in her loins.

"Let's see if I can jog your memory." Quinn pressed forward, capturing Honor between her body and the counter. She kissed Honor's throat and down to the hollow between her collarbones. Honor tasted as pure as sunshine and elusive as moonlight. "I'd wait forever for a moment with you."

Honor spread her fingers through Quinn's hair, holding her to her skin, cleaving to her body. "All the days of my life and beyond. All yours."

"Can we skip the barbecue?"

"I'm afraid not. My salad, remember?"

Quinn opened the buttons on Honor's polo shirt and kissed the soft pale skin between her breasts. "How long do you think we'd have before they came looking for us?"

"An hour?"

"More than enough time." Quinn tugged Honor's shirt from the waistband of her shorts and slipped one hand underneath. She stroked lightly, her thighs tightening when Honor shivered.

"Stop." Laughing, Honor grabbed Quinn's wrist and tugged her hand away. "Not when we have two hungry kids who've been waiting all morning to go to the barbecue."

"Oh, them." Quinn rubbed her cheek over Honor's shirt above her breast and grinned up at her. "Whose idea was that again?"

"You're as responsible as I am."

"Mom?" Arly raced into the kitchen and skidded to a halt. "Geez, you guys. It's not even noon."

"It's one," Quinn said, straightening and surreptitiously lowering Honor's shirt, shielding Honor so she could get herself back together. "Besides, is there some rule about that?"

Arly shoved both hands on her hips and frowned. "I don't know, but there probably ought to be."

Quinn studied her twelve-year-old daughter, trying to decide if she was really upset. Arly was at the age where sex was alternately intriguing and repelling. She and Honor had never made any secret about the nature of their relationship. Still, they tried to be affectionate without exposing the kids to more than they wanted to see.

Arly grinned. "Of course, it probably wouldn't work with you two."

"Enough." Honor lifted the salad bowl and held it out to Arly. "Take this while we collect Jack. Do you have everything you need for this afternoon?"

"I've got my bathing suit, and my iPad, and my phone, and—oh, Quinn, Robin called. You're supposed to bring the volleyball."

"Got it." Quinn kissed Honor quickly. "See you at the car."

Honor watched Quinn leave, still captivated by the tight, powerful lines of her body and the fierce focus in her deep blue eyes. She caught Arly watching her contemplatively. "Does it bother you? When we're affectionate?"

"Mom. Geez."

"Serious question, Arl."

Arly shook her head. "No, why should it? Quinn is cool, and she loves you."

"She loves all of us."

"I know. That's good. I love her too."

The tightness around Honor's heart relaxed. "I know."

"Nick Raymond told me about this party Friday night at Allison Knickerbocker's," Arly said in a rush. "He sort of asked me if I wanted to go."

Honor took the salad from Arly and set it on the kitchen table. She pointed to a chair. "Sit." She pulled out a chair and sat facing her daughter. "What did you tell him?"

"That I'd think about it."

"How old is he?"

Arly fidgeted. "Sixteen."

Honor had an image of Quinn throttling the boy. "So what did you think about it?"

"I thought I better tell you, and if I did you'd say no."

"Chances are the crowd is going to be Nick's age or even older, and that's too old for you. I know you want to have private time with your friends, and getting together with them is fine. But the rules are still the same. I need to know where you are and who you're with and what you're doing, each and every time."

"I know."

"And parties at people's houses with kids who are three or four years older than you are not okay. I'm sorry."

Arly studied her red Converse sneakers. "That's okay. I didn't really want to go anyways. I don't really like him all that much."

"I'm glad you told me, and you'll tell me every time something like this comes up, right?"

Arly nodded, still studying her sneakers. "I'm not sure I like boys."

"Okay."

"What if I like girls?" Arly raised her eyes and met Honor's with a hint of belligerence in the set of her jaw.

Everyone said Arly looked like her, with her blond hair and brown eyes, but there were times when she reminded her so much of Quinn. Her intensity, her strength, her determination. "Is that a problem, honey?"

"Not for me," Arly said.

Honor laughed. "Why would you think it would be a problem for me?"

"Sometimes parents don't want their kids to be like them."

Honor threaded her fingers through Arly's. "What I want is for you to do what makes you happy. What feels right for you. Boys, girls, it doesn't matter to me as long as they treat you right and make you happy."

"To tell you the truth, I'm not all that interested in anybody right now."

"To tell you the truth, I'm just as glad."

Arly jumped up, her worried expression fading. "So can we go to the barbecue now?"

"I think that's a great idea."

❖

"Hey, Hollis. Glad you could make it," Robin said. She wore cut-offs and a white apron adorned with a soccer ball on a skewer above the words *Serve It Up.*

"Thanks. Quite the crowd." Hollis handed Robin the wine she'd snagged from her kitchen on the way out the door. She hadn't thought about bringing anything until then—her social skills were pretty rusty.

The backyard of Robin and Linda's attached twin was crowded with men, women, kids, and dogs. And at least one ferret.

"Help yourself to anything you want. If you need anything, holler."

"Will do." Hollis wandered a few minutes and finally settled on an unoccupied garden bench underneath one of the large maple trees that dotted the yard. Three picnic tables were arranged in a horseshoe and covered with food, buckets of ice, and paper plates and cups. She scanned the gathering and picked out quite a few people she recognized from the hospital, although she didn't know most of their names. She looked again, more carefully, disappointment burning through her. She didn't see Annie. She checked her watch. If she stayed fifteen or twenty minutes, she could sneak out without seeming rude. No one would notice if she left.

"Hey, Hollis," Linda said, pausing with an armload of plastic ware. "Get something to drink—food will be up in a minute. There's alcoholic and non- in the coolers by the tables. Anything you see is fair game."

"Okay, thanks," Hollis said.

Linda waved her fingers and hurried on. Hollis sauntered over to one of the tables and grabbed a Guinness. As the weatherman had promised, the day was clear and hot. Afternoon temperatures in the eighties were expected.

"Hollis—just the person I need," Robin said from behind her.

Hollis turned. "What's up?"

"I need some help stringing this volleyball net. Come on."

"Uh, sure." Hollis followed Robin down the length of the sloping yard to a grassy area on the far side of a big rectangular swimming pool.

"This looks good," Robin said. "You hold one of the poles here and I'll get the other one in opposite you."

"Got it." Hollis gripped the flexible metal pole with the attached net and steadied it against her hip as Robin unrolled the rest of the net and walked twenty feet away. Robin worked the pole into the ground until that end was steady, and then Hollis put the net on some tension and got her end into the ground.

"Good job. Listen," Robin said, "how good are you at volleyball?"

"Huh, I don't know. I haven't played since high school, and it wasn't really my game then."

"But you've played before?"

"Like I said—about a million years ago."

"Well, that's about a million years more recent than most of the people here. You're on my team."

"Actual—"

Before Hollis could protest or come up with a plausible excuse, Robin was already powering around the yard, tapping people on the shoulder. It appeared she was going to have to play volleyball.

Forty minutes later, her T-shirt was soaked, her hair was matted to her neck, and their side was up two points. Robin was relentless, coaching the team with a combination of enthusiasm and dire predictions as to what might happen if they lost. Mostly it sounded like no one would get anything to eat if they weren't victorious, and at the moment, that was inspiration enough. Hollis was starving.

The serve came her way, she set the ball, and Quinn spiked it for a point. Robin yelled, "One more point." Kids ran around the perimeter of the court, cheering on their parents. Hollis heard her name called and glanced to her right. Callie, in a bright yellow sundress and green sneakers, waved and Hollis grinned.

"Hey, Callie." She looked for Annie but didn't see her. "Where's your—" A hard thud against her temple knocked her off balance and she went down. She rolled onto her back and tried to figure out what had just happened. The grass smelled sweetly of crushed clover and white fluffy clouds swirled overhead.

"Holy crap!" Robin leaned over her. "You really got nailed. You okay?"

"Yeah, I think so. I guess I should've been watching the game." Hollis rubbed her temple and felt a tender area as big as a lemon above her left eye. "Smarts."

"Hey, Hollis," Honor said, kneeling on her other side. "That was pretty impressive. Except I think when you hit the ball with your head you're supposed to be aiming for it to go back over the net. Or maybe that's soccer. How's your vision?"

"All systems go." Hollis pushed up to a sitting position. "Really, I'm fine. I just got caught by surprise, that's all."

"Well, we better put some ice on it." Honor cupped Hollis's chin and tilted her face up, studying her intently. "I think you're going to have a shiner."

"Oh, that's ridiculous." Hollis pushed to her feet and swayed, a little bit dizzy.

"Whoa." Robin grasped her arm. "You sure you're okay?"

"Yeah, really, I am." Hollis felt like an idiot, happy now that Annie wasn't there. How uncool could she be?

"Well, at least sit in the shade and I'll get some ice," Robin said.

"No, I can get it. You have a game to win." Hollis gave Robin a little push toward the field. "I don't want everybody on our side to go hungry just because I wasn't paying attention."

"If you're sure," Robin said.

"I'm sure. Really, I'm fine." Hollis hurried off the field so the game could continue and spied Callie staring at her with an uncertain expression. She knelt down beside her. "Hi, Callie. I wasn't watching the game and I got smacked with the ball, but I'm okay."

"It knocked you down."

"Yeah, it did."

"Does it hurt?"

"Well, it stings a little bit, but it'll be fine. Where's your mom?"

"She had a baby call last night. I stayed with Suzy and Dan and Gillian and Mark. I came with them."

"Having fun?"

"Yes. I'm going swimming soon."

"That's great." The wave of disappointment was back, stronger than before. Hollis didn't know what to make of it. She liked Annie and looked forward to seeing her, but the intensity of her reaction wasn't like her. "I'm going to go get some ice. You have a good time today, okay?"

"Okay."

Hollis found an empty lounge chair and, after securing a few ice cubes in a plastic bag, stretched out and pressed the makeshift cold compress to her forehead. It helped with the sting, but not the embarrassment. She couldn't believe she'd let herself get smacked by the ball. Her head throbbed, but she actually felt pretty good. The exertion had been a welcome switch-up from her usual workout on the bike, and she'd enjoyed being part of the team. She closed her eyes and drifted in the sunshine. When a weight on the lounge signaled someone had settled beside her, she opened her eyes. Annie smiled down at her. Hollis's heart gave a little jog.

"Hi," Hollis said.

"Hi yourself." Annie pushed the cold compress away from Hollis's forehead and studied her seriously. "Callie told me you got hurt. Are you all right?"

"I'm not really hurt," Hollis said hastily, dropping the icepack on the grass by the chair. She pushed her damp hair out of her face. "Just a silly accident. Nothing much."

"Hmm," Annie said, lightly tracing the bruise on Hollis's face. "I think you might be understating things. You've got a lump on your forehead and your upper eyelid is starting to turn purple."

Hollis held very still. She didn't want Annie to stop stroking her. The light caress sent tendrils of heat streaming through her. "All from a friendly backyard game."

Annie laughed. "I've been watching some of that game. If I didn't know they were all friends, I wouldn't believe it. Talk about competitive."

"Well, I guess you have to consider the crowd. Pretty much everybody here is competitive by nature."

"I'm glad it's not more serious." Annie dropped her hand and leaned away. "Have you had anything to eat?"

"I didn't get around to it before Robin commandeered me to play."

"I was just about to fix myself and Callie a plate. I'll get you one too. Anything you can't eat?"

"No, believe me, anything you bring will be welcome." Hollis rubbed her stomach. "I'm actually starving."

"Me too."

"Callie told me you got called out last night. Were you up all night?"

"Not quite," Annie said noncommittally. "I got a little sleep this morning."

"Just another typical Saturday night, then," Hollis said.

Annie nodded. "I guess you know what that's like."

"Oh, absolutely. I can have the quietest week in the world, but as soon as Friday afternoon comes around, it gets busy. Babies just seem to know when the sun goes down, especially if it's a weekend."

"You've got that right." Annie stood abruptly. "Well, let me get you that food."

Hollis watched her wend her way through the crowd to the table, take plates from a stack, and start filling them, quickly and efficiently. No one ever waited on her unless she was home. No one worried if she'd had enough sleep or enough to eat or had a chance to decompress after a big case. She liked things that way and hadn't missed it. Until now, when Annie reminded her how nice it was to have someone who cared.

CHAPTER TEN

Annie stared at the plate. She'd piled nine chicken wings onto it without even noticing. Glancing around, relieved no one was watching, she redistributed the wings between the three plates. She'd examined hundreds of patients in her life—women she cared about, women she'd come to love—and she'd never felt anything like the brief brush of her fingers over Hollis's forehead. Heat as bright as summer lightning had flashed through her hand, up her arm, and struck somewhere around her heart. Her body still pulsed. The dark blue depths of Hollis's eyes still threatened to pull her under. She was afraid to think of what her reaction meant. Her mind conjured answers, but her emotions, her heart, recoiled from the obvious explanation. She had no experience with something so simple that moved her so much. She'd thought she'd understood passion and desire and love when she'd been with Jeff, and she'd learned the hard way she'd been totally wrong. Now she didn't trust anything she felt, especially when she had no good reason to feel that way about someone she wasn't even sure she knew. When she looked at Hollis she saw two women—the one from her past who was tangled up in disillusionment, disappointment, and overwhelming loss, and the other, a stranger she had just met who stirred her in ways that defied common sense. Both Hollises were dangerous, and she vowed to be more careful about crossing boundaries.

"Mommy?" Callie tugged at Annie's hand. "Are we going to have potato salad? And what about corn? And Jell-O?"

"Jell-O definitely—after dinner." Annie stroked the red-gold waves that fluttered around Callie's innocent face. She'd do anything to preserve her trust and faith, even though she knew she couldn't protect her innocence forever. "And yes—salad and corn too. Come here."

Callie lifted her arms and Annie scooped her up. "Can you reach the big spoon? You put the salad on the plates."

Callie carefully scooped salad onto the three big red plastic plates.

"Excellent." Annie set Callie down and finished filling the plates. "Here's yours."

"Can I go eat with Mike and Jack and Sandy?"

Annie searched for Callie's friends. Robin and Linda sat at a big picnic table with a handful of children not far from where Hollis stretched out on the lounge. "Yes, but don't leave that table. I'll be right over there with Hollis."

"Okay." Callie hurried away, her plate balanced carefully out in front of her.

Annie started toward Hollis, her face warming when she realized Hollis was watching her, a somber, intent expression on her face. Annie felt exposed and didn't know why. She smiled and put on her sociable face. "I hope you're as hungry as you said."

Hollis smiled too, but her eyes held questions. Fleetingly, Annie wondered if Hollis could see through her mask of confidence and polite distance. Everyone else accepted her self-sufficient, self-assured façade so readily. Hollis made her feel naked, as if her innermost thoughts and feelings were displayed on her face like images on a big blinking billboard. She was alternately uncomfortable and attracted to the sensation of being so open. So seen. Searching for something to distract Hollis's unwavering focus from her, she gestured to the plate. "I went a little overboard."

"Good." Hollis sat up straighter and put her legs on either side of the lounge chair, making room for Annie. "I'm starved."

When Annie sat, she was very nearly in Hollis's lap, but she couldn't think of a good way to change position without making it obvious. So she carefully kept her bare knee away from Hollis's leg, even though Hollis wore jeans and probably wouldn't notice the glancing contact. *She* would notice. Just being this close to Hollis had electrified her to the point she feared sparks would dance from her skin.

"I didn't get us anything to drink," Annie said, putting her plate on the grass. She had to move. "I'll go get something now."

Hollis grasped Annie's arm. "Stay, it's my turn to hunt and gather. What would you like? Beer, wine…?"

"Just sparkling water, or if they don't have that, any kind of diet soda." Annie's muscles turned to stone—she couldn't move now if she'd wanted to. And she didn't, even though her head screamed *Run*. Hollis's fingers were strong and warm. The slight pressure from her fingertips harnessed all the errant electricity racing through Annie's body and sent it streaking straight to the pit of her stomach. The tingling in her depths blurred her reason, and all she knew was she didn't want it to end.

"You don't drink?" Hollis asked, her fingers loosely clasping Annie's wrist.

"No." Annie stared at Hollis's hand. No one had touched her so intimately in years, and Hollis didn't even know what she was doing. Annie gently drew her arm away. "Or smoke. Although I pretty much indulge in all the other taboos—dancing, music, fornication."

Hollis regarded her solemnly. "I thought your…sorry, I don't know the term."

"Community is good. Or sect."

"I thought your community was less restrictive than the Amish."

"In general, yes, but religious communities tend to become isolated, and as they do, they also become more insular. Ours was a community of only a few hundred people, and the elders were very rigid about many things, including gender roles. Women were meant for bearing children and tending to their men's needs."

"It must have been frustrating," Hollis said.

Annie laughed softly, surprised. "That's the first time anyone's ever put it that way. I don't talk about it very much—what's the point? The few people who know have tried to understand, but most of the time I get the feeling they're more repulsed. And silently blaming—as if I should have rebelled sooner."

"I don't feel that way," Hollis said. "I can see how much you've accomplished, and I can only imagine what it must have been like for someone as bright and outgoing and eager to make a contribution as you to be held back. I'm glad you found your way."

Annie looked away, her throat tight. If Hollis only knew how badly she'd lost her way, she wouldn't be so kind. But she didn't want to tell her of the mistakes she'd made. "I wish I were the person you seem to think I am."

"What part did I get wrong?" Hollis asked softly.

"I wasn't strong or smart or even brave. I was naïve, senselessly innocent. And, I'm a little ashamed to admit, overwhelmed by the world when I finally realized how much there was of it."

"You can't blame yourself for that. You didn't have a chance to prepare. Anybody would be off balance."

"Yes, but most people wouldn't have lost all sense of reality. I ended up grasping at the first anchor I could find—just to keep my balance. My foolishness, my weakness, could have cost me everything."

Hollis put her plate aside. "What do you mean?"

Sighing, Annie sought Callie sitting at the table with the other children. She was laughing, a white plastic fork in one hand and a pink tumbler filled with milk in her other. She was bright and joyful and miraculous. "I met a man and thought I was in love."

Hollis followed Annie's gaze, saw Callie with the other children. "Callie's father."

"Yes," Annie said, swinging her gaze to Hollis's. Meeting her eyes directly. "He was one of my teachers."

Hollis clamped her jaws together, keeping back an oath. She could only imagine how lost Annie must have felt, coming from an environment where she'd had no choices, no exposure to men except in rigidly controlled circumstances. "And you fell in love with him."

"I thought I had," Annie said, no bitterness in her tone, only resignation. "I know now what I really felt was need and gratitude— that a man like him would pay attention to someone like me—"

"Someone like you?" Hollis couldn't keep quiet. "You're kidding, right? You're beautiful. You're bright and warm and sexy. Who wouldn't be attracted to you?"

Annie blushed, a smile racing across her full red lips. "Well. I don't believe he ever actually said any of those things to me."

"Then he should have."

Annie laughed softly and some of the sadness left her eyes. "He showed me things, took me places I'd never imagined. So when he wanted to show me physical things, it seemed natural."

Hollis struggled to ignore the sinking sensation spreading through her. She'd never had any explicit reason to think Annie was a lesbian, but she'd let her own attraction make her think that was the case. She'd been attracted to straight women on occasion, but rarely. It wasn't a matter of physical appeal, but more one of personality. Subtle differences in desires and expectations always seemed to come through, but this time, she'd read the signals wrong. She put her own disappointment aside. This wasn't about her or what she wanted or hoped or didn't. This was about Annie. "Seems pretty natural to me, to be physically attracted to someone who's taken an interest in you and shown you new things, new experiences."

"I suppose," Annie said pensively. "It never occurred to me—not once—that I wouldn't want to be with a man when the time was right. Those things just aren't spoken of in our community."

"You mean being gay?"

"Yes. It never occurred to me I was a lesbian. And then I met Jeff and…well, I made quite a few mistakes." Annie laughed ruefully. "But I learned a lot too. I have Callie, I know who I am, and I know not to make the same mistakes again."

"When did you realize you were a lesbian?" Hollis asked, the weight of disappointment melting away.

"Not for several years after Callie was born. Several of my colleagues are gay, and when I saw some of my patients with their partners, I saw a different life than I'd ever imagined—one that wakened something in me. I realized the reason I felt so comfortable with them, so attuned, was because I was like them. So then I knew and another piece fell into place for me."

"Like I said," Hollis said softly, "you're amazing."

"You still think that, even after I told you this story?"

"Even more so."

"Thank you."

"I don't deserve any thanks. You did all the hard stuff."

"All the same—" A roll of thunder broke overhead and Annie looked up. "Uh-oh."

Huge black thunderclouds raced toward them from the east, obliterating the sun.

Someone yelled, "Storm coming," and a jagged bolt of lightning split the sky.

Annie jumped up and headed for Callie. Hollis barely made it to her feet before gigantic raindrops started pelting her. Within seconds, sheets of water poured down on them. Parents raced to find their kids, thunder roared, and lightning cracked. Hollis ran straight for Annie, who had Callie in her arms, and grabbed a beach towel off the back of an unoccupied chair on the way. She swung it around Annie's shoulders and over Callie's head. Wrapping her arm around Annie's shoulders, she yelled, "Follow me."

She led them toward the pool house, which was the closest shelter that wasn't a tree. Most everyone else had run for the house or the nearby garage. Hollis pushed open the door of the small shed, and they crowded into the twelve-foot-square space next to the pool equipment and shelves filled with neatly stacked containers of chemicals. She flipped the light switch, but nothing happened. "Power's out."

Another crack of thunder seemed to rattle the structure around them.

"Mommy," Callie said, her voice wavering, "I'm scared."

Annie brushed damp hair from Callie's face and stood with her in the open doorway. "It's okay, baby. It's just a big rainstorm. Sometimes when it rains this hard it thunders really loud. We're safe inside here." She used the towel to dry Callie's face and arms. When she was done, she handed it to Hollis. "It's pretty soaked. But you might be able to dry your hair a little bit."

"Thanks." Hollis briskly toweled her hair. Her T-shirt was beyond help—wet through and plastered to her in waterlogged folds. She wasn't concerned about being wet, though—she was too absorbed with Annie.

Annie's hair lay in ringlets along her cheeks and neck, and when a flash of lightning illuminated her face, her profile resembled that on a cameo carved from ivory. Her pale green top clung to her breasts and the arch of her collarbones, an eloquent invitation for fingers to follow their delicate curves. She was so beautiful Hollis's chest ached.

Annie turned away from the storm, her expression questioning. "Are you all right?"

"I'm good," Hollis said, though the brisk wind blowing through the open door raised goose bumps on her skin. "You're soaking wet, though." She used the driest corner of the towel to blot the water from Annie's face and the angle of her jaw. Annie's lips parted and her pupils flickered as Hollis leaned close. "Better?"

"Yes, thanks," Annie said, her voice husky.

Callie wriggled in Annie's arms. "I want to get down now. I want to watch the lightning."

"All right. Just stay right next to me." Annie kept one hand on Callie's head but her gaze locked on Hollis. "I appreciate you getting us to shelter."

"You're welcome," Hollis whispered, backing up a step, the towel clenched in her fist. Beyond Annie's shoulder, the sky lightened. "It's letting up."

"Yes. These summer storms never last long."

"No." Hollis hoped it kept raining. Nothing in the world outside this small cocoon had ever made her feel so alive.

Annie turned away and leaned outside, angling her head to check the sky. "I need to get her home and dried off before another wave comes through." She took Callie's hand. "Come on, baby."

"Right," Hollis said following her out into the light drizzle. Annie dashed across the yard toward the drive, and Hollis shoved her hands into her pockets, shivering in the cool breeze.

CHAPTER ELEVEN

At eight a.m. Tuesday morning, Annie drove to Kathy Murphy's home in West Mt. Airy, a short ten-minute drive from her apartment. Kathy still had almost four months to go before she delivered her second child. Today was a routine checkup. Annie liked seeing patients in their homes—the mother-to-be was most relaxed and confident in the familiar setting, and that safety helped ground the entire birth process in a positive light, from the progression of the pregnancy through delivery and aftercare. Kathy was waiting on the front porch in a white wooden swing hung from colorful braided ropes set in the ceiling, her five-year-old by her side and an open children's book covering their laps.

"Hi," Kathy called, smiling brightly. Her daughter Grace waved enthusiastically as Annie came up the walk.

"Hi." Annie smiled and waved back to Grace. "Beautiful morning."

"Isn't it? I love this time of year," Kathy said. "It's a great time to be pregnant."

Annie laughed. "That's the spirit. How is everything?"

"Fine. Well, almost." Kathy frowned for a second and pointed to her feet. "All except for that. I was hoping not to see that again until closer to the end. It's not even June yet and I'm swelling."

Annie kept her expression neutral as she glanced at Kathy's ankles. Both were swollen for several inches above the joint. Pedal edema was common in the last several months of pregnancy when the pressure in the abdomen from the expanding uterus and growing fetus impaired the return of blood and lymph from the lower extremities. Six months was early to begin seeing this much fluid collecting, though, and could signal problems. Annie settled onto the swing on the other side of Grace. "When did you start seeing it last time?"

"Oh, not much to notice until almost the last month, I guess." Kathy closed the picture book and lifted Grace down to the floor. "Honey, Nana's in the kitchen. I think she might like your help with breakfast, okay?"

"Okay." Grace scampered into the house.

"How have you been feeling otherwise?" Annie asked.

"A little more tired than I remember being with Grace, but then I didn't have a five-year-old to keep me running, and I'm five years older." Kathy laughed. "I can't go all day like I used to—I have to take a nap."

"Believe me, I know what you mean." Annie chatted with her for a few minutes about Kathy's family and her husband's new job and then said, "Let's go inside so I can check you over. I want to get a couple of blood tests too, just to make sure the swelling isn't going to give us problems down the road."

"Okay," Kathy said.

Annie went back to her car and got her med kit. Inside, she followed Kathy upstairs to the bedroom, checked her pressure and vital signs, listened to her heart and lungs, and drew blood samples for chemistries. "I'll call you when I get the results, otherwise I'll see you next month. Is the same time good for you?"

"I'm not planning on going anywhere," Kathy said. "Just have them call like they did the last time, a couple of days in advance." She patted her belly. "We'll be here."

"Then so will I."

After making a few more house calls, Annie drove to the birthing center to see patients scheduled for ultrasounds or other tests. She finished at eleven thirty and went to her small cubicle in the staff area to write up her notes. She checked her watch. Eleven forty-five. She'd be seeing Hollis at one.

She set her pen down on the open chart. No, she wasn't meeting Hollis today. She was meeting Dr. Monroe. She had to keep that in mind. As charming and surprisingly sweet as Hollis could be, their relationship had to remain strictly professional. What they needed to accomplish was too important to complicate with personal feelings, especially since Dr. Monroe was very likely to be more an adversary than the woman who had listened to her so intently two days before. Hollis had almost made her believe her experience with Jeff had been more a triumph than the disaster she'd always thought it to be.

She couldn't forget that Hollis and doctors like her often needed convincing that midwifes were capable and competent and had an important role to play in the care of women and their children—at the very least. Some were blatantly hostile. Annie closed her eyes and rubbed her temples. She really ought to call Barb and tell her she was the wrong person for this job. She didn't want to collaborate with OB doctors to begin with, and now she had to deal with someone who tangled her up inside and made her forget what had always been a clear and certain path.

"Headache?" Barb asked from behind her.

Annie jumped and spun around on her chair. "No—just thinking."

Barb leaned against the partition separating Annie's space from the two adjoining work areas. They were both empty at the moment. As the administrative director, Barb had an office of her own down the hall. She was dressed as usual in pressed pants and a crisply ironed shirt, low heels, and no jewelry other than her wedding ring and watch. In her mid-forties, she was an avid proponent of advancing the rights of midwifes to train and practice independently. Knowing Barb believed as passionately as she did in the cause helped Annie accept that sometimes compromise was a necessary step toward achieving a goal.

"Anything to report on the task force?" Barb asked.

"Not yet," Annie said. "We got…sidetracked on Friday and are meeting again today. I have to say, though, Barb, I'm still not convinced this is a good idea. So few of our patients ever need referral, I don't see why—"

"Last month when St. Vincent's closed in Manhattan," Barb reminded her, "thirteen New York City midwifes lost the legal right to practice because they had no physician group willing to support them in an emergency. It might be a matter of paperwork now, but we can't be caught in a position like that. We need to build our bridges now to secure our practice."

"Maybe instead of spending our efforts getting the support of a group that looks down on us, we should be publicizing the data that shows we provide better, safer care for pregnant women."

Barb sighed. "You know statistics are just numbers that show general outcomes. They can't be applied to every physician. There are plenty of wonderful OBs. We don't want to tarnish them any more than we want them to dismiss us."

"I know." Annie pushed her hair out of her eyes and ran her fingers through the thick strands. "I know. You're right. Honestly, I do understand. It just makes me so angry."

"And I understand that." Barb squeezed Annie's shoulder. "But you're the one I want on this. Let me know if this doctor looks like she's going to be an obstacle. We're not completely without resources, you know. The chairman over there is behind us, and if I have to, I'll put some pressure on him to get his people to fall in line."

"I'll let you know how it goes. Hopefully we won't have to go there," Annie said. The idea of putting pressure on Hollis or going behind her back made her instantly uncomfortable, and that was another of her problems. She couldn't be worried about Hollis when she should be focused on what she needed to accomplish.

"I'll let you get back to work," Barb said. "Remember, my door is always open."

"Thanks." Annie turned back to her desk and picked up her pen. She had work to do. Then she had a meeting with Dr. Monroe. She just needed to keep thinking of Hollis that way and everything would be fine.

❖

Hollis finished clinic only twenty-five minutes late and grabbed a couple of hot dogs from the street vendor outside the hospital on her way to her office. She had half an hour before Annie was due to arrive for their meeting. Whenever she'd had a minute between patients, she'd thought about Annie. She'd had a restless night, remembering standing in the rain with her, talking about things she never talked about, wanting to know more about Annie than she had any other woman, even Sonja.

Annie's story humbled and inspired her. Listening to Annie, trying to imagine her life, she'd realized as never before how lucky she had been. She'd grown up in a family where anything was possible. Even though she'd been the only girl, she'd never felt there was anything she couldn't do, and she'd never gotten the message from her parents or her brothers she shouldn't try because she was a girl. Rob had been the oldest, her role model, and he'd been as tough on her as he'd been on their four brothers. He'd been good at everything—the golden boy who never let his success tarnish his glow. He'd been second in his class, prom king, a star athlete. He'd married the prom queen right out of high school, as his father before him had done, and like his father, he'd joined Engine Company 447.

She'd wanted to be just like Rob. She'd had to play harder to keep up, and work harder sometimes, because everything was so clear for the boys. They grew up knowing who they were and who they would become—they'd be firefighters like their father, or police officers like their cousins, and none of them had wanted to be anything else. She could have been a firefighter—her father might have wanted her to pursue a safer career but he would have supported her if that's what she'd wanted. But she'd wanted something else and that had been all right too.

"Go for it, Hol, you can do it," Rob had said, and she'd believed him.

Annie hadn't grown up with many choices, but somehow she had found herself and her way. The price she'd paid had been steep, the path plagued with pain and disillusionment. Listening to Annie tell her story, Hollis had wanted to go back in time and change the young Annie's first experiences with a world she hadn't known existed. She *still* wanted that. She wanted to be the one to take Annie to the theater for the first time, and walk with her along the river at sunset, and watch her laugh at the antics of the ducks chasing bits of bread thrown by children in the park. She wanted to be the one who showed her how much there was to life, even though she knew that wasn't possible. She'd dealt with tragedy enough to know one could only go forward. The past was written and couldn't be unwritten, no matter how much she wanted to. Sighing, she walked into the office. This was her world, the one she had made, the one she knew.

Sybil gave her a quizzical look. "Problems?"

"What? No," Hollis said.

"So." Sybil's eyebrow shot up and she pointed to Hollis's face. "What happened to you?"

Hollis grimaced. "Volleyball."

"I don't know what I find more surprising," Sybil said. "That you were playing volleyball or that you managed to get hit by one."

"Ha ha." Hollis set the hot dogs down, picked up her mail, and leafed through it. "Freak accident. We were winning."

"Of course you were." Sybil smothered a smile. "Anything happening in clinic?"

"Nope. Everything's routine for a change."

"Okay." Sybil picked up an old-fashioned steno pad Hollis didn't think they even made any longer. Sybil probably had a private stash. "Medical records called about some overdue discharge summaries—I put them on your desk."

"I'll do them."

"Today, please."

"Right."

"Larry Anderson called from University, and they want you to do OB-GYN grand rounds there next month. I told them it would have to be the last weekend because you were full otherwise."

"Okay," Hollis said absently, tossing drug promotions in the trash and signing office copies of operative notes she'd dictated. "Remind me to pull slides that Wednesday."

Sybil made a note. "The chart you wanted me to get is on your desk too." She paused. "That's the same Annie Colfax you're meeting with in fifteen minutes?"

Hollis squared the paperwork she'd just signed and placed the neat stack in front of Sybil. "Yes. That's her. Thanks for pulling the chart."

"I didn't read it, by the way."

Sighing, Hollis rolled her shoulders to ease the sudden tightness. "She was a patient of mine briefly, four years ago. Emergency C-section."

"You know, it's not that much of a coincidence. You've got a lot of patients in the medical field. They know the score—it's only natural they'd want the best."

Hollis smiled ruefully, wondering what choice Annie would make today. Another thing she hadn't been able to choose. No wonder she was angry. "Thanks. You can send her in when she gets here."

"Of course." Sybil made a face at the hot dog bag leaking a faint orange substance. "Go eat your lunch. Those things are deadly enough when they're hot."

"I'm on it." Hollis carried the offending objects into the other room and settled behind her desk. Annie's chart sat alone by her right hand. She pulled it in front of her and stared at the closed manila folder with the plastic numerals along the side—Annie's patient number spelled out in six multicolored digits. She knew what was in the chart. She remembered examining Annie, remembered making the incision and lifting Callie from Annie's open uterus, and the bleeding that she couldn't stop. The bleeding that she'd been certain wouldn't stop unless she did something about it, and quickly. She didn't open the folder. She picked up the phone instead.

"Dr. Ned Williams's office, may I help you?"

"It's Hollis Monroe. Is he there?"

"Oh hi, Hollis, no, he—wait a minute, he just came in. Hold on."

"Hey, Hollis," Ned said. "You didn't miss much yesterday—barbecue got rained out."

"Yeah, it was some storm." The roll of thunder played in Hollis's head again and suddenly she was running with her arm around Annie, Annie's breast against her side, soft and warm. A surge of desire rose out of nowhere and she caught her breath. She'd only wanted to protect Annie and Callie, that's all. Memories played tricks sometimes, nothing more.

"What's up?" Ned asked. "Hollis?"

Hollis pulled herself out of the storm. "I need a favor."

"Sure."

"I'd like you to review a case for me."

"Litigation?"

"No. I just want a second opinion on the management."

"Sure? Who's the doc?"

"Me."

Ned was silent for a beat. "Okay. Mind telling me why?"

"It was a long time ago and I'd just like a second pair of eyes." The explanation was weak, but Ned was a friend and he wouldn't push. She didn't doubt her treatment then or now, but she suspected Annie did. And that ate at her. Maybe clearing the air on this once and for all was the first step toward working together. Or...anything else.

"Well, bring it around. I'll look through it in the next day or so."

"I appreciate it. Thanks, Ned." The second line rang. "I've got another call."

"I'll call you when I've had a look."

"Appreciate it." Hollis switched to her other line. "Hi, Sybil."

"Ms. Colfax is here."

Hollis slid Annie's chart onto the bottom of the stack, out of sight. "Thanks. Send her in."

CHAPTER TWELVE

Linda set her protein shake aside and picked up the ringing phone in the flight ready room. "Linda O'Malley. Go ahead."

"This is State Trooper Anthony Alaqua. We need transport for a twenty-five-year-old female, motorcycle versus truck."

Linda ignored the fluttering in the pit of her stomach. She hated motorcycle call-outs even more than the usual MVAs. The carnage wrought by machine versus man was so often devastating. But medevac runs were usually for major traumas or other life-threatening situations, and she was used to the shock of human tragedy by now. Still, she sometimes wondered if the horrors didn't leave some invisible scar on her soul. Beside her, the printer spat out the location and details of the accident, logged in at the site electronically by the first responder, and she pushed the pointless musings aside. This was what she did, and she wouldn't change it no matter the cost. "The coordinates are coming through now. Estimated flight time is twenty minutes."

"Good. We already have one DAS."

The roiling in her stomach surged. One dead at scene. Not just a minor bump and slide, then. "We'll push it."

"Roger that. Out."

Linda hung up, grabbed the printout, and hurried across the lounge to the closed on-call room door. She knocked sharply. "Jett? We need to roll."

The door opened and Jett McNally, the chief helicopter pilot, scrubbed a hand through her thick sandy hair. She'd been on shift six hours and had flown four times. She'd probably been catching a nap. "I heard the phone. What have we got?"

"Motorcycle accident. One to transport." Linda scanned the details. "Looks like head injury and multiple extremity fractures. Her vitals are shaky."

Jett's full lips thinned and her jaw tightened. "Okay. Wheels up in two. Rally the troops."

"Right. We'll meet you up there."

Jett, lanky and lean, yanked her flight suit off a hook in the cubby by the door and pulled it on over her black jeans and tight T-shirt. From the back she looked like a young guy, and she moved like a practiced soldier. She zipped up, grabbed her helmet, and disappeared. Linda liked and trusted all the helicopter pilots, but she secretly preferred flying with Jett. Unlike the others, who had come from civilian sectors, Jett had seen combat in Iraq and Afghanistan, and she was unflappable in an emergency. Linda loved being a flight nurse, but emergency medevac choppers often flew into unstable situations due to weather or terrain, and she flew easier knowing her pilot could handle anything. Especially now, with the baby coming. She pressed her hand to her abdomen, the fluttering settled a little, and she checked the on-call list hanging on the board behind the STAT phone. Good. Sammie Chu and Dave Burns, two of the easiest-going and solid members of the flight team, were up for trauma and anesthesia. After paging them with the code to report to the flight deck, she zipped into her own royal blue flight suit. The form-fitting suit was getting tight in the middle. She didn't have too many flights left. As she collected the rest of her gear, the exhilaration of heading into the unknown caught her once again, and she headed for the elevator to the rooftop flight deck with nothing on her mind but the upcoming call.

When she reached the roof, Jett was beside the big EC145 Eurocopter with a clipboard in her hand, completing her preflight check. She shot Linda a thumbs-up and climbed into the cockpit. The rear double doors slid open, and Linda stepped aboard, settled into the pull-down seat behind Jett, and strapped in. The engine roared to life and the overhead rotors turned, caught, and whirled. The belly of the chopper trembled like a beast on a chain, hungry for freedom. Linda peered out the open bay doors and watched a short, thickset man with a bullet-shaped, shaved head and a taller brunette in hospital greens sprint across the tarmac. Not yet noon and heat shimmered off the black surface like fingers of fire. Dave Burns, the nurse anesthetist on flight call, and Sammie Chu, the senior trauma fellow, clambered aboard at the same time.

"Hiya, what we got?" Sammie asked in her deep alto, the Texas twang still evident in her voice despite six years at PMC. She took the other half of the double seat next to Linda and pulled on her helmet.

"Motorcycle victim." Linda passed Sammie the field report.

"Hello, summer," Dave said and dropped into a jump seat across from Linda and Sammie.

Jett's voice came over the comm channel. "Flight crew, make ready. Wheels up in twenty seconds."

"All clear," Linda said into the mic in her helmet.

Everyone settled back, the doors closed, and the chopper lifted off.

Linda watched out the window as Jett made a lazy circle over the hospital and then arrowed northeast toward Route 309, the site of many of their vehicular call-outs, especially during the summer season. Eighteen minutes later, the crash scene came into view—a clot of vehicles blocking the northbound lanes. Fire trucks, police cruisers, and ambulances had all converged in a ring across the three-lane. A pickup truck was canted onto the median, its front end crushed, the hood popped open and steam billowing out as firefighters coated it in flame-retardant foam. Some distance away, dark skid marks snaked up the highway to where a big touring motorcycle lay on its side. A blue tarp covered a shapeless mound twenty feet farther down the road. A clump of people gathered nearby, presumably tending to the survivor.

A state trooper waved a flashlight, directing Jett to a makeshift landing site on the highway, and the helicopter descended, touching down with the barest of jolts despite the winds that had picked up as they'd flown.

"Clear," Jett signaled over the radio channel.

Linda released her safety belt and grabbed the med kit. Sammie and Dave grabbed their gear boxes, and they all climbed out and raced toward the circle of emergency responders.

Several people moved aside and Linda and Dave knelt by the patient. Sammie talked to a middle-aged man in a paramedic uniform a few feet away. The girl on the ground was slight, maybe five-one, a hundred pounds if that, dressed in jeans and a yellow, scoop-neck T-shirt—not exactly biker gear—and the lightweight clothes hadn't offered her much protection. Her left shoulder was raw with road rash and her arm was clearly fractured just above the wrist. Fortunately, her helmet, a minimal affair with no face or chin protection, was still in place. An open fracture of her left femur was obvious from the inch of bone protruding mid-thigh through a ragged rent in her torn jeans. The EMTs had already started an intravenous line in her right arm and splinted the fractured leg. Linda checked her vital signs while Dave assessed her airway.

"She's nonresponsive to verbal commands," Dave said, "and she's not moving much air."

Sammie squatted across from Linda and pressed a stethoscope to the girl's chest. "The truck changed lanes and didn't see them. Reports are this girl and the driver were ejected from the bike on impact."

"Was she ever responsive?" Linda asked, documenting the first set of vitals on her notepad.

"Unconscious when the EMTs got to her." Sammie frowned and moved her stethoscope an inch to the left. "Breath sounds are decreased on the left."

Linda said, "Her pressure's been all over the place, but it's steadily tailing down."

"What's hanging in the IV?"

"Normal saline."

"Run it wide open." Sammie draped the stethoscope around her neck and looked at Dave. "How's the pulse ox?"

"Crappy. 72 and drifting lower."

While Dave and Sammie conferred, Linda checked the positioning of the splint on the girl's leg and moved down to assess the pulses in her foot. The foot was mottled, faintly purple, and cold. "We've got no blood flow here, Sam."

"Looks like several broken ribs, possibly a hemopneumothorax too." Sammie grimaced. "Dave, you're going to need to tube her."

"You have to take this helmet off," Dave said. "I can't get to her airway this way."

"All right." Sammie duck-walked around the girl's prone body until she was leaning over her head from above. "Linda—stabilize her neck while we get this helmet off."

"Right." Linda bent over and held the girl's shoulders and neck in line with her spine while Dave and Sammie eased off the helmet. The position was awkward, and a muscle twinged in her lower back. She ignored it, concentrating on preventing the girl's neck from flexing. If her cervical vertebrae were unstable, too much motion could crush her spinal cord.

"Okay. Linda—hand me the C-collar," Sammie said.

Linda passed the molded plastic neck support to Sammie and straightened, trying to massage the cramped muscle in her back with the heel of her hand.

"You okay?" Sammie asked.

"Fine."

"I'm gonna have to get that tube in now," Dave said. "Pulse ox is 68. There's a number seven right on top in my box, Linds."

"I've got it." Linda pulled the curved plastic tube from Dave's kit and held it by Dave's left hand as he opened the girl's mouth and inserted the laryngoscope. She said to the first responders still crowded around, "Anyone got suction?"

"Here." The EMT who'd briefed Sammie passed a thin, flexible catheter to Dave.

"Thanks." Dave cleared saliva and blood from the girl's throat. "E-T tube?"

"Here you go." Linda positioned it in Dave's hand so he could slide it down the trachea.

He took it without shifting his focus from the oropharynx and eased the tube alongside the blade of the laryngoscope, past the base of the tongue, and into the trachea. Linda quickly checked for breath sounds. "Nothing on the left, Sammie."

"Yeah—I hear that," Sammie said, also listening for breath sounds. "She's got tracheal shift to the right. That left lung is down. Linda, open up a cut down tray and get me a number thirty chest tube."

Linda's pulse jumped. This was bad. The girl was too unstable to even get into the chopper, and the longer they were in the field, the worse her chances became. Quickly swiveling around on her knees, Linda reached for the surgical field trauma kit. The muscle in her lower back cramped again, harder, and she caught her breath, battling a wave of nausea. Ignoring the pulling sensation, she lifted the instrument pack from the bottom of the trauma box, extracted the two-foot-long chest tube, and tore open the clear protective wrapper. After folding open the outer layers of the sterile cut down tray, she pulled on a pair of surgical gloves, snapped the blade onto the handle of the scalpel, and waited for Sammie to ask for it. When Sammie did, she passed it, handle first, across the girl's chest, and Sammie made a two-inch incision between the fourth and fifth ribs in the anterior costal line.

"Kelly," Sammie said.

Linda slapped the oversized hemostat into Sammie's palm and got the chest tube ready.

Sammie pushed the Kelly through the thin muscles connecting the ribs and into the chest, spreading as she went to make room for the tube. "Okay, I'm in."

"Here you go—number thirty," Linda said.

Sammie twisted the tube through the hole she'd made in the chest wall and a minute later blood poured out onto the ground. While Sammie sutured in the chest tube and Dave hand-ventilated the patient, Linda ran back to the chopper to get a Pleur-evac drainage container from the storage bin. She sprinted back, the cramp in her back escalating with every step. The nausea worsened and she had to drop onto her knees next to Sammie to fight the light-headedness.

"Linds? What's wrong?"

"Not sure," Linda gasped, panting for breath. "Pulled something in my back."

Sammie connected the sucking chest tube to the vacuum container. "Head back to the chopper. We're about ready to transport."

"I'll sta—" Pain shot through Linda's lower abdomen. "Oh God. That felt like a contraction."

"That's it," Sammie said. "Go lie down, Linda. We're all right here."

Carefully, Linda stood, pressing her hand to her belly. She couldn't be in labor now. It was way too soon. Heart racing, she walked carefully back toward the chopper, afraid any sudden movement might make things worse. She signaled to Jett, who jogged toward her.

"What is it?" Jett asked.

"They're about ready to transport and they might need help." Linda grasped Jett's arm as another wave of pain rolled through her abdomen. "God. I'm having contractions."

"I've got you." Jett gently slid an arm around Linda's waist. "Let's get you inside. I'll radio ahead and tell them we're coming in. You'll be fine. We'll be back there in just a few minutes."

Linda glanced over her shoulder. Dave and Sammie were loading the trauma patient onto a litter. "She's in bad shape, Jett."

"Don't worry about her, that's Sammie's job. She's got it." Jett lifted Linda into the chopper and climbed aboard after her. "What do you need me to do?"

"I just need to lie down right now."

Jett guided Linda to one of the fold-down stretchers along the wall. "Okay, here you go. Sammie will be here in a second. Don't worry."

"Call Robin," Linda said as Jett strapped her in. She tried to keep the rising panic at bay. She wasn't going to lose this baby.

CHAPTER THIRTEEN

Y ou can go right in," Sybil said. "She's waiting for you."
"Thanks." Annie suppressed the urge to glance at her watch.
She knew she wasn't late. She'd been in the hospital lobby for fifteen
minutes, drinking a cappuccino she didn't need to kill time until her
appointment. She didn't want Hollis to think she was eager to see her
by arriving early, but she'd been too agitated to wait at the clinic any
longer, and she hadn't been able to concentrate enough to fill out the
ever-present insurance forms she *should* have been doing. Even a walk
around the pond didn't calm her nerves the way it usually did. Her
secret paradise was filled with lingering images of Hollis now, and the
warmth that flooded her as she pictured Hollis waking from sleep on a
park bench, soft and tousled, was more disconcerting than the unwanted
urge to see her again.

She stared at the plain wooden door, wondering what waited for
her on the other side, wishing it was as simple as a business meeting
with a doctor she didn't care about offending or hurting. Somehow
she'd wandered far away from the safe paths she always traveled,
where nothing but Callie and her patients mattered. Where the longing
for comfort from someone who truly knew her was rare and quickly
brushed aside. Well. It was up to her to get things back on the right
road. Nothing new there. She'd forged this life out of necessity and
the desperate drive to survive when everyone she'd trusted had turned
away. She'd been right then and she was right now. Business only. She
took a breath, grasped the handle, and pushed open the door.

Hollis was behind her desk in hospital greens. Her eyes were
shadowed, and the faint line of her surgical mask still creased her

cheeks. The desk was neat, although piled high with work—much like Hollis herself, who always seemed in control even when she was obviously exhausted. Like now.

"You look tired," Annie said, unable to stop the rush of concern. "Were you up all night again?"

Hollis stood as Annie closed the door and leaned on her desk, both palms flat on its plain brown surface. A smile flickered over her generous mouth. "Not quite. How have you been? No more storms?"

"No." Annie took the chair she'd occupied the first time she'd been in the office. "Nice and peaceful."

An awkward silence filled the space between them, space that had been anything but quiet the last time they'd been together. Annie struggled not to think of the moments they'd huddled together in the small shed with Callie between them, thunder and rain obliterating the universe. God, the things she'd told Hollis. How had she managed to reveal so much of herself without meaning to? Why was it so easy to talk to Hollis about things she rarely thought of herself? And why was she thinking of them now? Annie took a breath. "I realize we got off to a bad start the last time, and that was my fault. I apol—"

"Annie," Hollis said quietly. "We're past apologies now, aren't we?"

"I don't know," Annie said, hearing the brusqueness in her voice and the overture toward accord in Hollis's and not knowing how to change it. She wasn't certain she could deal with this Hollis—the one with kindness in her eyes and a hint of confusion swimming in their deep blue depths—today. "I suspect you and I are going to disagree, and we ought to find that out, shouldn't we? Isn't that why we're both here?"

"Why don't we both say what we have to say and then see where we are." Hollis dropped into her chair and pushed back a few inches from the desk. She crossed one leg over the other, her ankle resting on her knee. Her surgical clogs were dark brown, and Annie wondered if that was intentional, to hide the bloodstains.

"All right," Annie said, although she thought it might be anything but all right. Once they'd said aloud what was likely to divide them, once their differences—ethical, personal, fundamental—were irrevocably etched in the air, they wouldn't be able to pretend there was a middle ground where those differences wouldn't matter. They wouldn't be able to pretend friendship was possible—that something else might be possible…but then, there couldn't be anything else. So perhaps it was all for the best. She ought to go first before she changed her mind. "I told my boss—the regional director—that I didn't agree with establishing a joint working relationship with your group, even for high-risk patients. We already have a system in place to deal with emergencies, and the statistics have shown those methods are effective. To be blunt, Dr. Monroe, we don't need your permission or your support to practice a profession as old and well-established as yours."

"The state disagrees," Hollis said quietly.

"The state," Annie said, unable to keep the heat from her voice, "decides in favor of those with the money to buy opinions, and we both know which group has the advantage there."

Hollis didn't move except to steeple her fingers on her thigh. Her gaze never wavered, her expression never changed. Thoughtful. Remote. The distance between them was so vast Annie felt as if she were standing on the edge of a chasm and one misstep would plummet her into its endless depths. If she reached out her hand, she'd find no one to grasp it, no one to stop her fall. Unlike that weekend, when the ever-present solitude had disappeared for a few hours in the middle of a rainy afternoon, she'd be all alone again. The ache of loss was familiar—she remembered feeling the same hollow sadness after she'd delivered Callie and her world had imploded. The urge to get up and run from her past was so powerful she trembled. She grasped the arms of her chair to keep from bolting.

"I told my boss I thought it was a bad idea." Hollis smiled wryly. "Pretty loudly, actually. My specialty is high-risk pregnancies, and I know how quickly things can go bad. Lives can change in the blink of an eye, when there's no time for a phone call or to wait for an ambulance to transport a mother in trouble or an infant in distress to even the closest hospital. Sometimes we know when a mother is at risk for complications, but all too frequently it's the ones we thought were going to be easy that go bad. Those are the ones I worry about. Those are the ones you are not equipped to deal with. Why ask for trouble?"

"Statistics—"

"I don't *care* about statistics." Hollis's eyes darkened and her control fractured just long enough for Annie to catch a glimpse of fury—and something else, something wounded and bleeding—beneath her calm expression. "One preventable death is one too many."

"Who was it?" Annie asked.

"What?" Hollis pulled back in her chair.

"This is personal, isn't it?"

"Of course it's personal. Isn't it for you?"

Annie knew there was more, but Hollis was right. She was entitled to her secrets. "We're not going to disappear, Dr. Monroe."

"I know that." Although, taking note of the formal address for the second time in as many minutes, Hollis wasn't so sure. Annie had been girded for battle, shields up and sword drawn since she'd walked in the door, just as she'd been the first day she'd come to the office. She was that Annie now—defensive, angry, distrustful. Knowing what Annie had gone through in her past, Hollis understood a little better where those feelings came from, but the knowing couldn't help deflect the pain of being shut out. One misstep here and Annie would be gone. "Now that we've spelled it out, what are we going to do about the situation?"

"We could make it simple," Annie said. "We'll both tell our superiors it's not tenable. It's a win-win."

"Not a bad solution," Hollis said. Annie's answer to the impasse would avoid any more questions she didn't want to answer. She wouldn't have to worry about the attraction that grew stronger every time she saw Annie. But if Annie walked out the door now, if they solved their dilemma by simply agreeing nothing was possible, she'd probably never see her again. Oh, she might run into her on some rare occasion passing in the hall, but that hadn't happened yet and probably wouldn't happen often. She didn't want Annie to walk out of her life, and that might mean changing her mind about the clinic—at least in the short term. After all, they were only at the information-gathering stage. It didn't mean anything would change in the end. She could still vote against any formal relationship between the OB department and the midwifes. "I don't know about your boss, but I doubt mine will accept our decision without some indication we've explored all possible avenues of working together."

Annie grimaced. "Unfortunately, mine would probably feel the same way."

Hollis breathed easier. So they'd have a little more time. Right now, that was enough. "Okay. Why don't we at least do the initial fact-finding? Then we can both appease our bosses and still get what we want."

"What do you suggest?" Annie's tone held the slightest edge of suspicion.

"The only way we can justify a decision about the feasibility of an OB-midwife joint care center is if we assess our clinical practices. See how we mesh."

"Why do I get the feeling that your idea of assessing clinical practices means you'll be grading midwifes on their care? And by whose standards?"

Hollis barely managed to clamp down on a hot wave of temper. "Is that really what you think of me? That I won't be fair or objective?"

Annie closed her eyes briefly. "No. I'm sorry. No. I know you'll be fair."

The tightness in Hollis's chest eased. "How about we make sure it goes both ways? I'll spend time with you however you want—seeing patients with you in your clinic, assisting at births, doing follow-ups—whatever you say."

"And vice versa?"

Hollis nodded. "Although it'll play hell with your schedule. My patients tend to be even more unpredictable than the norm."

"You don't have to worry. I can handle a difficult schedule. I'm used to being available when my patients need me."

"I was thinking about Callie—"

"I appreciate that—" Annie paused and glanced down at her beeper. "Sorry, I've got an emergency page."

"Of course, you can—" Hollis frowned at the sharp knock on her door. Sybil never interrupted when she was in a meeting except in the case of dire emergency. "Come in."

The door opened and Sybil looked in. "I'm sorry, Dr. Monroe. The ER on two. Honor says she needs to talk to you right away."

"All right." Hollis reached for the phone. "Sorry, Annie."

Annie rose. "That's fine. I need to go take my call too."

"I'll call you when I'm free. We'll set something up."

"Fine." Annie followed Sybil out the door, tapping her phone as she went.

Hollis watched the door close behind her, thinking Annie couldn't get away fast enough. Shoving the twinge of disquiet aside, she picked up the phone.

"Monroe."

❖

"Hollis will be down in a few minutes," Honor said, checking the readouts on the monitor above Linda's bed.

"Did you get hold of Robin?" Linda asked.

"She's on her way. She just had to call Phyllis to pick up Mike after school." Honor took Linda's hand. Linda's fair skin was unnaturally white and her pupils huge, inky disks. Her pulsed raced. Stress reaction, and completely unlike her. Linda was a rock in a crisis—everyone's rock. Honor's heart twisted to see her so afraid. "Listen, you're going to be all right. There's no bleeding, the fetal heart tones are fine. It's probably just a false alarm, but we're going to do everything by the book. Are you hearing me?"

"If anything happens, you'll make sure Robin—"

"Okay, you're obviously not hearing me." Honor stroked the damp hair off Linda's forehead. When Jett had radioed that they were delivering two patients instead of one—the anticipated MVA, unstable and needing immediate surgery, plus a midtrimester female in early labor—Honor had known it was Linda without hearing the name Jett hadn't sent over the airways. She'd called Quinn for the trauma, and then she'd called Robin. And for the next ten minutes she'd paced, double-checking that everything was ready for Linda's arrival. Quinn had asked if she needed her to stand by, but she'd said no. Quinn would have her hands full with the multiple trauma patient, and Honor wanted to be the one to take care of Linda. Linda was one of the few people in her life she loved unconditionally. She'd lost Terry in this emergency room a dozen years before, and she wouldn't lose anyone else. "Robin is going to be fine because you're going to be fine. Nothing else is acceptable."

Linda laughed shakily. "I forgot how close to God ER physicians are."

"Well, best remember that in the future."

"I was being careful—"

"Of course you were. I know that. Robin knows that. Stop worrying."

Linda closed her eyes. "Okay. I'll let you play doctor, then."

Honor smiled. "Very wise. I'm going to step outside and wait for Hollis."

"You called her?"

"By the book, remember? If you need anything, you know where the buzzer is."

"You'll make sure Robin gets through the red tape?"

"I'll take care of it. Don't worry."

Honor stepped outside the curtain and scanned the ER. The automatic doors at the end of the hall opened, but the woman who strode through wasn't Hollis Monroe or Robin. The pretty blonde paused at the nurses' station, said something to the charge nurse, and then walked down the hall toward Honor. She stopped and held out her hand.

"Hello, I'm Annie Colfax. I'm Linda's midwife. Robin called."

Taken off guard, Honor hesitated for a microsecond before pulling the curtain aside. "She's right here. Go on in."

CHAPTER FOURTEEN

H i," Annie said, stepping up to Linda's bedside.
"Oh, you came," Linda said. "I'm so glad. Have you seen Robin?"

"No, not yet, but she called just a few minutes ago." Annie lightly gripped Linda's wrist. The vital signs scrolling over the monitors beside her bed all looked normal. Some of the burning in her stomach quieted. "I imagine she'll be here any second."

"God, this is a nightmare."

"If this is premature labor," Annie said gently, "the most important thing is early treatment, and you're getting that right now. I know it's hard, but try to relax."

Linda laughed shakily. "Tall order."

Annie squeezed her fingers. "I know. How did this star—"

"Sorry," the ER chief said, coming into the cubicle. She held a chart out to Annie. "Thought you might want this."

"Thanks," Annie said.

"We haven't been formally introduced. I'm Honor Blake. Are you with the Wellness Clinic?"

"Yes." Annie remembered seeing her at the picnic the day before with a good-looking dark-haired woman and two children. The younger boy went to Callie's preschool. The world suddenly seemed a lot smaller, and she flashed back to the community she'd left behind where, for better or worse, everyone knew one another. Sometimes that closeness offered comfort and strength, and sometimes it shaped the bars of an invisible prison. She shook off the touch of the past and scanned the brief notes and lab data on the chart. "I've been following Linda regularly since insemination. She's been doing fine." Annie turned back to Linda. The chart told her little—what she wanted was Linda's story. "How long ago did you first start having contractions?"

"About—"

The blue-and-white-striped curtain opened with a snap and Hollis strode in. Her eyes registered surprise when she saw Annie, but she quickly looked away and smiled at Linda. "Hi. Honor called me down to take a look at you. How are you doing?"

"I've been better," Linda said. "I was just telling Annie—Annie, this is Dr. Monroe—"

"Yes," Annie said, "we know each other." She glanced at Hollis, whose expression was pleasantly neutral, as if their acquaintance was merely in passing. Perhaps here, on the professional field, they were still strangers. An unexpected arrow of disappointment shot through her, and she mentally brushed the ache aside. She handed Hollis the chart. "Linda was just telling me what's been going on."

"Good," Hollis said, leafing through the few pages of intake notes. "Now she'll only have to repeat it all once."

"I'll wait for Robin," Honor said and stepped into the hall.

"Go ahead, Linda," Annie said. She wasn't really sure of the protocol now that Hollis was here, but she knew what she needed to do, and until someone suggested otherwise, she planned on doing it. Maybe Hollis's silence was part of their new clinical observation plan, but whatever the situation, she couldn't be distracted by it now.

Annie and Hollis flanked the narrow hospital stretcher while Linda recounted the medevac flight and the onset of the twinges she'd at first attributed to a muscle pull. Annie asked a few questions and noticed Hollis making notes in the chart. She was left-handed. Why hadn't she ever noticed that before? With an effort she looked away from Hollis's hands, but it was harder to ignore the shimmer of electricity that danced over her skin.

"And thinking back," Annie said when Linda fell silent, "you don't recall feeling this way previously?"

"No, God," Linda said, shaking her head. "You'd think I would have known right away."

"Not necessarily. A backache is pretty much a way of life for pregnant women at your stage. It's natural to think that's all it is." Annie glanced at her watch. "So all this started about an hour ago?"

Linda nodded.

"How many contractions do you think you've had all told?"

"At least five," Linda said.

Annie glanced at Hollis. The next step was to assess the status of Linda's cervix. If the contractions had caused the cervix to dilate prematurely, she was at risk for premature delivery. She'd need intravenous medication to help relax the uterus, and close monitoring.

"We're going to need to take a look," Hollis said, as if reading Annie's mind. "If the contractions continue or your cervix is dilating, I want to start some mag sulfate."

Linda's eyes closed for an instant and then she nodded. "Whatever needs to be done."

Honor poked her head in, "Linda, Robin's here."

"Tell her I'm okay," Linda said.

"You tell her," Honor said, holding the curtain aside.

Robin strode in, her dark hair damp with sweat, wearing a soccer T-shirt and shorts and looking as if she'd just come off the field. She leaned down and kissed Linda. "Hi, baby. How you doing?"

Her voice was soft and steady, and Annie had a fleeting moment of envy, imagining that kind of tender caring. She looked away and found Hollis watching her. She lifted her chin, chasing the dreams away. "Can we talk outside a minute?"

Hollis nodded.

"We'll be right back," Annie said to Linda. She followed Hollis into the hall and stopped a few feet away, out of earshot of Linda's cubicle. "If I saw her in the clinic, I'd examine her, and if the cervix wasn't compromised, I'd hydrate her and watch her to see if her contractions stopped before transferring her. The contractions might stop spontaneously."

Hollis was used to consulting with other physicians about patient care, but she was also used to calling the shots when and how she saw them. She valued the input of every other professional, but her instinct—and training—was to take charge when the case involved her area of expertise. If Annie hadn't been Annie, she wouldn't even be considering how to answer. And since Linda was the only one who really mattered, she went with her gut. "She's forty years old and this is a first pregnancy, so we don't have any history to go by. She's what—twenty-four weeks?"

"Twenty-three."

"So the fetus isn't viable. We've got a good shot at controlling this if we jump on it hard now. I'm not comfortable waiting. There's almost no downside to mag sulfate."

"*Almost* none." Annie checked behind her and lowered her voice. "But some studies have shown an increased incidence of neonatal death."

Hollis nodded. Annie knew her numbers. "True—but usually only in instances of multiple other complications."

"She's here now, and it's not my call." Annie waved a hand, taking in the bright lights and beeping monitors and atmosphere of urgency permeating the ER. "And this is no time for a turf war."

Relieved not to have to fight this out, Hollis nevertheless felt the distance grow deeper between them. Distance she couldn't change. "I'll get the nurses to set up for an exam and meet you inside."

"I'll explain what's going on to Robin and Linda," Annie said.

"Okay, thanks."

Annie turned away and Hollis walked over to the nurses' station where Honor was charting. "I'm going to take a look at her now, but I want to keep her here and give her a course of mag sulfate."

"I thought you might," Honor said, returning the chart to the rack. "I didn't know Robin called the midwife, by the way. I honestly hadn't thought of it."

"No problem."

"They usually hand off before the patient gets here."

Hollis shrugged. "We might be seeing Annie's group here a lot more. Dave wants us to set up something formal between our department and their group."

"Probably a good idea," Honor said. "It'll make things smoother in situations like this."

"I hope so." Hollis signaled to one of the ER nurses working Linda's section of the ER. "Can you set up for a pelvic in ten?"

"Sure, Hollis. Give me five minutes." The redhead paused. "Nice shiner."

Hollis grinned. "Thanks."

When the nurse moved away, Honor said, "So something tells me you don't agree with Dave about this new interdisciplinary thing with the midwifes."

Hollis shook her head. "I don't know how I feel about it. I guess that's what Annie and I will have to find out."

"I saw you two talking at the barbecue. It's good that you know each other. It'll probably make working together easier."

"Maybe." Hollis wasn't sure she could call her relationship with Annie personal. It had been so long since she'd had any kind of a relationship with a woman, she wasn't sure what one felt like anymore. She was a little out of practice. But she didn't need to worry about that with Annie. They weren't going in that direction.

"I'll call the pharmacy for the IV meds," Honor said. "If you need anything else, let me know. You're not going to admit her right now?"

"No, I think we can treat her down here for now. Give me a call if things change, though."

"Of course."

Hollis headed back toward Linda's room. She wondered how long Annie would stay. She was supposed to give a student lecture—she looked over her shoulder at the big plain-faced clock on the wall—in ten minutes. She'd be late. They wouldn't have a chance to talk, and she wanted to. She didn't want Annie leaving angry or upset when she might not see her again for days. The wait since Sunday had been distracting enough. She slipped back into the cubicle.

"It'll just be a minute."

"Robin," Annie said, moving toward the hall, "call me if you need anything when Linda gets home."

"Annie, wait," Linda called. "Could you stay? Just until—"

"Of course." Annie glanced at Hollis.

"Definitely," Hollis said. "We all need to be in the loop."

"Thanks," Annie said quietly.

The nurse rolled in an instrument stand with a sterile pack on top. She smiled at Linda. "Don't worry, Linds—you've got the best looking after you."

Linda looked from Hollis to Annie. "I know."

❖

While Hollis and Annie looked after Linda, Honor called down the order for the mag sulfate and went to check on Quinn and the motorcycle patient. The trauma bay was the usual scene of chaos. X-ray technicians scurried about getting portable films, anesthesia and respiratory therapy were assessing the airway and setting up the portable ventilator, nurses were drawing blood and inserting catheters, and Quinn was directing all of that as she examined the girl nearly buried by instruments and personnel. Honor pulled on a cover gown, cap, and mask and worked her way through the group around the bed to Quinn's side. "How does it look?"

"She needs a thoracotomy—all that blood's probably due to a lacerated lung and pulmonary vessels. Head injury is severe—we're waiting on neurosurgery to put in an intracranial bolt to monitor her pressure."

"Ortho?"

"Right here," a deep male voice said from nearby.

"Is the OR ready for you?" Honor asked.

"They're on standby." Quinn stepped away from the table. "How's Linda?"

"Hollis is with her now. She's stable, but Hollis wants to give her a course of mag sulfate just to be sure."

"Robin here?"

"Yes, she just got here."

"You okay?"

Honor smiled, gazing into Quinn's blue eyes above the surgical mask that covered the lower part of her face. That Quinn could soothe her, steady her, with just a look still amazed her. She lived on the edge every day, dealing with life-threatening emergencies and making decisions that affected more than just the life of her patient, and she did her job with confidence. But when she was weary, worn down from the pain and suffering that she couldn't change even when she did her best, Quinn was there, supporting her, loving her. Quinn never failed to give her what she needed even when she didn't know herself.

"I'm fine." Honor squeezed Quinn's arm. "Call me when you're done in the OR."

"I will. If you need me, you could always call in to the OR."

"Don't worry—just go do what you need to do. I'll be fine."

"Okay. I'll see you later."

Quinn turned away, and Honor watched her work for another minute before heading back to check on Linda. Hollis was just finishing her exam, and a nurse was hanging an intravenous bag of magnesium sulfate. Robin sat on the far side of Linda's bed on one of the exam stools, holding Linda's hand. Annie stood next to Robin, halfway between Linda and Hollis.

"How we doing?" Honor asked.

Hollis snapped off her gloves and tossed them into the wastepaper basket. "The cervix is closed. That's a very good sign. I want to keep it that way."

"That's great news." Honor smiled at Linda. "You heard that, right? Things look good. So I'm going to keep you here for a while so we make extra sure."

"Okay, thanks," Linda said softly, her fingers white where they gripped Robin's hand. "I don't want to go through this again. Whatever you say."

"What I say is, you'll be fine." Honor leaned over and kissed her on the forehead. "I'll be back to check with you a little later."

Annie moved closer to the bed. "I'll check back later too. If you or Robin need anything, call me."

"I'm so glad you were here," Linda murmured.

Annie smiled. "Of course I'm here. I'll talk to you soon." She glanced at Hollis. "You'll call me if there's any change?"

"Of course," Hollis said, watching the curtain swing closed behind Annie.

Chapter Fifteen

Annie left the ER the way she had come in, turning right at the automatic double doors and following the waist-high red line on the wall marked "visitors" back to the main lobby. She hadn't been a visitor in the ER, but she hadn't exactly been staff either. She'd felt a bit in limbo, unsure of her position in this new environment. Hollis had assumed control easily, and why shouldn't she? That was her territory. Annie had been the outsider. That was a position she *did* know well, and she didn't accept it without complaint any longer. Linda was still her patient, and she wouldn't be usurped. Not that she didn't understand the hierarchy of hospital politics or patient care. She accepted there'd be times she would have to step away when a patient needed care she couldn't give. But she wouldn't be sidelined because of red tape and someone else's rules.

And wouldn't Barb be glad to hear her say that. Laughing softly at her own shifting views of the big picture, she halted outside on the hospital's main walk to call the clinic and rearrange her afternoon schedule. She wanted to get back to the hospital to check on Linda in a couple of hours. Hopefully, Linda would be stable and ready to go home by evening, and she'd need to organize her follow-up care.

"Hi, it's Annie," she said when Barb answered. "I got delayed at PMC—one of my patients is here, early contractions. They're treating her in the ER."

"Does it look like she's going to stop?"

"I think there's a good chance she already has. The OB consultant started her on mag sulfate, though, prophylactically."

Barb was silent a moment. "What's your thinking?"

"I want to come back to check her status later, so if you don't mind, I need to take a couple hours now to pick up Callie from school. I didn't have anything scheduled except for a birthing class this afternoon. Okay if I have someone cover that for me?"

"Don't worry about it—Andrea is here. She can handle it. Take the rest of the day. How did the meeting go?"

"We were interrupted—we both got called for the same patient."

"That's a handy coincidence," Barb said.

"I guess that's one way of looking at it." Annie laughed. If she believed in fate, she'd think it was somehow conspiring to throw her and Hollis together in the most awkward situations possible. But as she didn't believe in much of anything beyond her own will any longer, coincidence was probably as good an explanation as any. "We had to coordinate our care on the fly, but I think we worked together all right, considering the circumstances."

"Good. Maybe that bodes well for future cooperation."

"Maybe." Annie had liked watching Hollis work. She was direct, confident, and compassionate. Her therapeutic approach was different than Annie's would have been, but not necessarily wrong. Not even all that aggressive. Plenty of practitioners would have agreed with Hollis's treatment, including some of Annie's midwife colleagues. If Linda had continued to have contractions, Annie would have recommended the same thing. The only difference was timing—and she did tend to be more conservative than most, opting to delay aggressive intervention as long as possible. Medical judgment wasn't always cut and dried—that's why it was called judgment. Hollis hadn't been wrong in her treatment, not today. Annie forcibly drew herself away from the pull of the past, recognizing that Hollis triggered emotions that should be long gone.

She'd never be able to go back and relive those events, she'd never be certain that what had happened couldn't have been changed. If only she'd been able to say yes or no, if only the choice had been hers, she could have lived with it so much more easily. Instead, all these years she'd been haunted by not knowing, her absence of memory creating a black hole that taunted her with uncertainty and doubt. Hollis's was the only face she could remember, other than the one who hadn't been there. Jeff. The lover who had lied to her, the father of the child he had urged her to abort.

Annie rubbed her eyes. The Hollis of her past was still bound to the pain and sorrow of so many losses, and that wasn't Hollis's fault. Being around Hollis now only raised more questions to which she had no answers, and she was tired of asking. She needed to stay focused on what mattered.

"So do you think you're going to be able to work with this doctor?" Barb asked.

"What?" Annie said. "Oh, yes. It's early yet, and if it turns out I can't, I know you can get someone who will be able to. Hollis is reasonable."

"Reasonable. That's an interesting word. So she isn't opposed to the concept?"

Agitated by her lapse into the past, Annie walked toward her car as she talked. The sky was nearly cloudless, a blue so pure it barely looked real. Hollis's eyes were that crystalline blue when she laughed. Annie jerked her gaze back to the concrete walkway shimmering in the afternoon heat. God, she needed to get Hollis out of her head. "Actually, I don't think she's in favor of a formal association, but she's willing to investigate the options."

Barb laughed. "She sounds a lot like you."

Annie fished her keys out of her shoulder bag and pressed the remote for her car. "I have no idea what you're talking about. We're absolutely nothing alike. She's an interventionist. I like to give the body a chance to take care of itself."

"The two aren't necessarily mutually exclusive."

Annie slid into her car and started the engine. "I know. But we're about as far apart as you can get on the professional spectrum."

"Well," Barb said, sounding philosophical, "maybe that's a good thing. At least we know you will have looked at this thing from every side when you two make a decision."

"Right," Annie said, thinking of the agreement she and Hollis had made to go through the motions of an exploratory review so they could render a report to satisfy their bosses, even though they agreed from the outset a working association wasn't really tenable. All they'd be doing was legitimizing a foregone conclusion. She sighed. She wasn't really going to be able to put her name to a decision she hadn't thoroughly investigated. She knew Hollis wouldn't be able to either. Hollis was too much of a professional. So was she, and there was more than just professional purview at stake—the bottom line was patient welfare. She'd just have to go into this with an open mind. A weight lifted just at having admitted as much to herself. "Right. I'll give it my best shot."

"I never doubted it. Keep me in the loop."

"Always." Annie rang off and dropped her cell phone onto the seat beside her. She ought to be a few minutes early picking up Callie. The idea of a surprise visit in the middle of the day and the expectation of Callie's uncensored delight made her smile. Callie was the best thing in her life. She regretted everything about her relationship with Jeff, except for Callie. Maybe that's why she'd never been able to put that segment of her past behind her—it was hard to dismiss her relationship with him as a mistake, something she wanted to forget, when the miracle of her life had resulted from it.

She pulled out, still puzzling over the tangle of her past. Jeff might have fathered Callie, but he was no part of Callie's life—not her past or her future. Jeff was her past too, if she'd let him be. She'd believed in him, and that had been her mistake. She'd paid for that naïve belief with a broken heart and a wounded spirit, but maybe she was the winner after all—she had Callie. Smiling, she headed for the exit and felt the past slip a little further away.

❖

Hollis jogged out through the ER loading area and headed for the medical education building across the street. With luck she'd only be a few minutes late. She cut through the parking lot, zigzagging between rows of cars, and skirted around the empty security office kiosk toward the street. She blinked in the bright sun, enjoying the few stolen moments in the sultry afternoon, relaxing for a second away from the harsh artificial lights and urgent clamor of the ER. A horn blared, shattering the calm, and sunlight glinted off metal in the corner of her eye. Her heart leapt into her throat and she jumped back, shielding her eyes with her hand. A car slammed to a stop inches from her. Heat wafted off the bumper and an image of splintered leg bones flashed through her mind an instant before relief squeezed out the terror. No pain. She was okay. "Sorry! Wasn't looking where—"

The driver's door burst open and Annie shot out. "Oh my God! Are you crazy? I almost ran you down." Annie clutched the top of the door. "Are you all right? You came out of nowhere!"

"Hey, my fault." Hollis forgot about the near miss. Annie sagged against the open door of the car, her eyes wide with anger and concern. The golden highlights in her hair danced in the gleaming sunshine. Even ruffled and mad, she looked all kinds of sexy. Hollis grinned, just glad to see her. "No harm done."

"That's what you think." Annie pressed a hand to her heart. "You just took about a million years off my life."

"You still look pretty good to me." The words were out before she could stop them, but then, why not? They were true. Annie was beautiful. Great to look at, but something more than her undeniable attractiveness teased at Hollis's mind like a whispered caress. Annie's freshness, her untamed spirit, captivated her. Annie made her think of things she'd long forgotten—lazy mornings and days filled with possibility, cool nights and promises under a canopy of stars. Annie made her feel like life still held surprises that weren't cloaked in pain.

Annie colored, her brows drawing down. "Could you be a little more careful?"

"Sorry—late for a class." Hollis tilted her head toward the street, keeping Annie in her sights. If she looked away a second, she'd be gone. Always disappearing, was Annie. "Got a lecture to give. What are you doing later?"

"What do you mean?"

"You're coming back to check on Linda, aren't you?"

"Yes," Annie said. "I'm picking up Callie right now. I thought I'd come back here around five."

"Good. I'll meet you in the ER. Might as well put this joint-care research to good use." Annie might shy away from a personal interaction, but she was dedicated to her patients. Another thing Hollis found appealing about her. Annie knew what she was about.

"All right," Annie said. "We should talk—"

Hollis was tired of everything being about their differences. She wanted to connect again like they had at the barbecue. She'd been wanting it since Annie had walked away. "Have dinner with me after."

Annie shook her head as if she was having trouble understanding. "What?"

"Dinner. No work. Just dinner."

"Thanks, but I can't," Annie called and started to get back into the car.

Hollis stood her ground. Annie couldn't run if she was in front of the car. She wanted to see her later—away from the distractions of the hospital and the demands of patients. Hell, she wanted a date. "Why not?"

"Callie—I have to leave her with a sitter to come back over here. I can't leave her all evening too."

"No problem." Hollis shrugged. "Meet me in the ER early—four thirty. We'll see Linda and then pick up Callie. Take her with us. That's not too late for her to eat, is it?"

"No, but she's four, Hollis. Going out to dinner with a four-year-old—"

"Will be perfect. She won't be fussy about where we go." Hollis waved and jogged backward toward the street. "See you later."

"Right," Annie muttered, sliding back into her seat as Hollis turned away and ran for the building across the street. She held her breath as Hollis dodged traffic and reached the sidewalk safely. "Later."

The woman was crazy. She obviously hadn't had the interesting experience of taking a four-year-old out to dinner. But then, maybe she had. Hollis had brothers and she probably had nieces and nephews. Annie didn't know because Hollis was very good at getting her to talk about herself but even better at not revealing much of her own story. That would have to change if they were going to see each other.

Annie drew a breath, dispelling the cloud that seemed to fog her brain every time Hollis was around. What was she thinking? The idea of seeing Hollis again made her heart race, which proved only one thing. She was alive and breathing. Hollis Monroe was a very attractive woman—who wouldn't get a little sidetracked by that killer smile and those devilish eyes and that tight, powerful body? God, she was gorgeous. So what? There were plenty of other hot, charming women around—just because she hadn't noticed any in, well, ever, didn't mean anything. She knew better than to be caught up in the thrill of attention from someone like Hollis—someone who made her feel attractive and sexy, as if she was the sole focus of their interest, as if what she thought and felt really mattered. Once, she'd been hungry for the kind of attention Hollis promised, starving to be seen and valued. She'd learned the hard way what happened when she lost all common sense over a handsome charmer who looked at her as if she was a beautiful, fascinating woman. She wasn't about to forget, no matter how many butterflies Hollis set loose inside her. She wasn't a cloistered girl any longer.

Dinner—or any other interaction that wasn't strictly business—was out of the question. She put the car in gear and edged toward the street, relieved to have sorted that out. She had Hollis and her own irrational response to her in perspective now. She gripped the wheel harder, willing her hands to stop shaking.

CHAPTER SIXTEEN

After signing over her last two patients to the night shift—a teen rule-out-appendicitis who needed a white blood cell count and surgical consult, and an octogenarian with right-sided weakness waiting for a bed on the medical floor, Honor slipped into Linda's cubicle. The lights had been turned down low and Linda appeared to be sleeping. Robin still sat on the stool beside the stretcher, holding Linda's hand and reading on her iPhone. She glanced up and smiled wanly. She looked tired, unusual for her. She was always on the go, always organizing some event or rallying a team, always full of energy. Honor reflexively scanned the monitors. No change from the last time she'd checked. Everything was stable. The tangle of uneasiness in her chest relaxed a fraction.

"She's doing great," Honor whispered. "Need anything?"

"No," Robin said softly. "I'm fine."

Linda's eyes flickered open. "What time is it?"

"A little after four," Honor said.

Linda frowned at her. "Why are you still here?"

"Because you are." Honor moved up beside the bed and rested her fingertips on Linda's shoulder. "How are you feeling?"

"Thirsty. Otherwise good."

"Here." Honor held the big Styrofoam container with the straw extending through the plastic cover close to Linda's face. "Drink."

"Thanks." Linda took a few sips and gestured toward Robin. "You could at least make her go home."

"Not likely. I think she might be waiting for a courtesy dinner tray. You know how good the food is here."

Linda made a face. "Please. Send her home before we have another patient."

Laughing, Honor squeezed Linda's arm. "Don't worry. I expect Hollis will be by anytime now to give you the green light."

"You think this is just a little bump in the road, then, nothing serious?"

"We'll have to leave that to the experts, but you know these things aren't all that uncommon." She glanced at Robin, then at Linda. "You know your flying days are done until this little item makes an appearance for good."

Linda nodded. "I know. I knew that was coming anyhow. It's fine. I was starting to get a little nervous going up, and that's no way to start out a flight." She sat up slowly. "But what about my spot down here?"

"You know you have one." Honor caught the flash of alarm, quickly hidden, on Robin's face. She remembered Quinn's worry when she went back to work soon after Jack's birth. Sometimes being the one to wait and watch was the hardest role. "But that's going to have to be Hollis's call too."

"And Annie's," Linda added.

"What are your plans there?" Honor asked, keeping her tone light. Now wasn't the time to pressure Linda, and she really didn't want to. Taking care of friends was tricky—she risked unconsciously using her position to influence Linda into thinking her way, and that wasn't fair. If she'd been in Hollis's shoes and had to make the OB call, she'd have had to step aside.

"What do you mean?"

"Are you still planning on the home birth?"

Linda glanced at Robin.

"Up to you, babe," Robin said. "Whatever you want, as long as it's safe."

"I still want to go through with it as planned, but I guess we'll have to see what the next few months are like." Linda traced her thumb over the top of Robin's hand. "Is that okay with you, baby?"

"It's a plan I can live with." Robin lifted Linda's hand and kissed her knuckles. "I'm sure Annie will keep a close watch on things."

"Knock, knock," Annie said and parted the curtain. "I think I heard my name."

Linda smiled widely. "Hi. It's good to see you."

"It's good to see you looking better." Annie glanced at Honor. "Things have been quiet, I take it?"

"Yes. No further contractions. She's only had the one dose of mag sulfate and everything looks good."

Annie patted Linda's knee beneath the sheet. "That's terrific news. Hollis will probably let you go home after she sees you."

"Praise Jesus," Robin muttered and everyone laughed.

"Bed rest tonight and tomorrow," Annie said. "No exceptions, okay?"

"Can you handle everything, sweetie?" Linda looked at Robin. "You've got work and the kids, and if I'm in bed..."

"Not *if* you're in bed," Annie said, pointing a finger at Linda. "We can have an aide come by for a few days to give you a hand."

"We should be okay," Robin said. "I can rearrange some phone conferences I had scheduled so I can look after the kids. As long as they're squared away, everything else is flexible."

"We can get you some help with that too, Robin," Annie said.

"I appreciate it. If I get jammed, I'll call."

Annie nodded. "Okay, then. I'll be by tomorrow morning to see how you're doing. If anything changes during the night you should call me."

Honor leaned over and kissed Linda's cheek. "You're in good hands. I'll be at home—I can be over in five minutes. If you need anything at all, you call me."

"I will, don't worry," Linda said.

Just as Honor rolled the curtain back to step into the hall, Hollis came in, a chart tucked under her arm. A storm of butterflies took up camp in Annie's midsection again. Hollis looked great. She'd changed out of scrubs into black trousers and a soft brushed-cotton dove-gray shirt. Her dark hair framed her face in careless waves that highlighted her angular jaw and arched cheekbones. Annie's throat went dry. "Hi."

Hollis grinned, her gaze fixed on Annie's for a long moment, before she turned to Linda and Robin. "How's everyone doing?"

"A whole lot better," Linda said.

"Good. Let me take a look at you and we'll decide what's next." Hollis did a quick exam and a bedside ultrasound. "All nice and normal." She glanced at Annie. "Talk to you outside?"

"Of course."

Annie followed Hollis out into the hall.

"What do you think?" Hollis asked.

"There's been nothing abnormal since she's been here. She ought to be all right to go home on bed rest."

"I agree." Hollis took Annie's arm and drew her to one side of the hall as a tech pushed a portable X-ray machine down the hall. She continued to hold Annie's arm lightly as she leaned casually against the wall. "She's in a high-risk pool now. She's not a great candidate for a home birth."

Annie wasn't surprised that this had come up already. She'd expected Hollis or Honor to question the safety of home birth, and she had given her answer some thought. "I agree she's high-risk, or at least at risk for something further to develop. But until it does, there's no reason not to continue with the care plan we've outlined. I'll be monitoring her, and if she has another round of significant premature contractions, she'll be more likely to deliver prematurely. In that case, I'd recommend in-hospital delivery too."

"So you're suggesting a wait-and-watch approach right now?"

"I don't see why not. She'll have closer monitoring with us than she'd get with standard OB visits."

"I see all my high-risk patients as often as needed," Hollis said abruptly.

"Sorry, I'm sure you do. I just meant—"

Hollis rubbed her face. "No, I know what you meant. It's no problem. Where will you see her?"

"At least initially, home visits."

"Whoa." Hollis shook her head. "Okay, maybe that is a little more attention than we'd give her. Is that standard?"

Annie smiled. "What's the matter, Doctor? Not in the habit of making house calls?"

Hollis grinned and the tightness around her eyes relaxed. "Sorry. Before my time."

Annie laughed. "Mine too, at least in the old-fashioned way. But we see more than half of our prenatal patients at home. It's actually quite efficient and helps prepare everyone involved, not just the mother, for the birth."

Hollis ran a hand through her hair, ruffling it even more. She looked tired. "Right. Okay. I guess we've got a plan, then."

"I guess we do." Annie covered Hollis's hand with hers. "Listen, if you want to take a rain check on dinner—"

Hollis straightened. "No way. Why?"

"You were up late last night. You must be exhausted."

"I'm okay. And I've been looking forward to this all afternoon. Don't back out on me."

Ridiculously pleased that Hollis had thought about her earlier, Annie nodded. "All right. I can pick up Callie and meet you—"

Hollis grasped her hand. Her fingers were cool and strong. "That's not how this works. I'll pick you both up at home. Let me finish here and I'll be over. Say thirty minutes?"

"Yes, fine," Annie said, just the tiniest bit flustered. She was still holding Hollis's hand and she'd somehow agreed to a dinner date. No, no. Not a date. She was *not* going out on a date with Hollis Monroe. Annie kept that thought firmly in her mind all the way home.

❖

Annie assessed her appearance in the walnut-framed mirror hanging just inside her front door. Realizing that was the third time she'd checked, she turned away, grateful Callie was the only witness to her foolishness. She couldn't believe she was this anxious about a simple dinner, one to which she was bringing along her four-year-old. Hardly a romantic outing. Obviously Hollis wasn't thinking of the evening as anything more than a friendly gesture, a collegial outing to break the ice. After all, they would be working together frequently, and getting to know each other was smart. Hollis was smart. Hollis should be there any minute. Annie plucked at the collar of her emerald-green silk shirt and smoothed the front down over her breasts, turning sideways to make sure it didn't balloon out above the waistband of her sable-brown pants. Her heels were just high enough not to be work shoes, but not so high as to be too dressy. Hollis had looked great in the tailored shirt and pants she'd been wearing at the hospital. The cut of the shirt showed off her shoulders nicely, and the drape of the pants over her butt—

Annie jerked her attention away from the mirror and her mind away from Hollis's butt. Really, her mind was wandering into places that were completely unlike her. This was hardly her first date...non-date…dinner with a woman. She'd had a date every few months or so and found them all pleasant. She wasn't antisocial, she'd just never felt the urge to get seriously involved with anyone. She hadn't met anyone who interested her beyond friendship, and why complicate matters?

Hollis felt complicated already.

Snippets of their conversations, the memory of Hollis's quick grin, her dark piercing gaze, ambushed her at the most inopportune moments, breaking her concentration, distracting her in the most—all right, she'd admit it—pleasant ways. The thrill that rippled through her when she thought of Hollis was exciting. And dangerous. She didn't want to be out of control. She didn't want to have feelings that might take her places she'd regret. As much as she wanted to forget Jeff, she remembered all too well the exhilaration his attention brought into her life, the anticipation with which she'd waited for him to call, the often dreamlike wonder she'd experienced when she was with him—as if she had wandered into someone else's life, a fairy tale in which the world sparkled and she was beautiful. God, how shallow could she get. And here she was obsessing over whether her blouse brought out the green in her eyes. History was not about to repeat itself—she wouldn't let it.

Resolutely, she turned her back to the mirror, twitched aside the lace curtain covering the leaded-glass window in the foyer door, and checked the street in front of the house. Again. She dropped her hand as if the curtain were on fire.

"Let's go outside, honey." Maybe if she moved around she could work off some of her nervousness.

"Wait," Callie cried. "I forgot Buttercup."

"All right. Go find her."

While she waited, Annie checked her bag to make sure she had her beeper, money in her wallet, her cell phone, and the pale pink lip gloss she'd tried for the first time. Just in case she needed a touch-up. *Stop. God, just stop!*

Callie came running down the hall with a small yellow bunny clutched in her left hand. She had declared the bunny to be named Buttercup and had taken to carrying it around everywhere in the last few days. Annie grabbed the extra car seat she kept by the door. "All set?"

"Uh-huh. We're ready for dinner."

"Good. Let's go, then." Laughing, Annie pulled open the door and stepped directly into Hollis's arms. The car seat clattered to the floor. "Oh!"

"Hey!" Hollis grasped her around the waist, and they ended up in a loose embrace. "Hi. Am I late?"

"What? No. I don't know. Are you?" Annie nearly rolled her eyes. Apparently her IQ had just plunged fifty points. Hollis's body was firm and warm and her mouth was very, very close. Annie took a deep breath and her breasts brushed Hollis's. Her nipples hardened. Oh. Bad. Very bad. "Sorry. Wasn't looking where I was going."

"That seems to be going around these days," Hollis murmured. She didn't let go. "I was afraid you were going somewhere without me."

"Oh. No. We were just going to wait outside." Annie slipped her arm around Callie's shoulders and pulled away from Hollis. She wished her shirt was looser. She wished her brain would start working again.

"Well, I hope you're both hungry." Hollis squatted and held out a small box of crayons and a coloring book with the main character from the movie *Brave* on the cover. "I thought you might like something to do while we're waiting for dinner."

Callie looked up at her mother. "Can I?"

"Yes." Annie's throat tightened. No flowers or wine for her. Hollis had brought Callie a present instead. Oh, Hollis was a lot more than charming. "Dr. Monroe is a friend."

Hollis looked up, her blue eyes swirling with midnight stars. "Thanks."

Annie barely resisted the urge to run her fingers through Hollis's hair. She couldn't remember ever wanting to touch anyone so badly. She backed up a step. "That was really nice of you, thank you."

"No problem." Hollis silently congratulated herself. She hadn't been sure what a four-year-old might be interested in, but she'd made a quick call to her sister-in-law, who informed her that every boy and girl over two had seen the movie. Fortunately, the Rite Aid half a block from the hospital had everything in the kids' section. Callie was already paging through it, chattering excitedly about which picture she wanted to color. Her delight made Hollis's heart lift. She probably should spend more time with Bruce's and David's kids, but sometimes being around them made her heart hurt, even though she loved them. She glanced at Annie. "Guess it's a hit."

"Good call."

Annie's voice was husky and her eyes had gone from summer green to the shadowy secret depths of the forest. Her full lower lip gleamed a delicate pink, moist and tantalizing. Annie looked as if she was struggling not to touch her, and Hollis tightened everywhere. She was pretty flexible in bed, but more often than not made the first move. Right at that moment, she would've been content to let Annie do whatever she wanted. Anything, just to keep that look in Annie's eyes. She straightened and cleared her throat. "I'm glad she likes it."

Annie was an inch away and her gaze seemed locked on Hollis's mouth. "She does. Very much."

Hollis's hands trembled. Her insides burned. She wet her lips. "I just took a chance. You never know until you try, right?"

"No, you never do."

Annie's voice was soft and sensuous and every inch of Hollis's skin hummed with pleasure. The sounds of children playing ball in the street faded and the still night closed in around them. "Annie, you look beautiful. I want—"

Annie's pupils flickered and the hazy desire in her eyes disappeared. Her gaze sharpened. "We should go."

Hollis caught herself a second before she would have put her hands on her. She hadn't been thinking, and she was always thinking. She wasn't impulsive—decisive, yes, but she always knew what she was doing and why. She'd asked Annie to dinner to get to know her and to find a way through the defensive shields Annie used to keep her at arm's length. She wanted in—inside Annie's walls, where the warmth of Annie's smile waited. She didn't know why, but she'd figure that out. Chemistry, probably. Something as simple as that. Trying to kiss her before they even had a single date wasn't very smart.

"Right. We should go." Hollis forced herself to move, even though she wanted to stay exactly where she was until Annie looked at her the way she had just a minute before. Carpe diem—too late for that now. She sucked in a breath and grinned down at Callie. "Hey. Do you like Mexican?"

Callie looked at Annie. "Is that a movie?"

"No, baby, it's food. Come on." Annie swung Callie's hand. "You're going to like it."

Hollis picked up the car seat, hurried down the steps, and opened the rear door of her FJ Cruiser just as Annie reached the sidewalk. "I'll have this secured in a second."

"Thanks." Annie stepped back as Hollis moved aside, careful that they didn't touch. "Come on, Callie, climb in."

Annie buckled Callie in and handed her the bunny and her new coloring book and crayons. She closed the door and settled into the passenger seat, grateful for the bucket seats. At least there was no possibility that her body would accidentally brush Hollis's. If Hollis got any sweeter before the evening was over, she was going to have a hard time remembering they were colleagues. After Callie was born, she'd shaped a safe, stable life, with no room for uncertainty. Hollis was a cipher whose very presence made her world tilt.

Hollis reached between the seats and squeezed her hand. "Everything okay?"

"Yes," Annie said evenly, gently easing her hand away. "Absolutely fine."

CHAPTER SEVENTEEN

"You sure Mexican's okay?" Hollis asked as they crossed the parking lot to Casa Ranchero, a low-slung, one-story restaurant painted in bright oranges, greens, and yellows. Annie had been quiet on the short drive. Her subtle withdrawal of her hand when Hollis had casually touched her was obvious too. Hollis wasn't sure where she'd gone wrong, but she'd pushed some button that had sent Annie backpedaling until they might have been strangers again. She didn't plan on letting that go on for very long. Annie was hard to figure, and usually Hollis read people pretty easily. So far Annie only seemed comfortable letting her see her professional side—there she was solid and sure, certain of herself and the best treatment for her patients. Hollis had nothing but respect for her, even though they were at odds philosophically. Personally, though, Annie was exactly the opposite—introverted, guarded, and wary. She'd slipped up at the barbecue, revealing things about Callie's biological father and her past, and now she seemed determined to avoid anything else touching on the personal. Annie had good reasons to be wary—just thinking about the people who had abandoned her made Hollis's stomach curdle. She knew what it was to lose a huge chunk of her heart, and she'd had a loving family to help her get through the first shock of it. Annie had had no one—just loss upon loss. Hollis hurt to think of Annie in pain.

"Hollis?" Annie said softly. "Something wrong?"

Hollis gave a start and realized she'd slowed until she was barely moving. She shook her head, feeling her face warm. "No, I'm really sorry. My mind wandered there for a minute."

"I understand. Mine does that a lot lately." Annie grinned ruefully. "Guess that's going around too."

"Well, I promise to stay focused the rest of the night." Hollis quickly squeezed Annie's hand but didn't try to hold it. Annie would have to declare the limits first. But she let go of her anger—Annie didn't need her anger. Annie probably didn't need her to fix anything at all, although that was her default setting. It's all she knew how to do—the only safe thing she could do. "Forgiven?"

"Of course." Annie reached as if to touch her cheek and then let her hand drop. "You're allowed one lapse an evening."

Hollis wanted to grab her hand and tug her close. She wanted to kiss the smile that lingered on Annie's mouth. "Noted."

Callie skipped a few feet ahead. "Is it dinner soon?"

"You bet it is." Laughing, Hollis hustled to the door and held it open for Annie and Callie. She followed them inside and a hostess came forward to greet them.

"No takeout tonight?" The busty twentysomething brunette in a low-cut white ruffled blouse smiled brightly, her dark-eyed gaze glancing briefly over Annie and Callie and settling on Hollis.

"Not tonight." Hollis stopped by at least once a week to grab a quick takeout dinner, and the brunette—*Kristi, with an i*, as she'd reminded Hollis on several occasions—was *very* friendly.

Kristi leaned down and smiled at Callie. "Hi there. That's a great coloring book you've got."

"It was a present."

"Well, it's super. Have fun while you're waiting for dinner." She straightened and smiled at Annie before turning pointedly to Hollis. Her mouth lifted flirtatiously. "She's adorable. Yours?"

Hollis glanced at Annie. "Ah—"

Annie leaned toward Hollis until their shoulders nearly touched. "All ours."

"Well," Kristi said, her expression midway between surprised and disbelieving, "let me show you to a table."

Wending between the tables in Kristi's wake, Hollis murmured, "Ours?"

"I don't know what came over me," Annie muttered, looking straight ahead.

Hollis laughed, pleased. Kristi took them to a booth at a window overlooking the canal that ran through Manayunk, a one-time blue-collar area that had benefited from urban revitalization and now hosted chic restaurants and eclectic stores cheek by jowl with neighborhood bars and coffee shops—the kind with long Formica counters and heavy white ceramic mugs, not the Italian espresso machine types.

"Enjoy your dinner," Kristi said with one last smile for Hollis as she set the menus in the center of the table.

"I imagine you get that a lot," Annie said, accepting the menu Hollis held out for her.

"No idea what you're talking about."

Annie laughed softly. "I'm sure you haven't. Any recommendations?"

"Everything's good. Want to start with nachos?"

"Great idea. You'll like these, Cal."

"Okay." Callie knelt on the seat next to Annie, her coloring book open in front of her and her crayons splayed out beside her plate. She busily colored while Hollis and Annie made small talk. The wait for dinner was comfortable, the conversation light and completely non-work related. Annie asked Hollis about her renovation plans, and when Hollis realized she was monopolizing the conversation she asked Annie what she did for fun.

Annie stroked Callie's hair. "You're looking at it. We've got after-school events and swimming lessons and—"

"Don't forget the zoo," Callie said, pausing in the midst of coloring.

"The zoo...often," Annie said.

"Sounds like you're pretty busy." Hollis noted the absence of any mention of a girlfriend. Welcome news. She also noted Annie seemed to take very little time for herself—her life seemed to be about her patients and her daughter. But then, neither did she, and she didn't even have a kid to spend time with. She was all about work. Maybe that ought to change. The thought made her uneasy, and excited in a way she hadn't been since before Rob...since before her family was torn apart and her girlfriend decided she wasn't any longer. "Okay—tell me one thing you like to do that no one knows."

Annie stared at her. "That's rather personal." Her eyes were dancing, as if daring Hollis to push a little.

"I know."

"Hmm," Annie said, tracing the tip of her finger over her lower lip.

Hollis's breath stopped in her chest.

"I am completely addicted to…"

"Oh, come on," Hollis groaned.

Annie laughed. "*Sons of Anarchy.* I tape every show."

Hollis laughed. Annie was always surprising her. "A secret biker babe, huh? What do you ride?"

"Nothing." Annie glanced out the window, her gaze growing distant.

"Is that not allowed? By the church, I mean?"

Annie shook her head. "No. Some communities are very progressive about machinery use—especially farm equipment. Motorcycles too. I've heard of churches that even have motorcycle groups who worship and ride together." She glanced at Callie, pain flickering in her eyes. "But that would be for the men. Some wives ride along, I imagine."

"Well, you don't strike me as the type who'd be happy being a passenger anyhow."

Annie turned from the window and regarded Hollis. "Is that what you think? That I like to be in charge?"

"Not that so much," Hollis said, taking another chance and wondering if she was about to push another hot button. "But I think you'd be happier making your own choices."

"Well, you're right there." Annie took a short, fast breath. "I'd rather be driving."

"So," Hollis said, treading carefully. "I happen to have a sweet Harley Street Glide, and I'd be happy to teach you how to ride it."

Annie's eyes widened. "Really? Really!"

Hollis laughed, her heart soaring on the wings of Annie's smile. "Sure. It's not hard to learn. We'll find an empty parking lot and I'll teach you."

"I don't know," Annie said, glancing at Callie, frown lines forming between her brows.

"And the first thing will be a safety lesson." Hollis reached across the table and took Annie's hand. "Hey. I wouldn't take any chances with you. Don't worry. I wouldn't let you go out unless I was certain you'd be all right."

Annie searched Hollis's face as if looking for what lay beneath. Hollis hoped she couldn't read the picture that had just popped into her head of Annie—her neck arched, her eyes closed in surrender—or sense the fierce urge she had to see that nothing and no one ever hurt her again. She took her hand away before her trembling betrayed her. "What do you say?"

"Yes." Annie nodded, certainty erasing the tiny lines in her forehead. "Yes. When?"

"Whenever you want."

"Good." Annie nodded. "And then I want leather pants."

Hollis choked on a mouthful of salsa and grabbed for her water. She gulped down half while struggling to erase the image of Annie in tight leathers straddling her. Not working. Sweat popped on her forehead. Every muscle in her body seized, some of them transmitting extremely pleasurable and highly ill-timed messages.

"Are you all right?" Annie asked.

"Fine," Hollis wheezed. She wiped her face with the corner of her napkin and forced a smile. "Sorry. Hot—the salsa. You're serious—you really *do* want to be a biker babe."

Annie grinned. "Da—darn right."

"Well, no point doing anything halfway, right?"

Annie's met Hollis's gaze. "No point at all."

"All right then." Hollis strove to sound casual while avoiding looking directly at Annie. Her circuits were already overloaded, and no amount of ice water was going to cool her down. "We can use one of the parking lots over at Textile for our training course. Work for you?"

"Mmm-hmm," Annie said, mentally reviewing her schedule and resolutely not questioning what she was doing. "I have a few patients to see and a home follow-up this weekend, but maybe after that. I could call you—and I'll make you lunch this time."

"That would be great. Thanks."

"Mommy, can I come?" Callie had put her crayons aside as soon as the nachos had arrived and, after demolishing her weight in chips and cheese, declared them her new favorite food. Now her eyelids were beginning to droop. Annie stroked her hair. "Mommy has to learn how to ride first, baby. When you're bigger, you'll be able to ride with me."

"When will I be bigger?"

"Every single day you grow up a little bit more, and before you know it, you'll be big enough."

"Will I get my own Harley when I'm bigger?"

Hollis laughed. "Guess she was listening."

Annie shot Hollis a wry look. "Always, even when you'd swear she was a million miles away." Annie shifted Callie onto her lap. "First, we'll get you a bicycle. That will be fun to ride."

"Okay." Callie put her head on Annie's shoulder and closed her eyes. Annie sighed. "Sorry, Hollis. I think I have to get her home."

"That's okay." Hollis signaled to the waitress for a check. "I think she did really well."

"And I think you're a really good sport."

"That's me." Hollis grinned. "Besides, it was fun."

Hollis took care of the check and they got Callie settled in the back of her car. Ten minutes later, Hollis pulled up in front of Annie's.

"Thanks," Annie said. "It's been a while since I went a whole evening not thinking once about work. I had a really good time."

"Ditto for me, on both counts." Hollis glanced into the backseat, where Callie slept soundly. "Are you...seeing anyone?"

Annie was glad for the dark because she knew she was blushing. "No."

"So—" Hollis switched off the engine and shifted on the seat until they faced each other. The twilight closed in around them. "I'd like to change that."

Annie scrambled for words, a nameless panic welling up in her chest. "I'm flattered. But—"

"Hey." Hollis held up a hand. "I didn't mean to put you on the spot. You don't have to explain."

"I'm usually not caught off guard." Annie frowned. Hollis always did the unexpected. She should have expected it. "We have the work thing to sort out. It's just not a good idea."

"Bad timing," Hollis muttered. "I know. I was telling myself the same thing earlier."

Annie warmed inside, not from embarrassment but from a ripple of pleasure she could neither deny nor explain. "Really?"

"Yeah. The whole situation is touchy, I get that. I just..." Hollis shrugged. "I haven't been seeing anyone either. Haven't been for a long time...well, dates now and then, but... Hell, I'm sounding a little bit like an idiot here, aren't I?"

"No," Annie said softly. Hollis had never talked to her about anything personal, and she didn't want her to stop now. She couldn't remember the last time she'd wanted to know more about someone, when she wanted the first fragile threads of connection to grow stronger, rather than to disappear. "Maybe we could just do the friends thing."

"Sure, that's the smart thing to do," Hollis said. "Only..."

"Only what? What, Hollis?"

Hollis reached over the space between the bucket seats and plucked a strand of hair away from Annie's cheek. When she sifted it through her fingers, Annie felt the tiny tug deep inside. She held her breath, unable to look away. Hollis's face was all she could see. So beautiful.

"I don't usually want to kiss my friends," Hollis murmured. She leaned closer, sliding her fingers around the back of Annie's neck. The slightest pressure from her fingertips drew Annie closer, until the moonlight sparkling in Hollis's eyes blinded her.

Panic grabbed Annie by the throat. She recognized this feeling—this drowning rush of desire, only so much more than she remembered. Another second and she would be lost. "Hollis, I can't."

"Okay."

Hollis's breath shimmered against her lips, warm and gentle. Hollis's fingers loosened and slid along her skin until her hand was gone, leaving Annie's skin to chill in the hot summer air. Annie shivered.

Hollis sucked in an uneven breath. "Sorry. I'm making a mess of this."

"No, you're not," Annie whispered. "I'm sorry."

"Don't be." Hollis eased back in her seat, and the silvery strands of their connection snapped and disappeared into the dark.

Annie hurriedly collected her bag from the floor in front of her seat, needing to get out of the car. Needing to get away from her own disappointment and the silence that grew cold and still between them. Unwanted memories warred with resurrected needs, made it hard for her to breathe. She didn't even know where the feelings came from, but she wanted to run like a night creature sensing danger. "Why don't we hold off on the motorcycle lessons. We're both busy."

"I'll help you with Callie." Hollis jumped from the car and came around the other side, opening Annie's door and then Callie's. When Annie unbuckled Callie's car seat, Hollis said, "Let me take her."

"I can carry her," Annie said.

"I know, but it'll be easier for you to get the door."

Hollis gently lifted Callie. Annie extracted the car seat and hurried up the walk, fishing her keys from her bag, aware of Hollis right behind her, carrying her daughter. She pushed the door wide, dumped her bag and Callie's toys on the table just inside, and spun around. Hollis stood on the other side of the threshold with everything that mattered to her in her arms. Callie's head rested in the crook of Hollis's shoulder, innocent and untroubled as only a sleeping child could be. Hollis's face shimmered in the moonlight, gentle and strong. Annie held out her arms. "Thank you."

Hollis passed Callie over. "Thanks for tonight. It was great."

"It was."

"I'll call you about setting up some time at the clinic." Hollis turned to go.

The door stood open between them. Annie could close it now and retreat into the safety of her life. "Hollis."

Hollis paused, turned back, her face in shadows.

"I'm seeing one of my new mothers tomorrow morning. Home visit. Are you free?"

"I can be."

"Maybe you'd like to see what I do."

"Good idea."

"I'll swing by and pick you up, then." Helplessly, Annie watched the chasm between them grow wider. "Is quarter of eight all right?"

"Sounds perfect. Good night, Annie." Hollis turned, walked down the steps, got into her car, and drove away.

Annie, her cheek resting against Callie's silken hair, stood in the open doorway watching until the red taillights winked out. She'd made the right choice, and by morning, when the bright light of sanity dispelled the unnerving spell of Hollis's touch, she'd believe it.

CHAPTER EIGHTEEN

Honor woke when Quinn sat up in bed. Blinking in the gray half-light, she rolled onto her side and traced the muscles in Quinn's back with her fingertips. "It's still dark out."

Quinn swung around on the edge of the bed, leaned down, and kissed her. "It won't be in fifteen minutes."

"Mmm." Honor curled around Quinn and laced her arms around Quinn's waist, running her palms over Quinn's abdomen. Quinn sucked in a breath and Honor smiled. She stroked the length of Quinn's thigh, her body stirring as muscles tensed under her hand. "You could have told her you'd ride after work tonight, you know."

"Too uncertain." Quinn swung her legs back onto the bed, settled against the headboard, and drew Honor into her arms. "I'm on backup call, and you know what summers are like."

"Triple the trauma admissions. Believe me, I know." Honor sighed and rested her cheek on Quinn's chest, basking in the soft, steady sound of her breathing and the unwavering beat of her heart. This was home—the heart of her existence. "You're awfully good to do this with her."

"Self-preservation." Quinn stroked Honor's back, lightly drawing strands of hair through her fingers. "She wants to ride in the breast cancer Ride for Life at the end of the summer, and there's no way she's going alone. It's ninety miles, and I'll have to work my ass off to get into shape."

Honor chuckled and pressed her lips to Quinn's chest. Strong muscles, soft skin. Miraculous. "I'd volunteer to go with you, but honestly, the idea of riding that far makes me want to run screaming in the other direction."

"You can cheer us on."

Honor laughed softly. "Always wanted to be a cheerleader."

"Those short little skirts are really hot." Quinn tugged Honor on top of her, entwining their legs.

"Forget it."

Quinn cradled her ass, guiding her over the familiar rise of her thigh. "Too late. The image is already in my mind. Do they still make pom-po—"

Honor bit Quinn's lower lip.

"Okay." Quinn arched beneath her, groaning softly. "No pom-poms."

Honor's head pounded with the pressure against her clitoris. Bracing her hands on either side of the pillow, she held herself just above Quinn's body, her breasts gently brushing Quinn's. Hot skin stroked her swelling clit. "This is not going to get you out onto a bicycle. And if you keep it up, I guarantee you're going to be uncomfortable while you're riding."

"Uh-huh. I'll chance it." Quinn kissed her again, a slow, deep, familiar glide of tongues, a teasing brush of lips.

Honor's mind went blank and her blood raced. She fisted her hands in Quinn's hair and pressed into Quinn, riding Quinn's hard muscles, propelling herself higher, striving for the crest. So soon, so good. "Oh my God."

"That's right, baby," Quinn whispered, one arm holding Honor tightly to her, the other guiding her hips. "I love when you do this."

Honor buried her face in Quinn's neck, muffling her cry as pleasure broke over her like sunshine bursting from behind clouds. She trembled and let herself fall into the firm certainty of Quinn's embrace.

"Oh yeah." Quinn rolled her over and rose above her, kissing her closed eyelids, her mouth, her neck. Her body was hot and slick and hard. "I love you."

Honor scored her nails lightly down Quinn's back and massaged the tense muscles in her ass. "I love you. Beyond everything. I wasn't even thinking of sex five minutes ago."

Quinn nuzzled her neck. "I was."

"I think that's the first thing you think of when you open your eyes."

Quinn laughed, kissed Honor lightly, and rolled off. She tangled her fingers with Honor's, her strong surgeon's hands gentle and sure. "Second thing. First thing is how right it is to have you beside me and the kids asleep in the other rooms. Then all I can think of is wanting you."

"Get out of this bed if you plan to go, otherwise you're going to have to think up—"

A door slammed down the hall and footsteps raced toward their room. A knock came on their door.

"Quinn? You up?"

Quinn pulled the sheet over Honor's nude body and grabbed the T-shirt from the chair beside the bed. She yanked it on over her head. "Yup. Just getting dressed."

"Five minutes," Arly said in a voice that sounded so much like Honor, Quinn could only laugh.

"I hear you," Quinn called.

"Meet you downstairs."

Quinn looked over her shoulder at Honor. "Too late. Hold that thought?"

"Darling," Honor said, "at the first opportunity. It's the first thing I think of in the morning too." She patted Quinn's ass when she stood up. "Have fun. Be careful."

"Always." Quinn stepped into sweats. "You want me to take Jack to daycare?"

"No. I'll drop him off on my way to Linda's."

"Okay. Let me know how she is. Love you."

"I love you." Honor rolled over and closed her eyes, the taste of Quinn in her mouth and her scent surrounding her.

❖

Hollis hit East River Drive on her bicycle just as the sun came up, pedaling in a fast, even rhythm alongside the few cars leading the rush-hour charge toward the city. On the river, sculls knifed through the dark water, the college crewers flexing and pulling as one as their coxswains called out the cadence. Ducks waddled on the green expanse between the twisting two-lane road and the river's edge. Runners strode along the paths paralleling the shoreline.

Ordinarily, this was her favorite time of day—when the air was fresh and the sky clear and the day stretched out before her filled with possibility. This morning, the clarion beauty of the early summer morning only served to darken her mood. She couldn't shake the disappointment of Annie's rebuff, and she couldn't sort out why she was so bothered. It wasn't as if Annie had cut her off—she'd just said she wanted to be friends. Fair enough. That should have been the end of the matter, but she couldn't let it go.

The first thing she did when she opened her eyes was replay the entire previous evening. What she'd said, or should have said, or more importantly, *shouldn't* have said. Hell, what had she been thinking? Annie wasn't like other women, and that was a big part of what fascinated her. Annie was self-sufficient, self-contained, and bent on self-protection—she had more walls than Hollis. Everything she said and did reinforced the no-touch zone that circled her like an impenetrable shell. She didn't want Hollis inside, and that was the only place Hollis wanted to be. She wanted to be the one Annie let in, even though that wasn't like her at all. Usually she wanted more distance, not less. She respected boundaries, she had a lot of her own. But when she was with Annie, she forgot about rules and boundaries and smart decisions. The world sparkled again, the air smelled fresher, the sky was bluer. Everything hummed with life in ways she'd forgotten.

Well, the world wasn't shining now. She shook her head, berating herself for her clumsy, premature moves the night before. The signs had been clear enough—go slow, use caution, take time to build trust. She hadn't done any of those things. A couple of shared meals, a few conversations. That wasn't enough to draw Annie out of her comfort zone. She'd let her wants cloud her judgment.

When was last time she'd done that? When was the last time she'd cared enough to even try? Well, she'd blown it.

A shaft of sunlight bounced off the water and the air ahead of her shimmered with tiny flecks of gold. Maybe not permanently, though. Maybe if she backed off and heeded the caution signs, she could work her way around to the right time to ask again.

Maybe. And maybe she ought to think twice about what she was doing. She sighed and rounded the circle in front of the Art Museum, halfway done with her morning ride. Maybe she'd be smarter to listen to Annie's message—she'd been doing just fine with the casual relationships she had. Annie wasn't the kind of woman she could treat casually. And really, anything else was just asking for trouble. She came around the parkway toward West River Drive and the return loop, her mind clearing. Maybe she should be grateful Annie had shut her down. Maybe she'd dodged a bullet. Maybe what she needed was a date with no strings, a pleasant night out to remind her of the priorities in her life. And what she wanted to avoid.

❖

Annie parked in front of Hollis's house at seven thirty, a good fifteen minutes early. She knew she'd be early, but she'd been too restless to sit in the park after she'd dropped Callie off at Suzanne's and too distracted to make casual conversation with Suz until Suz took the kids to school. She'd just wait out front and review her case notes.

When she turned off the engine, the sound of hammering drew her attention from the notes she knew by heart, and she shoved them back into her bag. She got out of the car, locked up, and followed the rhythmic pounding along the stone walkway circling Hollis's house to the back porch. Hollis stood on a wooden stepladder, nailing new trim around the porch windows. Her back was to Annie as she plucked nails from a leather equipment belt strapped low on her hips and quickly, efficiently drove in the nails. A navy blue tank top stretched across her sharply cut shoulders, and Annie followed the tapering lines of Hollis's back down to her waist where the tank disappeared beneath the waistband of her khaki work shorts. The backs of her legs were corded with muscle. Her dark hair lay in delicate curls at the nape of her neck, as if they'd recently been stroked into place by teasing fingers.

Annie stood at the bottom of the wide dark green porch stairs, giving herself a moment before she announced her presence. She'd spent a good part of the previous evening and most of the early morning trying not to think about the almost-kiss in the car. She still wasn't sure why the idea of Hollis kissing her alternately terrified and thrilled her, but anything that threw her off balance so badly came with a big warning sign. Still, she couldn't forget the pull of Hollis's piercing gaze or the way Hollis's fingers had gripped her neck, gentle and possessive. She'd ached in a way that was more sweetly painful than anything she'd ever known. Annie swallowed, her throat dry. Her heart thudded with nearly the same intensity as Hollis's rhythmic hammer blows. Just looking at Hollis brought the ache back, and she wasn't sure she wanted that to stop.

Suddenly Hollis looked over her shoulder. She paused, motionless, the hammer gripped loosely in her left hand and her gaze moving slowly over Annie's body. Finally, after what felt like an eternity while Annie stood as helpless as a forest creature under the eyes of a predator, Hollis said, "Hi. I'm sorry, I guess I lost track of time."

"I'm early," Annie said.

Hollis climbed down and slid her hammer into the loop on the side of her belt. The hammer swung against her thigh, reminding Annie of the gunslingers she had secretly admired in old movies as a child, only then she had imagined the rebels as wild, free women. The tank top clung damply to Hollis's chest, highlighting the curve of her breasts and her muscular abdomen. Annie pulled her gaze upward to Hollis's face.

"I'm early." Now she was repeating herself. Wonderful.

"I just need five minutes to shower," Hollis said. "There's coffee in the kitchen. Go on in and help yourself."

"All right, thanks."

Hollis turned, unslung her equipment belt, and placed it on a low plank bench under the kitchen windows. She disappeared through the screen door and Annie slowly followed. Keeping a professional distance was going to be harder than she'd expected, and something she had no practice at doing. She'd never let anyone get close enough that she'd needed to draw lines. She took a mug from a hook hanging underneath the glass-fronted wooden cabinet and poured herself a cup of coffee. Upstairs, water ran, and she pictured Hollis stripping and stepping into the shower. An image of her own soap-covered hands gliding over toned muscles and tanned skin leapt fully formed into her mind. She saw herself cupping firm breasts and sliding her thumbs over hard, heat-flushed nipples. She tasted the sweetness of Hollis's breath and quickened under the press of Hollis's mouth to hers. Hands trembling, she carefully set the coffee cup down.

Never once had she fantasized about sex with Jeff. She'd thought at the time what they'd shared was all that it should be. Later she'd come to appreciate other women and experienced physical stirrings that were wholly different and far sweeter than what she'd known. But this. This she had not imagined. This was far from anything she understood.

"Have you eaten?"

Hollis spoke from behind her and Annie swung around, startled. She didn't lose track of time, but today she had—fantasizing about a woman she hadn't even kissed. The woman she'd said no to, for good reasons she couldn't remember right now.

Hollis looked as good in dark pants and a light lavender shirt, set off by a narrow black belt and black loafers, as she had in a tank top and shorts. Her hair was damp from the shower and looked as if she'd just toweled it dry and carelessly run her hands through it. She probably had. She didn't need to do anything else. The wild look suited her, just as the holster had. No doubt she wielded her surgical instruments with the same confident nonchalance. She stood in the doorway rolling up her cuffs, watching Annie, her eyes shadowed, guarded.

"I had Cheerios with Callie about an hour ago," Annie said.

Hollis smiled. "Then you've got to be hungry. How do you feel about eating bagels in the car?"

"Our first stop is only a few blocks from here. We've got time to actually eat like civilized human beings." Annie laughed. "Well, like medical people anyhow. Ten minutes should be plenty of time."

"Good. Cream cheese?"

"Sure."

Hollis brushed by her, opened the refrigerator, and passed Annie a container of cream cheese. "Knives are in the drawer by the sink."

"I remember," Annie said, opening the utility drawer.

Hollis took a bag of bagels from the counter, opened it, and asked, "Cinnamon raisin, oat bran, pumpernickel, or everything?"

"Cinnamon raisin," Annie said.

"Coming up."

A minute later Annie followed Hollis out onto the porch and leaned against the railing. The bagel was fresh, the day was bright and beautiful, and Hollis was the most stunning woman she'd ever seen. She concentrated on her bagel. "You're up early working on the porch."

"I got up to ride, and when I got home…" Hollis shrugged, looking out over the yard. "Restless."

"You're a serious cyclist."

"It usually relaxes me." Hollis set her coffee cup down and brushed crumbs from her hands. "Do you ride much?"

"I did, when I was younger. I didn't have a car and it was a lot faster than walking. I never really rode for pleasure, though." Annie put her cup beside Hollis's on the railing. "Callie wants a bike. Any recommendations?"

"There's a good local bike shop on Germantown Avenue—I could take you over..." Hollis's jaw tightened. "Well. I can tell you where it is."

Annie knew she shouldn't, but she couldn't help herself. She lightly gripped Hollis's forearm. "I'd love it if you could consult. I want to make sure she gets the right thing, and honestly, I have no idea what kids' bikes are like these days."

Hollis stared at Annie's hand on her arm. A touch didn't necessarily mean anything, but tell that to her body. She'd been revved since she'd turned around and seen Annie watching her, and the look in Annie's eyes hadn't been saying stay away. Her skin was about to blister from the heat of Annie's fingers. "I'd like that."

"Hollis, I'm sorry if—"

"No. We're good." She hated knowing she'd made Annie uncomfortable. She cupped Annie's jaw and traced her thumb over her cheek. "It's okay. I got a little ahead of things last night. My fault."

"No fault," Annie whispered. "I'm just not—"

"No more apologies. It's all right." Hollis picked up both cups. "I'll take these inside. We should probably go."

"Yes, we should," Annie said, knowing it wasn't all right at all.

CHAPTER NINETEEN

"My first patient—Emmie—is a stay-at-home mom, so her schedule is flexible. Linda is right on the way, and I thought we could check in with her and Robin first."

"Good idea," Hollis said. "Just do whatever you'd usually do. Pretend I'm not here."

Annie laughed. "I'm a midwife, not a magician."

"What—you're saying I'm a distraction?" Hollis grinned when Annie's milky skin turned rosy, the way she imagined it would when Annie was aroused. Hollis shifted, stretching her legs, her trousers suddenly feeling too tight. Not a good way to start the day, but she liked the twinge of arousal a lot more than she had the dull ache of disappointment she'd awakened with. She liked how Annie made her feel. She liked feeling again, wanting again.

"A distraction? Not at all." Annie flipped her blinker crisply and turned down School House Lane. "I'm simply noting that you are not the type to be ignored."

"Oh yeah?" Hollis murmured, enjoying the game. "What type is that?"

Annie pulled to the curb and shut off the engine. "The forceful, commanding type."

Hollis almost choked. Geez, she hadn't expected that and definitely hadn't expected to get a rush from the way Annie sounded saying it. Like she might enjoy Hollis being in charge. "Thanks. I think." She jumped from the car as Annie got out and pulled her bag and a med kit from the backseat. "Was that a compliment?"

"No," Annie said, turning to stride up the stone walk. "Just an observation."

"Huh. Sounded like a compliment," Hollis muttered as she hurried after Annie. She grinned when Annie's laughter drifted back to her. She glanced up. The sky hadn't changed since her ride a few hours earlier—still crystalline blue and cloudless—but the day seemed brighter. Beautiful.

She'd cleared her schedule for the morning in preparation for shadowing Annie. She was looking forward to the experience—that probably explained her sudden upturn in mood. Professionally, she was intrigued. The home-birth movement was well-established in Europe—had been for centuries in some countries—and was growing in the U.S. by leaps and bounds. Articles for and against the practice were appearing in lay publications and medical journals. Thousands of mothers proclaimed the many advantages. She didn't feel threatened or competitive, but she was acutely curious. If she was missing something, she wanted to know. Maybe she'd learn something spending time with Annie. That was likely the cause of the anticipation churning in her belly.

Annie climbed the stairs and rang the bell. Looking at her started an ache in Hollis's chest she really didn't want to think about. She hurried up the stairs to join Annie, glad for the diversion of work.

Robin smiled when she opened the door and saw Annie and Hollis. "Now everyone's here. Come on in."

"I know I said late morning," Annie said, following Robin down the hall, "but you were on our way, and I figured with the kids, you'd be up."

"Been up, got the crew off, and was just making some breakfast. You two eat?"

Annie looked at Hollis. "We're good, I think."

"Yeah, thanks though." Hollis slowed a little, letting Annie take the lead. She considered Linda her patient now, but this was Annie's turf, and she was just here to observe. Funny, the role didn't bother her as much as she would have thought a few weeks ago.

"Honor's here," Robin added, stopping at the foot of the staircase. "Go on up—first open door on the left. I'll be right there. Coffee all around?"

"None for me," Annie said.

"That would be great," Hollis said. She followed Annie, taking in the black-and-white family photos that covered the cream-colored walls, mostly of Linda with various children. Hollis picked out the towhead she'd seen with Robin in the park. Callie's friend Mike. The other two in many of the photos were just as blond, but five or six years older. The display reminded her of her mother's house—and all the photos with her and the guys. She'd been the smallest, but Rob always made sure she didn't get buried by hoisting her up when she was small, and when she grew taller… The pang of pain caught her unawares and she turned sharply away.

Annie stood at the top of the stairs, watching her. "What is it?"

Hollis shook her head. "Nothing."

Annie's look said she didn't believe her, but after a moment when her eyes softened with sympathy, she walked on.

Grateful for the call of duty, Hollis slipped into the bedroom after Annie. The room was large with wide windows on two sides. Through those opposite her she got a glimpse of a large maple and the long grassy yard where she'd played volleyball. The trilling call of robins nesting in the branches outside the open windows floated into the room. Honor Blake sat in an easy chair next to the bed where Linda, in a white T-shirt proclaiming *I'd Rather Be Lucky Than Good* in purple letters, was propped up on several pillows. She looked rested—her color was better and her eyes had lost the patina of fear they'd worn yesterday.

Honor stood. "Hi, Annie, Hollis. I'll get out of your way—"

"No, please stay if Linda doesn't mind." Annie crossed to the bed.

"Stay, Honor," Linda said and Honor sat back down. "Hi, Annie. Hi, Hollis."

"Hi," Annie said. "How are you feeling?"

"Much better." Linda glanced at Honor, then Annie. "In fact, I feel perfectly fine. I was wondering—"

"Oh no, you don't," Annie said. "Bed rest for today at least."

Honor laughed softly. "Told you."

Linda gave an exaggerated sigh. "I was afraid you were going to say that. Bathroom privileges?"

"Let me take a look at you first."

Hollis took the cup of coffee Robin handed her as she came in. When Robin set the tray on a large oak dresser, Hollis lifted a small bright blue pitcher with hand-painted daffodils on the side and poured cream into her cup. "Thanks."

"Any time." Robin glanced at Linda. Her easy smile slipped a little. "Thanks for coming."

"Annie wouldn't have it any other way. Try to relax."

Robin sighed. "Man, I'd much rather have them."

Hollis laughed and sipped her coffee, watching Annie talk easily with Linda and Honor while performing a quick, thorough physical exam. When Annie finished, she pulled a chart from her shoulder bag and scribbled a few notes. Everything Annie was doing she would have done in the outpatient prenatal clinic at the hospital, but she had to agree, this was a much more relaxed, personal environment.

Annie finished her notes, pulled a straight-backed oak desk chair closer to the bed, and sat down. "Everything seems normal, and it's now been twenty hours since your last contraction. Here's my offer— you can go from the bed to that bathroom over there with assistance and back again. No showering, no bath, no quick trip downstairs to make lunch. The rest of the time you're in bed."

"Done," Linda said fervently. She tilted her chin toward Robin. "Besides, she's not going to let me get away with anything else."

"Damn straight," Robin said. "You want more tea, babe?"

"I'm good for now." Linda looked past Annie to Hollis. "Things not exciting enough for you over at the big house?"

Hollis grinned. "Not half as much fun as this."

Linda shook her head. "You're not going to be very popular if you start suggesting the OB staff should make house calls."

"Trust me, that's not on my agenda. I'm not going to risk my life." Hollis nodded toward Annie. "Besides, Annie's crew has that well covered."

Annie rose and packed up her bag. She'd been focused on Linda, but she'd felt Hollis behind her, sensed her watching. She hadn't been self-conscious, not in any kind of professional way, but her skin had tingled knowing Hollis was looking at her. She wasn't usually anxious, but every nerve jangled when Hollis was nearby. Her skin was hypersensitive, her blood rushed faster, and a seething urgency deep inside threatened her concentration. She couldn't think about all that now—she had more patients to see. She rapidly repacked her bags and turned to Hollis. "Anything you'd like to add, Dr. Monroe?"

Hollis drained her coffee cup and placed it on the tray. "No, I think you've covered everything."

Pleased, Annie said to Linda, "If anything changes between now and tomorrow, call. Even if you think it's nothing—anything that worries you—anytime, I'm a phone call away."

"We know." Linda grasped Annie's hand and squeezed. "When can I go back to work?"

Annie laughed. "God, medical people. I don't know yet. Let's see how the next few days go. One thing at a time."

"I know," Linda sighed. "But God, bed rest!"

"Hopefully, just one more day of that." Annie nodded to Honor. "Nice to see you again, Dr. Blake."

"I'll see you at birthing class. I'm going to second for Robin."

"I'll look forward to it."

Robin led Annie and Hollis out into the hall and closed the door. "I want Linda to have what she wants around this baby, but I don't want to take any chances. How safe is the home birth going to be, really?"

Annie expected Hollis to recommend hospital delivery and was surprised when Hollis remained silent. A faint nod from Hollis signaled she should field the question.

"Dr. Monroe and I talked about this last night," Annie said. "Until and unless Linda has other complicating signs, there's no reason to change the plan for her to give birth here. We've still got quite a ways to go, and things might change. That's why we're going to watch her carefully. After the next few days, I'll see her every week or sooner if we need to. If there's any sign of complications, then we'll switch plans immediately and have her deliver at PMC."

"Okay." Robin let out a long breath. "I'm really glad the two of you are taking care of her. Thanks."

Annie smiled. "Of course."

"Don't mention it," Hollis said.

On the way to the car, Annie said, "Thanks for the backup in there."

"Did you expect me to try a power play?"

Annie paused by the car. "On some level, I think I did."

"You know," Hollis said, "we're playing without a rule book here."

"Yes, I know. I can't say I like it much."

"No, neither do I." Annie went around to the driver's side, unlocked the car, and climbed in.

She waited while Hollis buckled her seat belt. "Linda is an unusual circumstance—we've been forced into a joint-care situation in the middle of an emergency. Ordinarily that wouldn't happen."

"You're right," Hollis said. "We'd be seeing patients jointly, but you'd have the lead unless problems escalated."

"You'd be all right with that?" Annie hadn't expected such an easy concession. Hollis wasn't like most of the OBs she ran into—but then, Hollis wasn't like anyone she knew. She had a healthy ego, but she didn't let it get in the way of what really mattered. "Playing backup wouldn't bother you?"

"I've got plenty to do," Hollis said. "Are you going to fight me if I think it's too to risky for a patient to continue with the home-birth plan?"

"I don't know. I suppose it depends on whether I agree."

"Well, that's why we're doing this." Hollis shrugged. "This kind of intensive follow-up is time-consuming and expensive, though."

"Time-consuming, yes," Annie said, starting the car and pulling out, "but we don't charge for every follow-up visit, and even when we do, our scale is less than yours."

"Okay, remuneration aside, it's a lot more work for you."

"Yes, I suppose, but that's exactly why we feel comfortable following high-risk patients." Annie signaled a turn onto Lincoln Drive. "We see them so frequently and in such different circumstances, we usually can identify the onset of complications at a very early stage."

"What happens if you're not available? Someone else takes your place?"

Annie frowned. "Yes, but it's not ideal and I don't like it. That's why I take call even when I'm not on call." She smiled over at Hollis. "I'm sure you know what I'm talking about."

Hollis laughed. "Oh, I do."

"See," Annie said lightly, "we have more in common than you thought."

"I know," Hollis murmured, looking forward to the next few hours. Spending time with Annie, working or relaxing, filled her with equal parts excitement and contentment. She steadfastly refused to consider why. She just wanted the feeling to continue.

As Annie visited the pre- and postnatal patients on her list, Hollis quickly appreciated that Annie's patients trusted her completely. Hollis could see why. Annie was fast and efficient, giving each patient her undivided attention and calming anxious loved ones at the same time. She was a natural caregiver.

A little after eleven, Annie said, "That's it for the home calls. Do you want me to drop you at home or the hospital?"

"Home is good. What's on for you the rest of the day?"

"I'm going to pick up Callie for lunch and then deliver her to a friend's until I finish in clinic this afternoon."

"I have clinic tomorrow. Do you want to come along?"

"Yes. We should sit down and compare our schedules and work something out for the next—I don't know, what do you think? Two weeks?"

"Better make it a month, at least," Hollis said. "We don't want anyone to accuse us of rushing to judgment."

Annie rolled her eyes. "No, God forbid."

"Meet me for lunch tomorrow? We'll work something out."

"All right." Annie pulled up in front of Hollis's and shut off the engine. "I liked working with you today."

"Yeah," Hollis said, wishing the morning didn't have to end. "I did too. You're good."

Annie laughed. "Not what you expected?"

"Not exactly. I expected you'd be confident. But you've got...the touch. You connect with people—and they feel it. It's like a surgeon having good hands. Some people have it, others never get it. Can't teach it. That absolute sense of caring can't be faked, and you have that."

Annie caught her breath. Hollis couldn't possibly know how much that meant to her. "Thank you."

Hollis made no move to get out of the car and Annie didn't want her to. The windows were down and a warm breeze sifted through the front seat, ruffling Hollis's hair. Annie was reminded of summer days on the farm and the smell of fresh-cut hay and the utter stillness of the air, as if she could reach out and grab handfuls of the steamy heat and wrap it around her fingers like strands of cotton candy. She'd felt so vastly alone then, under that endless blanket of blue sky and sun, that she'd ached for something she couldn't name. The ache pulled at her now. Hollis was so close. So real.

"Callie hasn't..." Annie's voice broke and she gripped the wheel. "Callie hasn't stopped asking about a bike since last night."

Hollis released her seat belt and turned toward her, her knee brushing Annie's. "You ready to get her one?"

"She'll need training wheels, right?"

"It depends on her balance and how comfortable she is on the bike." Hollis smiled. "But she inherited your touch—I was watching her color. She's got really good coordination. I think she'll pick it up pretty quick."

Annie's heart fluttered. She hadn't believed it could do that—not unless she was on her way to the ICU. Hollis had noticed Callie color. Hollis really looked. Hollis saw her. The fluttering settled lower in her belly, grew heavier. More insistent. She thought of Hollis's hand on her neck and a pulse tripped between her thighs. She took a breath, kept her voice light although she trembled everywhere. "I guess I'll probably have to get a bicycle too, then."

"It's a great way to spend time together." Hollis smiled. "Once Rob taught me…"

Hollis's smile faded. There was no mistaking the look, the same one she'd seen on Hollis's face in the stairwell at Linda's. Pain, raw and untempered. "Rob?"

"My oldest brother." Hollis averted her gaze. "He taught me— well, pretty much everything."

"He sounds great. Is he—"

Hollis's chin shot up. Her eyes were two dark pools, completely opaque. "He's dead. He was in the South Tower."

"Oh God, Hollis. I'm sorry." Annie took Hollis's hand. Her fingers were icy. She pulled Hollis's hand into her lap and cupped it between both of hers, rubbing gently as if that would help. She knew the cold was somewhere much deeper than she could touch, but she had to try. "I'm so sorry."

"He wasn't even supposed to be anywhere around, but I…" Hollis shuddered.

"What?" Annie moved closer and brushed her fingers through Hollis's hair. "What?"

"I was supposed to meet him for breakfast, and we were going to go house hunting. His wife was pregnant and he wanted a bigger place." Hollis leaned her head back and closed her eyes. "I canceled at the last minute. I'd spent the night at my girlfriend's and we were still… I figured Rob and I could always go another day."

"You couldn't know—"

"Rob was always there for me. Always." Hollis's jaw clenched. "But I couldn't drag my ass up to meet him, so he went to the fire station to hang with the guys. He rolled out when the call came. He was probably one of the first on scene."

Hollis's anguish ripped at the fabric of Annie's soul. She didn't have words to ease that horrible pain, but she ached to try. She stroked Hollis's hair. "Come on. Let's go inside."

"I'm okay." Hollis pulled away. Her eyes were wounded, haunted.

"Hollis—let me come inside. I'll fix us some lunch."

"No," Hollis whispered. "I'm not good company now. I'll see you in clinic."

"Hollis, wait—"

Hollis pushed open the door and a few seconds later, she was gone.

Annie understood Hollis wanted to be alone, didn't want to let Annie or anyone inside. She shouldn't care, but she did. Being shut out cut deep. She hadn't thought she'd ever let anyone get close enough to hurt her again, but she knew Hollis could. She drove away, grateful for the pain—taking it as a warning. She'd lost sight of all she'd learned for a short time, but she was clear now. She wasn't going to give anyone the power to hurt her, not even Hollis.

CHAPTER TWENTY

Floor rounds were running late, and Hollis didn't have time to think of Annie or dwell on the wounds their conversation had opened. Every time Annie's face, soft with sympathy and, later, hurt, swam into her consciousness, she grabbed another chart and concentrated on taking care of other people's worries. That had worked to keep her pain at bay when things got bad for almost ten years, but not today. Today she had to struggle to block Annie out. She had three post-op checks left when she got a STAT page. She grabbed a wall phone and dialed the extension. Ned's secretary picked up.

"Hold just a moment, Dr. Monroe," the secretary said. "He's right here."

"Hi," Ned said. "I've got a near-term mother in the office with placenta previa. Can you see her?"

"Is she bleeding?"

"A little spotting—that's what brought her in. No contractions."

"The previa is new?"

"Yeah—this is her first baby, but she's had a couple of misses."

"Send her to the ER and have them call me. I'll be down as soon as she arrives."

"Thanks. Appreciate it."

An hour later one of the ER attendings paged her. "Got Ned's patient here. She's not bleeding now but we typed and crossed her. Just in case."

"Good. Tell the blood bank I want four units standing by. I'll be down in five minutes."

"Name's Ellen Goodwin. Bay twelve. Thanks, Hollis."

Hollis found Ellen, a thirty-five-year-old African American

woman with bright deep brown eyes, waiting anxiously with her partner, Sheri, a fortyish blue-eyed blonde with a quick smile.

"Hi, I'm Dr. Monroe—Dr. Williams asked me to stop by and see you."

Introductions were made and she did a brief exam. "I'm just going to review your MRI and I'll be right back." Five minutes later she returned and pulled a stool over to the bedside. "You have what we call placenta previa. Part of the placenta—the vascular tissue that carries blood and nutrients to the fetus—is lying so low in the uterus, it's covering the cervix."

"Is the baby in danger?" Ellen asked in a surprisingly calm tone.

"Not yet," Hollis said. "But there's a risk of more bleeding, and if that happens... Do you know the sex yet?"

Ellen smiled. "Yes—we're picking out boy's names."

"He could be in trouble if you start bleeding and don't stop."

"What about Ellen?" Sheri asked.

"We never like to have a mother bleeding—and uncontrolled hemorrhage is a risk in this situation."

Ellen took Sheri's hand. "What do you suggest?"

"The baby is close enough to term to be delivered. I recommend an elective C-section first thing in the morning."

"Tomorrow?" Sheri breathed the words as if in shock.

"Yes. This way we can control the delivery and get the placenta out before there's a lot of blood loss—usually. You need to know there's still a risk we'll lose more blood than we'd like."

"And then?" Ellen still looked and sounded calm.

"Then you may need blood transfusions or, worst-case scenario, I'll have to remove the uterus to stop the bleeding."

Sheri's face went white. Hollis pulled over a chair. "Why don't you sit down, Sheri."

"I'm fine," Sheri said, sitting abruptly.

"We want more children," Ellen said.

"I understand," Hollis said. "That would be my last option."

Ellen nodded. "Fine. Let's go ahead."

"All right." Hollis stood. "You'll be admitted tonight. I'll schedule you for eight a.m. Bright and early tomorrow you'll have this baby."

"Thank you," Ellen and Sheri said together.

By the time Hollis had filled out the paperwork, it was close to seven. She grabbed a pizza from Giovanni's on the way home and ate it out of the box on the back porch. The house was dark and still. Her mother kept telling her to get a dog. Maybe she should.

After wrapping the remains of the pizza in foil for breakfast, she changed into a sleeveless T-shirt and cut-off jeans and went to work. She kept busy until almost eleven, working on the house. She tore out a wall where she'd mentioned to Annie she wanted to put a powder room, pounding at sections of old plaster and lathe that left her coated in a fine white dust, and shored up the sagging beams with new vertical posts. She quit when her back was too stiff to swing the hammer and heft the chunks of debris out the back door any longer. She'd worn gloves to protect her hands, but her forearms ached and she needed to rest them before surgery the next day. She took a long hot shower, hoping the pulsing water would relax her. It didn't.

She lay in bed in the dark, with only a sheet covering her hips and the windows open to catch the faint currents of air. The temperature outside hovered in the low seventies and sweat soon misted her skin. She stared at the ceiling, at the wavy patterns of light and dark made by moonlight filtering through the branches of the hemlock outside her window. She thought she could make out the shape of a monkey riding a tricycle.

She'd managed not to think of Annie for twelve hours. She thought of Rob almost every day, but in a distant way, as if through a curtain of rain. The instant her mind conjured up his face or a conversation or a memory of time they'd spent together, the curtain thickened and images dissolved, shielding her from the full force of the pain. Her shields had failed her when she'd seen the photographs of Linda's family and remembered her own family and the special bond she'd shared with Rob. That little break in her defenses had been the beginning, maybe, but Annie was the one to break through all her barricades. Annie crossed her barriers like they weren't even there, and that scared her. She was in danger of becoming attached, seriously attached, and attachments could be deadly. When they broke, or worse, were severed by random tragedy, they left you bleeding with no way to stop the hemorrhage. She'd vowed never to put herself in that position again, and she was in very real danger of doing just that.

She tossed and turned, too hot in the warm night air. Finally she got up and took another shower, and still, she couldn't relax. She pulled on a T-shirt and blue-and-white-striped boxer shorts and walked barefoot down to her front porch in the dark. She sat in an Adirondack chair with a worn canvas cushion, alone in the night. Cars occasionally passed, and now and then she heard the distant peal of laughter or a deep rumble of conversation from an open bedroom window. She ached, as lonely as if she were marooned on some faraway planet.

She wasn't alone—she had family she could call, but what could she say? Everyone grieved over Rob. Everyone bled. But only she carried the guilt. She dropped her head to the back of the chair and rubbed her eyes. She'd told Annie things she'd never told anyone. She'd made her last confession a week before the world exploded and hadn't been back to Mass since. She might be forgiven her sins, but she wasn't ready to accept absolution. Rationally, she knew she wasn't at fault for what had happened to Rob, but she'd played a part in the tapestry of fate that had put him there that morning, all because she'd put someone first over him, because she'd taken him for granted. He'd always been there, and she'd just assumed he always would be. The next time would be time enough—and she never had another time. She'd never be able to say all the things she'd felt her entire life but never thought she needed to say.

Still, she'd confessed to Annie—the words pouring out as if from a stranger's mouth. Why, she didn't know. Annie would offer her forgiveness, not recognizing the magnitude of her transgressions, and maybe that was why she'd confessed what she'd never said out loud.

Annie. Annie with the understanding eyes and tender touch. If things were different, would she have taken Annie to meet Rob? *Look at the woman I found—isn't she amazing?* Rob would have flicked her a high sign behind Annie's back—*Yeah, you did good, Monroe.* But things were what they were—Rob would never see his own child, and Annie didn't deserve her ghosts.

Rob's loss had left a huge gaping hole in her life, a sorrow she couldn't put aside. So she'd done the only thing she could—she'd withdrawn into a self-protective shell and buried herself in her work. Now Annie had cracked the shell, and she wondered if all the careful artifice of her life would fracture next.

Finally, exhausted, she made her way up to bed and lay face-down on top of the sheets, naked, alone, and accepting she had no answers.

❖

The next morning, Hollis stood in a lukewarm shower until the grogginess was gone. She had a cup of coffee and was at the hospital by seven, alert and with nothing on her mind but Ellen Goodwin. At seven thirty she went to see her in the pre-op area.

"Hi, Ellen. Sleep okay?"

"Fine. How about you?"

"Like a rock." Hollis smiled at Sheri. "How are you doing?"

Sheri rubbed Ellen's arm. "I'm fine. We're excited. It can't be too soon."

Ellen squeezed Sheri's hand. "We've tried and tried and didn't think it was ever going to happen. Now we're almost there."

"Good. Not much longer." Hollis signed some of the paperwork on Ellen's chart and placed it at the foot of the stretcher. "The anesthesiologist will be coming to take you back in just a minute. I'm going back to scrub, but you may be asleep by the time I get into the room. They'll start an epidural, but you'll be sedated so you may not remember everything that happens." She looked at Sheri. "As soon as things quiet down a little in there, I'll have the nurses call out to let you know how things are going. Don't be concerned if you don't hear anything for forty-five minutes or so. Sometimes we get a slow start."

"I understand. Take as long as you need. I just want them both to be healthy."

"Good enough. I'll talk to you as soon as I come out."

"Thanks, Dr. Monroe."

Hollis squeezed Ellen's knee. "Ready?"

"More than ready."

"Me too."

Hollis walked back to the OR and told the nurses she was ready.

"I'll page anesthesia," Sue Gregory, the scrub nurse, said. "Anything special you need?"

"I don't think so. Who's on call for neonatology?"

"Karl Provik."

"Good. I'll let you know when to call him."

"Okay, Hollis, thanks."

Hollis scrubbed, Sue gowned and gloved her, and as soon as anesthesia was ready, she stepped up to the table and Sue passed her the scalpel. She made the Pfannenstiel incision just above the pubic symphysis at the junction with the lower abdomen. She cut down through subcutaneous tissue and divided the rectus. The uterus looked fibrotic, somewhat pale, as if it hadn't been getting enough blood. She was glad they hadn't waited. She made the incision in the uterus and Sue sucked up the amniotic fluid as it gushed out. The color was good—clear, no signs of fetal distress. She widened the incision with one hand inside and palpated the baby's head. She delivered the baby and clamped the cord.

"You can call Karl," Hollis said and passed the baby boy to the waiting nurse. When she turned back, blood filled the uterus and poured over into the abdomen. The surgical field leapt into sharp focus, as if a color TV show had suddenly switched to black and white.

"We've got bleeding," Hollis said. "Better get up another suction and start the Pitocin." Sweat broke out on her brow and she blinked it away. "Kelly clamp."

Someone wiped her face. The bleeding slowed but didn't stop. "Load up the number two silks and have someone get her partner on the phone."

"Do you want the hysterectomy tray, Hollis?" Sue asked.

Hollis looked up at the clock. "In a minute."

❖

At noon, Annie decided Hollis wasn't going to call about meeting her for lunch before clinic. She was surprised. She'd known all along they were asking for trouble trying to build some kind of personal relationship—she hesitated to call it friendship, whatever lay between them had seemed from the onset to be something different—when they had to work together under such stressful, volatile conditions. But she'd assumed Hollis could handle it—just as she was handling it.

True, she'd had a lousy night's sleep and been grumpy at breakfast. She'd just managed to put on enough of a smile to fool Callie, and fortunately all she'd had scheduled for the morning was paperwork. No one minded when she bitched about that. Now she sat at her desk watching the clock, giving Hollis another five minutes to call. Four minutes had passed when she finally rose, disgusted at herself for putting all the power in Hollis's hands. She needed to be in clinic if she was going to make a decision that she hadn't wanted to make in the first place, and she was damn well going to have the information she needed. She closed down her computer with a few sharp punches to the keyboard, snatched up her shoulder bag, and spun around, nearly colliding with Barb.

"Going to a fire?" Barbara asked with a faint smile.

"Something like that," Annie muttered.

"Should I ask?"

"No," Annie said with a sigh. "Nothing major, really. Just a slight miscalculation on my part, corrected now."

Barb gave her an uh-huh look. "Okay. Whatever you say."

"I'm going over to PMC for clinic. Unless something comes up, I won't be back this afternoon."

"No problem. Let's get together the beginning of next week and talk about how this is going."

"Sure," Annie said.

"Don't forget, if you're running into roadblocks, I might be of help with that."

"Nothing like that," Annie said. "I'll talk to you later."

She hurried away, not in the mood to talk about Hollis. She definitely wasn't going to tell Barbara about the tangle the two of them had created when both of them should've known better. Well, she couldn't speak for Hollis, but she could certainly speak for herself.

She drove and parked in the hospital parking lot, thinking as she backed into a space of the morning she'd almost run over Hollis. Of the insolent way Hollis had planted herself in front of her car and refused to move until she'd gotten Annie to agree to have dinner with her. The way her deep blue eyes had sparkled with a touch of arrogance and a hell of a lot of charm. Did she have to be so good-looking? Did she have to be so damn nice? Annie switched off the engine and rolled down the windows, making the most of the halfhearted breeze. Hollis was charming. And Hollis hadn't done anything she wouldn't have done, given the circumstances. Hollis had suffered a terrible loss, and there was no statute of limitations on grief. Her pain had been palpable. So dense and fresh all she could think about was putting her arms around Hollis and holding her, getting between her and the memories that hurt her so much.

"As if I could," Annie muttered. "As if she wanted me to."

That's really what had put her in such a bad mood—Hollis didn't want her close. Perfectly understandable. She was the same way. So what was the problem?

"Absolutely nothing."

Annie grabbed her keys, pulled her bag from the car, and locked up. Striding rapidly toward the hospital, she vowed that when she saw Hollis, she was going to act as if absolutely nothing had happened between them—because really, nothing had. They'd each shared a few things they probably wished they hadn't, but that was over—in the past now. She could do this.

She got directions to the clinic from the guard at the door and found the clinic area a few minutes later. A pile of charts stood on a high counter and several pregnant women sat in a nearby waiting area watching television, corralling children, and talking amongst themselves. Annie glanced up and down the hall but didn't see any sign of Hollis. A red-haired man in a lab coat and scrubs sat behind the counter making notes in a chart.

"Excuse me," Annie said, "is Hollis Monroe here?"

"No, she's held up with a patient. Can I help you?"

Annie tugged her lip with her teeth. No telling when Hollis would be back. "I'm not sure. I'm Annie Colfax, from the birthing center. I was supposed to see patients here with Hollis this afternoon."

"Well," he said, rising, "I'm Ned Williams." He held out his hand, giving her a look as if he knew her. "One of the obstetricians in the group. I'm filling in for her this afternoon. You're welcome to join me."

"You wouldn't mind?"

"No, not at all."

"Okay," Annie said, storing her bag underneath the counter. She followed Ned down the hall to the first room, where he passed her a chart and gave her a brief summary of the patient.

The afternoon passed quickly. Ned was friendly and informative, although he lacked the personal charm that allowed Hollis to have such instant rapport with her patients. And she really needed to stop thinking about Hollis. Close to five, she gathered her things and waited while Ned took a call. She heard him say, "Thanks, Hollis," and she pretended not to notice her pulse jump.

"Thanks again, Ned." She held out her hand. "This afternoon was great."

"Glad to have you along." Ned shook her hand and leaned on the counter. "I'll tell Hollis you were here. She spent most of the afternoon in the OR with one of my moms in trouble. I definitely had the better day."

"Thanks, but I imagine I'll catch up with her tomorrow sometime."

"Good enough. Have a nice night."

"Yes," Annie said absently, "you too."

She glanced at her watch on her way out to the parking lot. Too late to do much cooking tonight. She needed to pick up Callie in twenty minutes. She wondered how long Hollis would be at the hospital. She wondered if she'd eaten.

"Hollis can take care of herself," she muttered, unlocking the car. But she couldn't forget the pain in Hollis's eyes.

She slid into the car, pulled out her iPhone, and instructed Siri, "Find me the number for the restaurant Casa Ranchero."

CHAPTER TWENTY-ONE

Hollis walked out the emergency room doors and blinked at the brightness of the early evening sky. Somehow, the artificial lighting in the hospital never seemed as brilliant as daylight. Sometimes she would go twenty-four hours without seeing the sun, and the long days of summer were a bonus—it was almost six p.m. and the sun hadn't yet set. She slowed just to feel the last warm rays on her face. The glass doors behind her whooshed open, and a group of nurses and techs came through, talking excitedly about weekend plans as they hurried past. She didn't have any weekend plans. She didn't have any plans at all.

She rarely gave any thought to how she would spend her free time. Until recently, she'd been perfectly content. Now she chafed, feeling aimless and untethered, as irritable as if she had an itch between her shoulder blades she couldn't reach. When she contemplated the night ahead, the hours stretched endlessly. She was too keyed up to consider sleep anytime soon, too damn tired to think about cycling, and she couldn't ride her motorcycle when she was this distracted. That left her without much in the way of options. She'd walked to work, so at least she'd have a few minutes to enjoy what was left of the day. She'd just grabbed jeans from her locker when she'd left the ICU and wore her scrub shirt for the short walk home.

"Hey, Hollis!"

Hollis turned and saw Honor. She slid her hands into the pockets of her jeans and waited for Honor to catch up. Her blond hair was loose and she carried a red nylon backpack over one shoulder. Dressed in beige pants, a pale yellow shirt with blue stripes, and running shoes, she could pass for one of the medical students.

"Hi," Honor said. "I'm glad I saw you leaving. You walking home?"

"Yeah."

"Mind company?" Honor asked, falling into step.

"No. Glad for it."

Honor gave her a quizzical look. "Rough day?"

Hollis sighed. "Yeah, but nothing out of the ordinary. I'm just…" She shook her head. "Never mind. Just need to catch my second wind."

"Well, if you're not busy for dinner you can come on over to my place. Phyllis—my mother-in-law—always cooks enough for an army."

"Oh, thanks. I appreciate it, but—"

"Some other time, then," Honor said, saving Hollis the embarrassment of making a lame excuse.

"I'll take you up on it," Hollis said, surprised to realize she meant it. "Does Quinn's mother live with you?"

"Quinn's mother?" Honor hesitated. "Oh—Phyllis. She has the twin next door and pretty much keeps us all afloat. But she isn't Quinn's mother, she's Terry's, my first partner."

"Oh." Hollis flushed, hoping she hadn't committed a faux pas. The few times she'd seen Quinn and Honor together, they'd looked as if they'd been together forever.

Honor must have read her mind. "Terry was killed about twelve years ago, when I was a resident."

Hollis caught her breath. "I'm sorry."

"Thanks." Honor smiled wistfully. "She was my first and I thought my only. I'm incredibly lucky to have two such amazing women in my life."

"Can I ask you a personal question?"

"Sure." Honor gestured to a bench in the shade of a huge oak at the edge of the park. "Let's take a minute. It's a beautiful night."

Hollis sat beside her, too heart weary to ask herself what the hell she was doing. "How long…how long did it take to feel like you could breathe again?"

"It felt like forever." Honor rested her fingertips on Hollis's arm. "And I guess forever is a really personal thing."

Hollis scrubbed at her face with both hands. "Yeah. Sorry, I don't know what—"

"I met Quinn about six years after Terry died, and at first I couldn't really see her." Honor laughed softly. "But my God, I could feel her. She filled up my life from the instant we met."

Hollis's chest tightened. "Were you scared?"

"Terrified." Honor turned the wedding band on her ring finger. "Of risking. Of losing her. Of everything. But I couldn't let her go."

"She's lucky you were brave," Hollis said softly.

"Mmm, I don't know that I was. I think falling in love with her helped me find some parts I'd lost and didn't even know were gone."

"Thanks for telling me," Hollis said.

"Do you mind me asking who you lost?"

"My older brother. 9/11."

"Oh God, that's horrible." Honor squeezed Hollis's hand. "I'm so sorry."

Hollis didn't know what else to say. She didn't even know why she was talking about Rob, except Honor Blake was the kind of woman who inspired trust. Her kindness was healing. "Thank you. For"—Hollis waved toward the park and the street and the dying day—"this. Talking helped."

"Good. Anytime." Honor took Hollis's hand and, as they started to walk, added, "Now I've got a quick question for you. Business this time."

"Shoot," Hollis said.

Honor brushed an errant strand of hair away from her forehead and shielded her eyes against a blazing shaft of sunlight that slashed low across the horizon, as if the sun were making one last desperate attempt to avoid setting. "Annie gave Linda the okay to go back to work this morning, and she's already bugging me to put her in the rotation. If I don't give her a slot in the ER, she'll talk someone, somewhere, into letting her float. Honestly, I'd rather keep her close in case there's any trouble."

"I'm sure if Annie cleared her, she's okay for regular floor work. I just don't want her flying. What do you think about putting her on half shifts instead of a full eight?"

Honor smiled. "For starters, I think she'll complain. Then I think she'll make my life a misery wanting to pick up overtime when someone calls in sick or we get busy. I can put her on eight hours and make sure she's not on her feet the whole time. I'll screen the cases she's taking if I have to."

"How about four days a week—that will give her enough downtime to get off her feet and recharge. I think as she gets closer to term, she'll be grateful not to be working that much."

"That I can do. How long do you think you'll let her work—until eight months?"

"Let's play it by ear. I'm sure Annie will be keeping a close eye on her."

Honor waved to a tall man in a blue work shirt passing on the opposite side of the street. He held the hands of twin girls about Callie's age. "How's that working out? With Annie?"

Hollis's stomach clenched until she realized Honor was asking about the exploratory committee. "Fine so far. Better than I expected, really."

"Annie seems very competent."

"Yes. Hopefully the rest of her group is like her." Hollis glanced into the park where kids and adults gathered near the pond. She didn't see Annie—too late, probably. The pang of disappointment annoyed her. "I doubt it, though. She's pretty unusual."

"Medicine is changing," Honor mused. "We've got a lot more PAs in the ER than we did five years ago. Every division has physician assistants and nurse practitioners handling primary-care duties. We'd be in trouble without them."

"Are you suggesting we OBs are holdouts? Dinosaurs?"

"I didn't say that." Honor laughed. "Although a few of you…"

Hollis grinned. "Yeah, okay. Maybe so."

"I understand the concerns," Honor said, pausing at the corner at the far end of the park. "But the bottom line is offering the best patient care, and multidisciplinary teams have definitely improved that in cancer care and rehab."

"That's the approach Annie and I will be taking—so I guess we'll find out." Hollis pointed to her house on the opposite corner. "I'm over there."

"It's ridiculous we're only a few blocks away and we haven't gotten together before this," Honor said. "How about dinner Saturday night? Nothing fancy—we'll grill something. Bring a guest."

"All right," Hollis said before she could fabricate an excuse. She wasn't looking forward to a long weekend of her own disgruntled company. "I'll be stag, though."

"I'm glad you can make it. Is six okay? The kids are famished by then."

"Yeah, I know," Hollis said, thinking of Callie. "Sure, it's fine."

"'Night, then."

"'Night." Hollis waved and jogged across the street. Just as she reached her front gate, a car pulled to the curb and someone called her name. She wasn't sure she hadn't imagined it, but she spun around, a rush of excitement surging in her chest.

"Hi, Hollis!" Callie waved out the window of Annie's Volvo.

Hollis walked over, bent down, and peered inside. "Hey, Callie. How are you doing?"

"We brought dinner."

"Did you?" Hollis looked past Callie to Annie, who stared at her uncertainly. "Hi. You're full of surprises."

Annie blushed. "I took a chance you might be hungry."

Hollis glanced into the backseat and saw the takeout bags. A panoply of delectable scents reached her and her stomach rumbled. She laughed. "I guess I am. You two want to come in?"

"I thought maybe we'd have a picnic in the park," Annie said. "We've got another hour of light left. If you're not too tired, I mean."

Hollis wasn't tired all. For the first time since she'd walked out of the hospital, she looked forward to the evening. "What do you need me to bring? I can grab—"

"Just you," Annie said, the smile Hollis loved replacing the uncertainty in her eyes.

"I'm at your service, then. Let me carry the goods."

"I'll take you up on that." Annie ducked her head and unbuckled Callie, hoping her relief wasn't obvious. She hadn't given herself time to think about what she was doing once she'd made the phone call to the restaurant. She wasn't usually impetuous—not any longer. She didn't do things on the spur of the moment, especially not with other people—other people who had somehow come to occupy the very center of her thoughts. Of course, she didn't really know what she did in those circumstances because there hadn't been anyone like that.

Not for so long, and not for who she was now. She was a different person now. At least she hoped she was, or she was doing something completely crazy.

"I want to help carry the goods too, Mommy," Callie informed her.

"Well, sit tight until I come around the other side, and then you can get out and help Hollis."

"Okay. Hurry."

Smiling, Annie stepped out of the car and looked across the roof at Hollis, who was watching her with an expression halfway between amused and that other look she got—the dark, contemplative one, where Annie imagined she saw hunger licking around the edges of a swirling fire. The look that made her burn inside. She swallowed. "I suppose I should've called."

"No," Hollis said, "you did exactly right." She glanced down and grinned. "Can I let her out? She's about to bust."

Annie laughed and her uncertainty faded. "Yes, please." She closed the door and hurried around to the sidewalk. Hollis leaned into the backseat, her jeans stretched tight over her very handsome ass. Callie danced from foot to foot, grinning as if she were about to get a Christmas present.

Hollis straightened with her hands full of bags of food and saw where Annie's gaze had been riveted. Her eyebrows rose and she smirked. "Everything okay?"

"Just fine." Annie willed herself not to blush—and thought she'd managed it—but Hollis's eyes sparkled with satisfaction. Damn her— she *knew* how hot she was. Annie laughed. "And you know it."

"Never hurts to hear." Hollis handed Callie a plastic bag. "Here, Cal—you got the food. I'll carry the sodas."

"Okay!" Callie gazed at Hollis with an expression of awe, and Annie's heart stopped in her chest. What if she was making a horrible mistake? She had more than just herself to think about. But she wasn't doing anything—just a friendly dinner—oh, that was so much BS too. Oh God, what was she doing?

Hollis balanced the cardboard tray with sodas in one hand and closed the car door. "This is nice. Thanks."

The pleasure in Hollis's deep voice dispelled the last of Annie's misgivings. "It's not all that much. I wasn't sure what you liked, so you're having the same thing again."

"That's perfect. You remembered." Hollis's right hand drifted down to rest on the top of Callie's head, the way Annie's always did when they walked together.

The gesture was so touching Annie felt tears rise to her eyes. Oh, there was something terribly wrong with her. This wasn't her. She turned her face away. "We should go before it gets too dark, and you need to eat." She held out her hand to Callie. "Come on, baby. Let's go."

Hollis came up close to her side. "I'm starving."

"Yes," Annie murmured, carefully not looking at her. "I am too."

Once across the street, Annie asked, "Over by the pond?"

"Sounds great," Hollis said.

Annie found a patch of grass in the sun on the far side of the pond. They weren't alone, but they might as well have been for all anyone else mattered. All she could see was Hollis, sprawling in the grass, passing food to Callie and murmuring instructions. She was so good with Callie. She was so good with everyone. And she was so damn good to look at, even with the creases of fatigue around her eyes and the shadows that flickered in their depths.

"Why don't you relax—let me take care of the food," Annie said, grasping Hollis's wrist.

Hollis glanced up, her blue eyes sparkling, and a lock turned deep inside the fortress Annie had built to protect herself. Doors swung wide and Annie sensed her secrets slipping away.

"Something wrong?" Hollis asked softly.

Annie shook her head, afraid of what would come out if she spoke. "No."

"For a minute there, you looked frightened."

"No, not that." Annie smiled at Callie, kneeling by Hollis's hip. "Happy."

"Yeah." Hollis settled next to Annie, stretched her legs out on the grass, and handed Annie a burrito. "Happy can feel that way sometimes." She opened her burrito and took a bite.

Annie ate in silence, occasionally wiping Callie's chin with a paper napkin, feeling sublimely content. "I think I'm in heaven."

"Me too," Hollis said. "How did you know to do this?"

"I took a chance. When you didn't come to clinic—"

"Oh cra—" Hollis glanced at Callie and bit off the curse. "I'm sorry. I got held up and I never thought—"

Annie slid her fingers down over the short sleeve of Hollis's scrub shirt to her bare arm. Hollis's skin was hot, the muscles underneath her fingertips solid. "It's okay. I heard you were held up—Ned told me."

Hollis frowned. "Ned? You went to clinic?"

"Yes. I spent the afternoon seeing patients with him. He's very nice."

"He is, sure." Hollis frowned.

"What?"

"Sometimes he—"

"Mommy," Callie said, "is it okay if I feed the ducks?"

"Remember the rules. Just a little bit." Annie opened her bag handed Callie a small plastic bag filled with bird food. "Don't throw it all in at once and don't go anywhere except right in front of us."

"I won't." Callie raced down the slope and squatted at the edge of the water, carefully opening the plastic bag and meticulously throwing one morsel of food at a time into the water.

"Sometimes he what?" Annie asked when Callie was out of hearing.

"Did he hit on you?"

Annie stared. Hollis looked angry. Jealous? A little frisson of pleasure shot through her. "No, of course not."

"Why of course not? You're beautiful, and Ned always notices beautiful women."

"Well, he was perfectly professional." Annie fussed with the remainders of the food, hoping to hide her confusion. She didn't have any reason to want Hollis to be jealous, but she liked the possessive tone in her voice. She'd never felt anything like that in her life.

"So what *did* Ned say?" Hollis asked.

"I heard him talk to you on the phone just as I was leaving, and he said you'd been tied up all day. That's all. Rough case?"

Hollis leaned back on her elbows and sighed. "Yeah. A routine—well, as routine as any section for me ever gets—went bad. A placenta previa."

"Term?"

"Almost. Just diagnosed, so I scheduled her for an elective section this morning. Just got the baby out and all hell broke loose." Hollis shook her head. "Blood everywhere. I couldn't get the damn artery clamped and—" She grimaced. "Annie, I'm really sorry. I didn't think. Talk about insensitive—"

"You're anything but that." Annie leaned onto her side, keeping one eye on Callie, and took Hollis's hand. "Hollis, this is the business we're in. You don't have to apologize. I'm fine. Tell me."

Hollis let out a breath. "Right. Anyhow, it didn't go the way I wanted it to."

"Are they all right?"

"I think so. The baby's good. I spent the afternoon in the intensive care unit with the mother after surgery. She was unstable for a while and we had to transfuse her. She looked a lot better when I left an hour ago."

"Did she—did you have to—"

"I got the bleeding stopped. I'm not sure it will ever be smart for her to get pregnant again, but that's down the road." Hollis squinted out across the water, her expression bleak. "I came within a hair of doing the hysterectomy, but when I called out to talk to her partner, she asked me to wait as long as I could."

Annie caught her breath. *Wait as long as she could.* She tried to imagine the position Hollis must have been in—the patient bleeding, possibly in danger of dying, and a loved one asking her to wait as long as she could. How long was long enough? What was fair to everyone, and how did Hollis carry that burden?

"So you waited and it worked," Annie said.

Hollis looked at her, her eyes worried. "It did, this time."

"You must be happy, then."

"Mostly I'm tired." Hollis hesitated. "Look, Annie, there's something you need to know about Ned."

Annie frowned. "What?"

"Right after you and I first met, when you were so angry about the surgery I performed, I asked Ned to review your case. I didn't think the two of you would likely cross paths—hell, I'm sorry."

"Why?"

"What? I didn't mean to breach your privacy—"

"No, not that." Annie waved a hand impatiently. "I'm not embarrassed that he knows, although he never let on that he recognized me. Why did you ask him to look at my case?"

Hollis sighed. "I thought if you had an independent opinion you might feel better about the outcome. He said—"

"I don't care what he said," Annie said, the realization lifting a weight from her spirit. "You did what you thought you had to do."

"I want you to know he agreed. Maybe it doesn't make any difference now—"

"Thank you." Annie brushed her fingers through Hollis's hair. "Thank you for caring enough to do that. It means a lot to me."

"You mean a lot to me, Annie." Hollis caught Annie's hand and kissed her palm.

Hollis's lips were warm and incredibly soft. Annie cupped Hollis's neck, felt the blood rush under her fingertips, felt soft skin, the faint sheen of perspiration. Hollis looked at her, waiting, giving her the choice. It was so simple to make. So terrifyingly simple. Annie leaned closer and kissed her.

Chapter Twenty-two

Hollis didn't believe Annie was really going to kiss her, but at the last second, she did. Hollis's mind went completely blank. She'd been raised to think on her feet—indoctrinated by a family of alpha males and one iron-willed matriarch to bounce back no matter what came her way, to keep a clear head, to fear nothing. She'd chosen a career that tested her a hundred times a day. She didn't falter when faced with unexpected situations, never panicked at critical junctures where her wrong decision could mean the difference between success and unimaginable disaster. And now she couldn't think. Couldn't move—all because the warmest, softest, sweetest lips she'd ever known whispered over hers.

The kiss seemed to go on forever, at least it felt as if her heart stopped for that long, but when Annie drew back it had probably only been a second or two. Hollis blinked and the sun was still in the same position hanging low over the horizon. Her hearing returned and she was surrounded by the sounds of children laughing, dogs barking, the murmur of conversation floating across the pond. Callie still crouched at the water's edge, carefully tossing food to the ducks. Everything was exactly as it had been, only everything had changed.

Annie's face was inches away, so close the amber flecks in her deep green irises glowed with reflected sunlight. Her lips were still parted, moist and full. Hollis held her breath, absorbing the roaring in her head into every cell. Imprinting the memory.

"Well," Annie said with merest hint of breathlessness, "I didn't see that coming."

"Neither did I," Hollis said, and her voice sounded rusty and unused. She glanced down and saw Annie's fingers curled around her wrist. She didn't remember Annie's hand moving from her neck. The press of Annie's fingertips to her nape still radiated in warm currents down her spine. She quivered inside and her hips tensed in anticipation. She turned her hand over and laced her fingers through Annie's. The kiss had ended, but something else had begun—something she was afraid to examine and terrified of losing. "I don't even have a next move."

"Well," Annie said again, color rising into her face. Her neck flushed a delicate rose as far down as the pale skin in the open collar of her white shirt. "Should I apologize?"

"I can't imagine what for." Hollis pictured the silky skin of Annie's throat under her lips, imagined kissing her way down to that soft, pink expanse framed by the snow-white triangle of Annie's shirt. Her fingers trembled to caress flesh. Her thighs tensed with sudden pressure. Her nipples peaked, hard and aching. Such a delicate kiss and she was burning.

"I didn't think if you wanted—"

"I wanted," Hollis said quickly. "Oh yeah, I most definitely wanted."

"That's good, then." Annie smiled crookedly.

"Yeah. Good. Excellent." Hollis ached to kiss her back. She didn't. She'd never be able to kiss her for just a brief second, and they were outside surrounded by kids and dogs and ducks and Callie was fifteen feet away. She wanted Annie naked, she wanted her undone. No, she definitely couldn't kiss her out here. Maybe not anywhere until she found her sanity. "Why?"

"Why what?"

Annie still hadn't moved away and her body swayed toward Hollis. If Hollis leaned just a little, Annie's breasts would…

Hollis sucked in a breath and edged away a fraction. "What made you…you know…just now."

"Oh." Annie laughed and pursed her lips. "You looked like you needed a kiss. A little tired, a little sad. You're usually so indomitable."

"Wow. That's…it wasn't a pity kiss or anything, was it?"

Annie's eyes widened. "I'm not doing this right at all. *I* needed to kiss you—I couldn't help it. You…make me feel all sorts of things I don't usually feel."

Relief and pleasure stirred in Hollis's belly. "Is that right."

"That's very right." Annie laughed.

The husky, sexy sound went straight to Hollis's groin. At this rate she was going to burst into flames. "Jesus, Annie, have a heart here."

"What?" Annie asked in a tone that suggested she knew exactly what she was doing.

"You have a really sexy laugh."

Annie caught her lower lip between her teeth, an altogether innocent move that had Hollis's thighs twitching.

"About the kiss. One more thing," Annie said.

"What?" Hollis managed to get out.

"I really like your ass."

Hollis felt her mouth drop open. "Okay. You took me by surprise before, but now I'm speechless."

Annie's smile grew into a look of playful satisfaction. "What? You've never had a woman tell you you've got a great ass before?"

"Uh…" Hollis shook her head. "Actually, no."

"Well, you've been wasting your time on women who don't deserve you, then."

Hollis grinned. "Maybe so. Whatever the reason, thanks."

"Thanks?"

"For the kiss."

"I wasn't kidding about wanting to kiss you." Annie shook her head. "I'm tired of not admitting what I feel. I've been thinking about kissing you for days."

Hollis kissed Annie's knuckles. "I'm not tired or sad now. I'm just happy to be here with you."

"You know," Annie said, looking suddenly serious, "I was thinking while you were telling me about your patient today, that it's not fair to put those kinds of decisions on you. It's not fair that you have to accept the anger and pain and displaced blame from patients like me."

"It's not about being fair. I signed up for it," Hollis said.

Annie smiled wistfully. "I doubt very much you signed up for guilt by proxy."

Hollis brushed her thumb over the corner of Annie's mouth. "Annie, you have every right to be hurt and angry and disappointed about what happened to you. None of what you went through was fair, and I'm part of that. I know when you look at me, you think about that night." She blew out a breath. "I wish we could go back—"

"No." Annie pressed her fingers to Hollis's mouth. "No. I don't want to go back. I don't want the past crowding into the present any longer, but I don't know how to change it."

"That kiss was a nice start."

Annie glanced down the slope. Callie was still engrossed with the gaggle of ducks that paddled back and forth in the shallow water a few feet in front of her, plucking seeds and corn from the surface of the water. "I guess my timing could have been better."

"Your timing is great." Hollis shrugged. "Well, almost perfect."

"Oh?"

"I could've done with an hour or so more of that kiss."

Annie's face flooded with heat and she swallowed. So could she. She wanted more right now. She wanted her hands in Hollis's hair again, she wanted to see that dazed look in Hollis's eyes and know she put it there. That idea was so far from anything she'd ever desired, she couldn't even find a context for it. "I'm not sure I have a worthy follow-up."

"After a kiss like that, I find that hard to believe."

"The kiss was barely a kiss."

"Oh no, it was definitely a kiss." Hollis inched closer until her thigh brushed Annie's, her face inches away, her eyes dark and intense. "And I'd like more."

"Should we talk about work? Is this a problem?" Annie half hated herself for asking, but she had to. She had to find her footing in a landscape she no longer recognized.

"Work is work. *This* doesn't have anything to do with it."

"Neither one of us can leave work at the office," Annie said. "That's not what we do. It's not who we are."

"This doesn't have to interfere."

"I don't even know what this is."

"Then let's find out."

"We should have a date. Shouldn't we?" Annie asked.

Hollis grinned and she looked younger, and impossibly beautiful. "What? What did I say?" Annie desperately wanted to kiss her again. Why did they have to be outside surrounded by people? And Callie?

"I like you taking charge," Hollis murmured.

"I'm hardly doing that," Annie said, growing more self-conscious every second. She really didn't know what she was doing. Her infrequent dates were more group things with friends, where she was unofficially paired off with someone and could keep her distance, not a one-on-one evening out. Keeping Hollis at a distance had been impossible from the start. And she didn't want to. "I could probably get a sitter Saturday night. We could go—"

"Damn," Hollis said. "I already—"

"That's all right," Annie said hastily. Saturday night, of course Hollis would have plans. Just because she was free every night didn't mean someone as desirable as Hollis would be. "I'm being presumptuous. I—"

"Annie," Hollis said firmly, "I'm having dinner with Honor Blake and her family. Come with me."

"Oh, I couldn't do that."

"Why not? They're neighbors. You know Honor." Hollis rubbed her palm over Annie's arm. "It's just dinner with friends. Please. I want to see you."

"Hollis, there's something you should know."

Hollis regarded her steadily, calmly. "Okay."

"I…" Annie sighed, not even sure what she wanted to say. "I'm not at all sure this is a good idea."

"I know. Neither am I. We'll take it nice and slow." Hollis glanced quickly at Callie and kissed Annie before Annie knew what was happening.

Hollis's mouth was soft but sure, her lips moving with silky pressure over Annie's. She tasted of sunlight and spice, and Annie was suddenly famished. She nodded, her mouth still against Hollis's.

"Okay?" Hollis drew back reluctantly, wondering how she was ever going to be able to take it slow.

"Okay," Annie breathed. Tonight, for just this moment, she didn't have to know what she was doing. She glanced toward the water and Callie. "I ought to get her home." She smiled. "You look like you could use a bit of a nap too."

"I haven't been tired since the second I saw you pull up. What do you say we go bicycle shopping Saturday sometime."

"You sure?"

"Absolutely."

Annie nodded, ridiculously pleased to be seeing Hollis again so soon. "You relax right now. I'll clean this up."

"Actually," Hollis said, rising, "I think I'll feed some ducks."

The sound of Callie's laughter and the deep, sensuous tone of Hollis's voice kept distracting Annie while she wrapped leftovers and collected trash. She paused to watch Hollis point something out to Callie in the water, saw Hollis cradle the back of Callie's neck in a casually protective gesture, felt her heart twist. When she had everything together, she joined them.

"Look, Mommy. Tadpoles." Callie pointed at dozens of tiny torpedo shapes darting furiously in the shallow waters by the edge of the pond. "Baby frogs."

"Wow, look at them all," Annie said, smiling at Hollis.

"By the end of the summer they'll be as big as Kermit." Callie looked at Hollis. "Right?"

"Some of them," Hollis said. "Yep."

"We'll have to watch them and see," Annie said. She took Callie's hand and they walked back to Hollis's. After she buckled Callie in and stowed away the food bags, she turned to Hollis, who stood by the side of the car waiting. "Well, why don't you call if you're free—"

Hollis mouth covered hers with possessive insistence, hot and just short of bruising. This kiss was nothing like the first time Hollis had kissed her—that had been tender and gently searching. This was sure and claiming. Annie swayed and gripped Hollis's scrub shirt in both hands. Arms came around her waist, dragged her close. Hollis's chest was firm, her thighs lean and tight.

Annie pulled away. "Can't breathe."

"Sorry," Hollis muttered, her eyes flashing dangerously.

"I'm not. Just—" Annie kissed her, one hand sliding into her hair, the other grasping her shoulder. The world dissolved in color—brilliant reds, sensuous purples, mesmerizing greens. She was falling, floating, swirling. Annie broke the kiss, releasing Hollis's arm and grabbing the top of the open door to steady herself. "Saturday?"

"Yes."

Hollis looked as if she was going to kiss her again. If she hadn't had Callie with her, she might have let her, and that was probably a very bad idea. She needed time to get a hold on reality again. She stroked Hollis's jaw. "Call me."

"I will."

"Good night, Hollis."

"Good night, Annie."

Hollis didn't move, and Annie was careful not to touch her as she closed the door and skirted the front of the car to the driver's side. She really didn't trust herself right now—and that was new. New and confusing and thrilling. As she drove away she looked into the rearview mirror.

Hollis was still watching.

❖

When Honor walked in, the house was quiet. She smelled dinner but she didn't hear the kids. She dropped her bag by the sofa on her way through the living room. "Phyllis?"

Quinn was in the kitchen, barefoot in jeans and a faded red T-shirt, putting aluminum foil over casserole dishes that sat on the counter.

"Hi." Honor slid her arms around Quinn from behind and kissed the side of her neck, snuggling up against her. "I didn't expect you to be home so early. Where's Phyllis?"

"She's next door with Jack." Quinn turned and leaned back against the counter, pulling Honor into her arms as she moved.

"All night?"

"Mmm-hmm."

Honor threaded her arms around Quinn's neck and kissed her properly. When she finished, she murmured, "Where's Arly?"

Quinn grinned. "Sleepover at Angie's. Spontaneous thing after soccer practice. I said yes."

"Who's chaperoning?"

"Missy Frangipani and Donna Brundage."

"Lord bless them."

Quinn chuckled. "So that leaves you and me."

"I notice you just put dinner on hold." Honor kissed Quinn's chin. The slow stir of anticipation was familiar, familiar, but ever new.

"It should stay warm for at least an hour."

"Maybe two."

Quinn cradled the back of Honor's head, wrapping a handful of hair around her fingers, tugging gently until Honor's chin came up. She kissed her throat and worked her way down, opening Honor's shirt with the other hand. She kissed between her breasts and slipped open her bra. Slowly she moved her mouth over the slope of Honor's breast and bit lightly at her nipple. Honor's fingers tightened on her shoulders.

"Quinn," Honor warned. "Dangerous. Very dangerous."

"Not so much," Quinn murmured, and turned Honor until her back was to the counter. Sliding her hand lower, she opened Honor's narrow leather belt, then the button on her pants, then the zipper.

Honor's breath came faster, her vision tunneling until the room disappeared and all that remained was the sunlight on the side of Quinn's face. She ran her fingers through Quinn's dark hair. "I love you."

Quinn knelt and looked up, her smile lazy and powerful. "I love you. Hold on."

Honor gripped the counter and watched Quinn lower her clothes and push them away. She watched Quinn run her hands over her abdomen and down the outsides of her thighs, trailing up her calves and between her legs. She watched Quinn's mouth skim over her skin, tenderly, possessively, lifting her higher as she kissed ever lower. She watched Quinn take her in, take her home. She watched until she couldn't keep her eyes open anymore, but she saw Quinn, in her mind, in her heart. She always saw Quinn.

Quinn stood and scooped Honor into her arms, cradling her close and walking back a few steps to a chair at the long kitchen table. She sat and cradled Honor in her lap. "Welcome home, by the way."

Honor kissed her neck and sighed. "A very nice welcome home too."

"Think you can make it upstairs?"

"I need thirty seconds until I find my legs again."

Quinn chuckled. "Take your time. We've got all night."

"I know. A miracle." She rested her cheek on Quinn's shoulder. "I invited Hollis Monroe to come over Saturday. Dinner."

"Okay. I told Robin to come over with Linda and the kids too. That's not a problem, is it?"

"Don't see why it should be. We're all neighbors."

"Good enough, then."

"Let me try standing," Honor said, kissing Quinn's jaw. "I want you upstairs, naked, so I can have my way with you."

"If you can't make it, I'll carry you," Quinn said fervently.

Honor laughed and took her hand. "I'm quite sure I can manage."

CHAPTER TWENTY-THREE

Hollis worked on the house while the light lasted, sweating in the warm evening air as she nailed up trim, replaced floorboards on the porch, and scraped siding in preparation for repainting. She wasn't working to fill the time or exhaust herself enough to sleep as she often did. She was sawing and hammering and carrying stacks of lumber to keep her mind off the way her body hummed with the aftereffects of Annie's kiss. The rhythmic hum of the saw and steady cadence of hammer hitting nails crowded out her thoughts for moments at a time, but always when the physical exertion waned, the fire ignited by that kiss came surging back. Under the surface of her skin the stirrings of desire persisted like the bass line pulsing beneath the melody of a familiar song.

She stepped back, squinted at the 45° angle joining the two pieces of trim she'd just set around a porch column. Looked good. She rubbed her hand over her chest, massaging an ache she couldn't touch. Even as she struggled for balance, for a little distance, she replayed the exhilaration of the moment she'd pulled Annie into her arms. Annie. She wanted her. No denying it, not when her body was strung tight, clamoring for more of the heady sensation. Going slow would be a challenge. She hadn't craved like this since she'd first discovered sex, and those unschooled urges were only pale imitations of this consuming hunger.

She understood lust, but this wasn't that. She wasn't a hermit, or a monk. She dated a few women who enjoyed sex after a pleasant evening and who didn't expect anything more beyond that, and that suited everyone just fine. But Annie wasn't one of those women. Annie wasn't someone she could touch casually, wasn't a woman with whom she could share a few hours of physical pleasure and then leave with a quick kiss and an *I'll see you later*. No, Annie was far more special than that.

Hollis put her hammer aside and sat on the top step of her back porch. Her yard bordered the street, separated from the sidewalk by a hedgerow and at the end farthest from the neighbor's yard by a wooden fence. Even though she caught glimpses of cars passing and people walking by through the gaps in the hedge, she was invisible to them, alone in the slowly diminishing twilight. She rubbed the back of her neck. Her skin still tingled from where Annie's hand had rested. The whole front of her body vibrated from the sensation of Annie pressed against her when they'd kissed—when she'd held Annie close. She hadn't known she was going to do that, which was pretty damn surprising all by itself. She didn't do things spontaneously. Not where women were concerned, not anywhere in her life. But Annie had been about to get into her car—about to disappear—and she hadn't wanted her to go. She'd had more she'd wanted to say. *Thank you for bringing me dinner, thank you for remembering what I like to eat, thank you for letting me share your daughter. Thank you for making me feel my heart beat for the first time in so long.*

She hadn't had the words, and the hunger had been riding her hard. She'd wanted the softness of Annie's mouth against hers again, wanted to taste her again, wanted to hear the soft sound Annie made in her throat that she wasn't even aware she made when they kissed. That little murmur of pleasure shot through Hollis like an arrow, and she wanted nothing more than to coax Annie into making it again and again. She wanted it now like an ache in her soul. Hollis propped her elbows on her knees, laced her fingers behind her head, and closed her eyes, torturing herself with sweet memories. A hurricane raged inside her as she recalled every second of their too-short kisses, every inch of flesh where their bodies had too briefly touched. What was she going to do about this need she had for Annie?

This need gnawing at her wasn't going to be fixed by a few kisses or a night or two of hot sweaty sex. She wanted Annie fiercely. She wanted to be over her, she wanted to be inside her, she wanted Annie to open for her, to wrap her arms around her, to pull her deep, deep inside.

Hollis shot to her feet. The sun was gone, twilight had drifted away, and night had fallen. The kitchen light behind her glowed pale gold, casting molten shadows on the porch. She thought she might be looking at another sleepless night, but one far different than those that usually plagued her. She was restless and agitated, but not from some vague discontent. She willed the night to be over so she could wake up and go to Annie. Annie, a woman who had the power to leave her defenseless. Helpless. Vulnerable. She didn't care—and that scared the hell out of her.

❖

"When is Hollis coming?" Callie asked at nine on Saturday.

Annie placed a glass of orange juice in front of Callie. "I don't know, baby. We have to wait until she calls. She might have to go to the hospital first, remember I told you that?"

"I know, but I've been awake for a long time already."

"You woke up extra early, so it makes it seem like you've been awake even longer than usual."

Callie pushed her glass around on the tabletop, her expression contemplative. "If I sleep longer, I have to wait less?"

"Sometimes." Annie kissed the top of Callie's head. Her hair smelled as sweet and delicate as freshly opened rose blossoms. "She'll be here soon, baby."

She hoped. She was as anxious as Callie. She'd been keyed up ever since leaving Hollis, and a good part of her agitation had been physical. She recognized it, despite how long it had been since she'd experienced anything even close to unrequited desire. The sensations tormenting her had been that and so much more. Pure physical longing was a new experience—she'd been dependent on Jeff, although at the time she hadn't recognized her attraction for what it was. He'd been her guide in a strange and unsettling new world, and she'd mistaken need for something deeper. This fire in her blood was altogether different. She couldn't stop thinking about Hollis's mouth, her hands, the hard length of her body. Just the woodsy-citrus scent of Hollis's skin made her twist inside.

She hadn't gotten much sleep and had awakened at the first trill of birdsong outside her window. She generally rose with the sun, enjoying being up and about as the world awakened, but today the instant she'd opened her eyes expectation rushed through her, so intense she'd gasped out loud. Her thighs had tightened and her nipples had throbbed. The flush of instant arousal was so unexpected, so unusual, she'd clutched the sheet in both hands, afraid the slightest movement might make her explode. She'd gone to sleep imagining Hollis stretched out above her, and she'd awakened wanting her everywhere. She was a wreck.

"Mommy?"

Annie jumped, aware of the spatula in her hand and the pancakes browning on the griddle. She steadied her voice. "Yes, baby?"

"I think Hollis is here."

"What?" Annie spun toward the screen door leading to their small back porch and postage-stamp yard.

"I guess I'm too early," Hollis said through the screen. She leaned a shoulder against the doorjamb, one hand in the pocket of black jeans, a white shirt open at the neck, the sleeves rolled up her forearms. She looked sexy and a little dangerous. She looked gorgeous. "I'll wait—"

"No," Annie said quickly. Too quickly. How uncool could she be? "You're not early. Come in."

Hollis grinned, liking the way Annie flushed, liking her a little off guard and flustered. Guess she wasn't the only one who was nervous. "I went to the front door first—didn't see any signs of life. I don't want to interrupt—"

"We're having pancakes and bacon." Annie gestured to the table and the plate of bacon she'd just placed there. "What did you have?"

"Um. Half a slice of cold pizza?"

Laughing, Annie pointed to the table. "Get in here. Sit."

"Well, if you put it that way." Hollis hurried inside and stopped a few inches from Annie. "Hi."

Annie tumbled right into her eyes, went in over her head in an instant, and wasn't sure she'd ever surface. When she came back to her senses, she brushed her lips over Hollis's cheek, needing the tiniest taste to ease the urgency filling her chest. "Hi."

Hollis's eyes darkened and she stroked lightly down Annie's side, her fingertips coming to rest just above Annie's hipbone. "You sure this is okay?"

"Is that a trick question?"

"You look great."

"Sit, Hollis," Annie murmured, wishing like hell she'd put on something sexier than a plain old green tee. "Breakfast."

"Right." Hollis glanced at Callie, knelt by her chair, and said, "Hi, Callie. You ready to go bicycle shopping with Mommy and me?"

"Yes, we have been waiting."

"Have you." Hollis glanced up at Annie, then back at Callie. "Well. Let's have breakfast so we can get going."

Hollis rose, purposefully not looking at Annie until she'd made her way around to the far side of the table. If she looked at Annie another second, she'd have to touch her again, and as electrifying as that was, the little bit of physical contact was making her crazy. She wanted more. She made herself sit across from Callie while Annie finished cooking. Watching Annie was almost as good as touching her. She moved gracefully, with certainty, the confidence she displayed with her patients instilling her every movement, no matter what she was doing. And she looked fabulous in low-riding black pants and a white tank under a scoop-neck emerald-green tee. Hollis didn't have to work hard at all to imagine sliding up behind her, tugging her firm, curvy ass against her crotch, and kissing the back of her neck. From there she'd tease the T-shirt from her pants and skim her hand...

Hollis jerked her gaze away from Annie's ass. She was going to burst out of her skin if she didn't stop thinking about sex. Sex with Annie.

Annie turned and stopped with a spatula holding a golden pancake poised in midair. She stared at Hollis. "What?"

Hollis shook her head. She couldn't say what she was thinking. She didn't know where they were going, but she wasn't letting her hormones drive. She couldn't. She didn't trust herself to think rationally, not where Annie was concerned. "You need me to do anything?" When Annie's eyes widened, Hollis added quickly, "For breakfast. Help with breakfast."

"Oh. No. Almost there." Annie pulled plates from a cabinet, flipped pancakes onto them, and carried them to the table. "Here you go."

"Mommy, you forgot the syrup," Callie announced.

"Would I do that?" Annie passed the bacon to Hollis, grabbed the syrup from the fridge, and settled at the end of the table with Callie on one side and Hollis on the other. "Okay, you two. Eat."

Hollis's knee bumped Annie's and the ripple of heat that shot up her leg made her jump. She glanced at Annie, who was supervising Callie's syrup pouring. "Sorry."

"That's all right," Annie said, not looking at her.

Hollis concentrated on the very good pancakes. She was hungry, but her stomach was in knots. Maybe she needed a time-out. Maybe she should take her hormone-addled brain and her amped-up body for a walk around the block before she did something really stupid.

Annie smiled at her. "Everything okay?"

Hollis forgot why being unable to think of anything except Annie was a bad thing. "Everything is perfect."

❖

Hollis drained the last of her coffee and set the cup beside her plate. "That was fantas—"

The theme song from *Sons of Anarchy* played, and Annie looked toward her leather bag sitting on the far end of the kitchen counter. "I'm not on call, but I should probably get that."

"I'll get the dishes."

Annie dashed for her cell and Hollis stacked plates. As she carried them to the sink, she heard Annie say, "No, that's all right. When? Yes, I'll take care of it. Thanks."

Annie lowered her phone and sighed. "That was the service. One of my patients called and thinks she's in labor. I need to call her." She glanced at Callie, who was looking anxiously from Annie to Hollis. "Baby, why don't you go grab one of your coloring books while Mommy makes a call."

Callie swiveled and said to Hollis, "Are you staying?"

"Yep."

"Okay." Callie hopped down and bounded from the room.

"I'll wait outside," Hollis said, heading for the back porch.

Five minutes later, Annie joined her. "I'm really sorry, but I'm going to have to see her. This is her second baby, and her first labor was short. If she's started, she might go fast."

"Nothing to be sorry about," Hollis said.

"Callie is going to be disappointed." Annie smiled wryly. "Me too."

"Look," Hollis said, "how about if I take Callie to look at bikes. Then, when you're free, you can decide if you approve of her choice."

Annie looked toward the kitchen where Callie colored at the table. "Hollis, she's a handful sometimes. I could be gone half the day, maybe more."

"So tell me who you'd get to look after her, and if it gets really late or Callie wants someone more familiar, I'll take her there. But I think we'll be fine."

"She'd love it if you took her bike shopping, but it's a lot to ask."

"I volunteered, remember?" Hollis took Annie's hand. "Really. I want to. I'm not going to do anything except hang around over at my place and probably end up pounding in a few more nails."

"You're sure?"

Annie's fingers slipped through Hollis's, and the action was so natural and felt so right, Hollis's heart gave a little jolt of happiness. She tugged Annie closer and looped an arm loosely around Annie's waist. "I'm sure."

Annie's eyes sparkled and she kissed Hollis swiftly on the mouth. "Thank you."

"Maybe you can do that again, later," Hollis said, refusing to listen to the voice of caution roaring in her head.

"Maybe." Annie's smile widened and she brushed her free hand over Hollis's chest. "Maybe I will."

CHAPTER TWENTY-FOUR

"What do you think?" Hollis said, "Black or purple?"

Callie marched between the two bikes, studying them intently. She glanced at Hollis. "I bet I can ride without the training wheels."

"If your mom says okay, we can try it and see what you think."

"Which color do you like?"

"Hmm." Hollis folded her arms. "The black is pretty cool with the silver letters, but purple is pretty. Do you like cool or pretty?"

Callie giggled. "Pretty."

"Then I'd definitely do the purple. But I think you have to ask Mommy too."

"Mommy likes pretty."

Hollis laughed. "Okay. Well, when you come back with her—"

"Mommy," Callie cried and raced away.

Hollis turned. Annie was just coming through the door, the sunlight behind her making her hair shimmer with red-gold highlights. Annie bent down, wrapped her arms around Callie, and gave her a big swinging hug. The joy in Annie's eyes when she looked at Callie pierced Hollis's heart, and the afternoon suddenly took on an amazing glow.

Annie looked her way and smiled. "Hi."

"Hi," Hollis said, striding up to her. "That was fast."

"Her contractions stopped. I'm not sure she won't start again, but she's got a good support system, and they know to call me if they need me to come back." Annie's eyes drifted over Hollis's body and returned to her face. "How have you two been doing?"

"Great." Hollis leaned forward and kissed Annie's cheek. She was just so happy to see her. "Glad you could make it."

"Me too."

Hollis wanted to whisk her out of the store, away from people, away from everything, to someplace where they could be alone. Where she could take the clasp from Annie's hair and let the shining mass of curls fall loose around her shoulders, where she could slide the shirt off her pale, smooth arms, where she could guide her down and lie beside her and stroke her soft skin. She clenched her hands to keep from touching her. She hadn't yet been invited to do any of those things, and the sharp edges of her own lust sliced like razors beneath her skin.

"Find a bike?" Annie's voice was husky, the expression in her eyes making Hollis think Annie could read her thoughts.

"She's picked out a couple." Hollis dropped her hand on Callie's head. "Why don't you show your mom the two you like?"

Callie tugged on Annie's hand. "Come on, Mommy. Hollis says I don't need training wheels."

Annie raised a brow at Hollis. "Does she now?"

Hollis coughed and shook her head slightly. "I believe what I said was we could *see* how she handled a bike with no trainers. *If* you agreed."

Annie grinned at Callie. "Uh-huh. Clever kid of mine."

"Come on," Callie urged, and Annie followed her down the aisle.

Hollis hung back watching them as Callie excitedly pointed out the bicycles. Annie listened intently, nodding occasionally, her fingers resting on the back of Callie's neck. They were beautiful, the two of them. Hollis remembered Annie that first night in the hospital—she'd been so much younger, so traumatized, so terrified. So alone. The heat of fury raced through her when she thought of all the people who should have been there for her and weren't. She remembered lifting the baby from Annie's body and the blood and the stark icy moments when she'd fought for Annie's life.

She'd done the same thing she'd done in the OR that night dozens of times before and hundreds of times since, but looking at the two of them now, she wondered if she'd ever done anything that mattered so much.

Annie spun around and gave her a questioning look. Hollis shook off the memories and joined them.

"Everything okay?" Annie murmured.

"Yeah," Hollis said.

"What were you thinking of?"

"How beautiful you are." Hollis leaned closer. "How much I want to kiss you."

Annie blushed, looking unexpectedly shy. "There's that Monroe charm at work again."

"Just the truth." Hollis glanced down at Callie. "So? What did you decide?"

Callie grinned. "The purple one."

"No trainers?"

"Will you be there?"

"You bet. We'll take it outside so you can try it right now if you want. Are you ready?"

"Yes!"

Hollis glanced at Annie. "Okay with you?"

"She's determined, so I'd say we're ready."

"Excellent."

While Hollis went off to find a sales clerk, Annie took Callie outside. "Are you having fun, baby?"

"Hollis is going to teach me how to ride without the training wheels. Mike doesn't have any."

"Well, Hollis is a really good bicycle rider, and if you want to try, then I think you should."

"You're going to get a bike too, right? So you and me and Hollis can all go on our bicycles together?"

Annie's throat tightened. Callie had taken to Hollis so quickly, had trusted her so easily. And why not? Hollis was easy to like, easy to be with, easy to need. Already, Hollis invaded her thoughts day and night, kept her body poised on the edge of exploding, and now Hollis was becoming something even more perilous—Hollis was slipping into her life, as naturally as if she belonged there. Even her daughter was falling in love with her. Annie's breath caught. Oh no, she wasn't falling in love. She wouldn't. Callie was a child, naïve and innocent, but she wasn't. She warmed, thinking of Hollis's eyes on her, Hollis's hands slipping over her side, her mouth so hot and sure.

What are you thinking of?

How beautiful you are. How much I want to kiss you.

Annie shivered. She was very nearly lost already, and she couldn't afford to be—she'd worked so hard to build a life where she'd never again be dependent on anyone else, where she could make her own choices and never rely on someone who wouldn't be there for her. She would never be blinded by her own need masquerading as love again.

The door behind them opened, and Hollis came through with a young woman pushing the bike Callie had chosen. It seemed so big—a child's bicycle, and Callie was just a baby. Callie ran toward Hollis and Annie saw that she wasn't a baby anymore. She'd already begun to grow up. Hollis steadied the bike and Callie climbed on. After Hollis made a few adjustments so Callie's feet reached the pedals, she knelt down beside the bike and murmured to Callie. Callie nodded vigorously and Annie walked closer.

"Remember, no matter where you are," Hollis said, "you always look around to make sure there are no cars or people or other bicycles coming. Okay?"

"Okay," Callie said seriously.

Annie held up the helmet the sales girl passed to her. "And you'll wear this every time you're on your bicycle."

Callie cut a look at Hollis. "Do you wear one like this?"

"Yep. Every time. Mine looks just like this one, only mine is red."

"Okay." Callie grinned. "This one is prettier than Mike's."

Laughing, Hollis fitted the helmet to Callie's head and adjusted the straps, then tapped lightly on the top. "All right, you're ready to go. Remember what I told you about how you stop, right?"

"I remember." Callie looked up at Annie. "Mommy, can you stand on my other side?"

"Sure, baby."

Annie lightly pressed a hand to Callie's back and looked over Callie's head at Hollis, whose left hand rested on the handlebar. Hollis gave Annie an encouraging grin.

"Okay, Callie," Annie said, pulling her gaze away from Hollis. "Start pedaling."

Annie and Hollis ran alongside Callie, who wobbled at first but soon found her center. Five minutes later, Callie announced she was fine on her own and Annie stood back with Hollis while Callie carefully rode the bike in a circle around the big parking lot.

"I can't believe how big she seems now," Annie murmured.

"I know. I was just thinking about how small she was when I delivered her."

Annie caught her breath. Whenever memories of that night caught her unawares, she remembered pain and fear and the hands of strangers. A face came into focus, surrounded by bright lights that hurt her eyes, distorted by the red haze of agony. Hollis's face. Hollis's voice. *Trust me.*

She had no memory of the operating room or Callie's first breath, her first cry, her first instinctive drive to suckle, but she hadn't been alone as she had always believed. Hollis had been there. Hollis had been the first one to hold her child. And now Hollis was here, coming dangerously close to the places she protected with all her will. Still, she wanted a piece of that memory. "Was she beautiful?"

"Gorgeous," Hollis murmured, watching Callie as she laughed and steered in a big, almost-steady circle. "She had a full head of hair, I remember—red-gold wisps of fire—and she was strong, Annie, like you. Perfect." She looked at Annie. "I'm sorry you didn't see her in those first moments."

Annie shook her head. "It's okay. I have her. I'll have her every day for the rest of my life." She touched Hollis's wrist—a brush of thanks. "You were there. You took care of us both. I should have thanked you the second I saw you again."

"No need—"

"Thank you, Hollis, for my daughter."

Hollis swallowed. "You're welcome."

Annie smiled, feeling sad but somehow right. A circle had been closed, a chapter finally completed. It was time to let go, and maybe it had taken knowing Hollis for that to happen.

"Mommy," Callie said breathlessly, barreling down on them. "Can I have—"

"Brakes, Cal," Hollis called and caught the handlebars before Callie mowed Annie down.

"Oops," Callie said, working the brake to stop the bike. "I'll remember next time. Mommy, can I have this one?"

"Looks like it's yours already." Annie nodded to the clerk. "Go ahead and write it up."

Annie paid, and Hollis helped her load the bike into the back of her Volvo. "Thanks." Callie climbed in and Annie closed the door.

Hollis slipped an arm around her waist. "Six o'clock okay?"

Annie took a breath. "I'm going to pass on dinner tonight, Hollis. I'd rather be free if my patient goes into active labor."

Hollis regarded her through appraising eyes. "What happened?"

"What? Noth—"

"Annie," Hollis said softly.

"I'm sorry." Annie brushed away a strand of hair the wind blew into her eyes. Hollis deserved better. "You've been wonderful and I owe you so much."

"You don't owe me anything." Hollis's voice was still calm but her eyes had grown wintery.

"I do, of course I do."

"I don't want your gratitude." Hollis swept a hand down Annie's arm. "I know you feel it—the connection. I know you know I want you."

Annie glanced into the car. Callie was engrossed in one of the children's books Annie always kept in the console for emergency entertainment. What did she feel? Hollis stirred a great many things she had never expected and wasn't at all sure she wanted, but one thing was certain—the desolation of finding herself utterly alone was something she never wanted to revisit. She took a breath. "Hollis, we're already friends. Callie is fond of you."

"Is that what you're worried about?" Hollis frowned. "That Callie will get caught in the middle somehow?"

"Partly, yes. But I've never—" Annie sighed, knowing she was blushing. "Casual relationships just aren't my style."

"What makes you think I want a casual relationship?"

Hollis's fingers drifted up and down Annie's back, and the touch was like a live wire coiling beneath her skin. Annie tightened, want flooding through her. No, she wouldn't be able to do casual with Hollis. "I'm not in the market for anything else."

"I'm not Jeff, Annie." Hollis's voice was chillingly flat. She pulled keys from her pocket and bounced them once in her hand, searching Annie's face.

"I'm sorry," Annie whispered. She couldn't take the chance of losing herself again. She just couldn't.

Hollis's eyes shuttered closed. "Someday you're going to have to trust your feelings."

Annie hurried around to the other side of the car, wincing when she heard Hollis roar out of the parking lot and into the street. She didn't look after her, couldn't watch her leave.

Trust her feelings? No, better not to have them at all.

CHAPTER TWENTY-FIVE

T hanks," Hollis said, accepting the cup of coffee Honor handed to her. She settled into the curve of the wooden deck chair on the back porch next to Quinn. She'd almost canceled the dinner invitation when she'd gotten home from the bike shop, still reeling from Annie's rejection. The day had been so goddamned perfect she'd been blindsided. She'd let down her guard and she'd paid for it. She had good reasons for not letting people get close to her, and Annie had proved her right. Opening herself up, letting herself care, was an invitation to be hurt, and when the people she loved inevitably disappeared from her life, she bled. Annie had made her forget about her vow not to bleed again. Annie, with her warm touch and knowing eyes. Annie, together with Callie's infectious joy and innocent excitement, had cracked open the shell surrounding her heart and teased her with the promise of happiness. She hadn't been looking for happiness, she'd been content with the life she had. She ought to thank Annie for the reminder. Maybe she would, when the pain dulled and she could think rationally again.

"You two want some pie?" Honor asked.

"No, thanks," Hollis said, forcing herself to stay in the moment. "Dinner was so good I didn't leave any room."

The raucous evening with Honor and Quinn and their kids, and Linda and Robin and theirs, had helped keep her mind off Annie. Linda and Robin had already left, Arly had taken Jack over to their grandmother's next door, and the quiet left in their wake was soothing if a little hollow. Damn it—she missed Annie and Callie. God, it hurt.

Quinn looked over her shoulder at Honor. "Need help in there?"

"No," Honor said, brushing her fingers over the back of Quinn's head. "There's not much to do. I'll be out in a minute."

"Sounds like you and Arly have been doing some pretty serious cycling," Hollis said to Quinn. Night was coming on quickly, and the backyard was a mass of shifting shadows as the moon rose over the large maple trees.

"Pretty serious for me," Quinn said. "Arly's the natural. She never gets tired. I'm going to have to work some to keep up with her on a ninety-mile haul."

Quinn didn't sound like she minded the challenge.

"I thought I'd ride in it too," Hollis said. "It's been a while since I've done anything of that distance, though."

"We've still got a couple of months to put in some hours. How much do you usually ride?" Quinn asked.

"Twenty miles or so, four or five times a week."

Quinn snorted. "Sounds like you'll be fine, then. I'm lucky if I can get out three times a week. But Arly's got her heart set on this ride, so I'm going to make it, no matter what I have to do."

Hollis cradled her coffee cup in both hands, remembering the glint in Arly's eyes and the excitement in her voice when she'd explained over dinner how Quinn was training with her so they could ride in the Ride for Life together. Arly's enthusiasm reminded her of Callie's earlier in the day, when she'd picked out her bike and climbed on for the first time. Hollis envied Quinn that bond.

"You're welcome to ride with us, if you want," Quinn said. "Give me a little more incentive to keep up."

"Doubt you'll have any problem," Hollis said. Quinn might not be a seasoned cyclist but she looked to be in great shape. She coached a couple of soccer teams—she had to be. "But if you're looking for another team rider, I'd like that. I know you don't know me, but I've been riding all my life. If you want me to take Arly out when you can't make it, I'd be happy to do that."

"Hell, Hollis," Quinn said. "Arly's twelve, and a smart, responsible rider. I'd be fine with her going out with you."

"Thanks. How is she with early-morning rides?"

The screen door opened and closed behind them, and Honor sat down on the far side of Quinn. "I caught the tail end of that. Arly is a doctor's daughter." She smiled at Quinn and took her hand. "Two doctors. She's used to getting up early."

"She ought to be back from her grandmother's soon," Quinn said. "You can talk to her about your schedule then."

"Okay," Hollis said.

"In fact," Quinn said, rising, "it's time to put Jack to bed." She leaned down and kissed Honor. "Relax—you worked hard doing dinner. My turn."

Honor stroked Quinn's arm. "See you soon."

When Quinn disappeared down the stairs and across the yard toward the adjoining twin, Honor moved over into Quinn's chair, her own cup of coffee in hand. "I'm glad you came tonight."

"Me too. Thanks for asking me." Hollis looked out over the yard, took in the picnic table, the climbing set, the barbecue. Signs of a full life. "You've got a great family."

"Thanks." After a moment, Honor said quietly, "How are you?"

Hollis's immediate reaction was to say fine, but Honor had offered her friendship, had opened her home to her, had shared her family with her. She didn't have to pretend with her. "I'm not really sure. I'm trying to figure out what to do about a woman who says she's not interested."

Honor laughed softly. "Is that a rare occurrence?"

Hollis laughed too, Honor's gentle teasing making it easier for her to talk. "Actually, I don't really know. I don't usually get into situations like that with women. Most of my relationships are kind of casual friendships. Nothing that requires any negotiating. But—" She stopped, wanting to protect Annie's privacy.

"But this isn't like that," Honor finished for her.

"Exactly. She says she doesn't want a relationship, but how can she know if she won't even try?"

"Do you? Want a relationship, I mean."

"Not long ago I would've said no." Hollis sighed and tilted her head back, watching clouds sluice across the surface of the moon, glowing silver around the edges as they trapped the moonbeams inside. "Now I think—I'm not sure what I think. I just think I can't stop thinking about it."

"Well, I'm not exactly a relationship expert—considering I've only had two serious relationships in my life—but I'm guessing you wouldn't be so interested if you didn't feel something coming back from her."

"I told her to trust what she feels today, but I think what that really means is trust me. And she doesn't."

"Maybe given some time, she will."

"Maybe." Hollis sighed. "And maybe she's right to back off."

Honor squeezed Hollis's knee briefly. "I can't imagine waiting is easy—it wasn't for me and I thought I *wanted* to get away."

"Sorry to dump all this on you," Hollis said, feeling foolish. She didn't get hung up on women. Especially not women who walked out on her. "Probably smartest of me to let it go. Sometimes it's better not to rock the boat."

"Sometimes you're right—and sometimes the boat needs rocking. I guess what really matters is that you can tell the difference."

"I think this time the decision's been made for me."

❖

The baby arrived at five fifty-nine Sunday morning with barely a fuss. She was, her father declared, as calm and quiet as her brother had been noisy. By seven, Annie was on her way to Suzanne's to pick up Callie. She hadn't slept, and she was exhausted in body and soul. The usual post-delivery exhilaration had faded quickly in the face of her thoughts of how she'd left things with Hollis. She'd made the right decision, she was certain of it, but she hadn't expected the aftermath to hurt so much. The icy pain in Hollis's eyes when she'd walked away had haunted her all night. Now all she wanted was to collect her daughter, get some sleep, and forget the ache that accompanied every breath.

She parked in front of the white clapboard twin, climbed the wooden steps to the porch, and rang the doorbell. A minute later Suzanne, a small curvy blonde, opened the door. "Hi. How did it go?"

"Wonderful. Healthy baby girl. Once Pam's labor got going, it didn't take her long." Annie rolled her shoulders but couldn't dispel the tightness. "I didn't wake everyone up, did I?"

Suzanne laughed. "God, no. The kids have been up for an hour, and Dan and I just started making breakfast. Come on, your timing is perfect."

"Oh," Annie said, "I'll just collect Callie and take her home. You've had her long enough."

"Are you kidding? She's easy, and she helps keep my two out of trouble. Believe me, I love having her. Besides, you know we always cook plenty. Go on back, sit down, and I'll get you some coffee."

"I'm too tired and too hungry to resist. Thanks."

When Annie reached the kitchen, Callie launched herself into her arms with a welcoming cry. Annie wrapped her up and hugged her close, her fatigue and disillusionment falling away. She buried her face in Callie's hair and drew deeply of the clean, pure scent of childhood. Usually, all it took was a few minutes with Callie for her to remember what was important in her life. Today, her contentment was undercut with sadness. Tired, she was just tired.

Callie wiggled lose, vibrating with energy. "I told Mark and Gillian they could see my bicycle. Can we show them my bicycle?"

"I don't see why not," Annie said, stroking Callie's hair. "Can we wait until after breakfast? I'm really hungry."

"Okay."

"Thanks, Dan," Annie said when the tall, thin man with skin the color of burnished teak gave her a cup of coffee. She sipped it gratefully and slumped into a chair at the long wooden table. She'd been too busy most of the night to think of Hollis for more than a minute or two, and her work had helped her push her sadness aside. But she didn't have work to do now, and Callie's enthusiasm about her bicycle brought every minute of the day before back to her in vivid relief.

Hollis had been so good with Callie, and Callie was obviously enchanted with her. Unfortunately, so was she. Fortunately, enchantment was transitory.

She managed not to think of Hollis for the rest of the meal. After making plans with Suzanne and Dan to meet at her place later for lunch and an outing to the park with the kids and their bicycles, she took Callie home.

"Mommy is going to take a nap. You can play on the back porch and in the backyard, but not out front. You don't go out the gate, okay?"

"I won't."

"Doesn't matter if I'm sleeping, I'll know if you budge."

Callie laughed. "Okay. I won't. I promise."

Annie lay down on the bed fully clothed, not even bothering to close the blinds in her room. Despite what she'd told Callie, she was far from ready to fall asleep. Her mind was racing. Hollis's voice played through her mind.

Someday you're going to have to trust your feelings.

She did trust her feelings, but she trusted her experience more. Before she could over think her decision, she grabbed her cell off the dresser and called Barb.

"Annie?" Barb said, obviously having checked caller ID. "Problem?"

"Not really," Annie said. "I'm sorry, Barb, but I'm not going to be able to finish the work on the exploratory committee for you. I'm not the right person for it. For what it's worth, I think if the rest of the group is anything like Hollis Monroe, they won't be difficult to work with."

"So you're endorsing the joint-clinic project?"

Annie hesitated. She thought of Hollis in the ER with Linda, remembered Hollis telling her about her struggle to avoid surgery on the bleeding mother, remembered Hollis with her that night years before. *Trust me.* "I don't know what all the other physicians are like, but Hollis is ethically beyond reproach and I think her input will be invaluable."

"Well, that's a ringing endorsement." Barb paused. "So you're behind formalizing the association?"

Annie sighed, never having believed she would say this. "My vote is in favor."

"And yet you can't tell me why you want to be replaced?"

"Let's just say it's personal and leave it at that."

When she ended the call, Annie closed her eyes, hoping for sleep. She ought to feel better, now that everything was settled. Maybe when she woke up, she would.

CHAPTER TWENTY-SIX

Just before nine on Monday morning, Hollis walked down the hallway of the OB outpatient clinic, preparing herself to see Annie. She hadn't stopped thinking of her the entire weekend. She'd never expected to get all tangled up with a woman this way, so hungry for her she ached, and she'd spent a lot of time reminding herself why she'd avoided intimate relationships for almost ten years. Sonja had walked out on her during one of the worst periods of her life. Rob's wife had walked out on his memory, tearing a hole in their family and leaving even more sorrow in her wake. Everyone had been devastated, but Hollis had been destroyed. She didn't care if her heart never recovered—she never planned to give it to anyone again. She knew better than to get attached and she'd momentarily forgotten, but she had things in perspective now. She knew what she was about. She and Annie got along well. They respected each other professionally. Hell, she even felt connected to Annie's daughter. Callie was a bright flame who brought joy to her spirit every time she looked at her. There was no reason, absolutely none, that she and Annie couldn't have a meaningful friendship. She could handle it. So could Annie. They were adults.

Feeling settled, satisfied with her decision, she rounded the corner and stopped at the counter fronting the nurses' station. An instant pang of disappointment twisted through her when she didn't see Annie, but she quickly pushed it aside. A large stack of charts waited for her attention at the end of the counter. One of the OB nurses came out of a patient room and put another chart on the stack.

"Hi, Jackie," Hollis said, reaching for a chart. "Is Annie Colfax here yet? The midwife?"

Jackie gave her an odd look, and a woman sitting at the desk on the far side of the counter— a small blonde Hollis had taken to be a utilization review nurse or consulting physician—rose and held out her hand.

"Hi, I'm Suzanne Turner. I'm the midwife from GWWC. I'll be taking Annie's place."

Hollis dropped the chart onto the counter. "What do you mean, taking Annie's place?"

"We had to rearrange the schedule—she's overcommitted. Besides," Suzanne said brightly, "our supervisor thought it would be a good idea for us to rotate personnel while we're in the information-gathering stage."

A cold fist of anger settled in Hollis's chest, pushing down on her diaphragm, making it hard for her to take a breath. Annie was walking out on her. Without even a good-bye. How could she just walk away? Like they'd never touched, never shared something special. For a second Hollis couldn't think—couldn't feel anything except betrayal. But Annie wasn't Sonja, wasn't Nancy. Annie had a heart, if only she'd believe it.

Hollis almost turned and left, but the stack of charts caught her eye. Every one of those files represented a woman who needed her—a woman waiting behind a closed door or in a hard plastic seat in the waiting area. Waiting for her.

Hollis picked up the chart she'd dropped. "Let's get started, then. We've got a full morning."

❖

Callie came running down the sidewalk, waving a colorful sheet of paper like a flag. Seeing her unvarnished joy lifted some of the misery from Annie's heart. "Hi, baby. What have you got there?"

"Look what I drew today!" Callie thrust the paper forward and Annie dutifully took it.

The plain sheet of construction paper was covered with a vivid crayon drawing in the sprawling perspective of a child. The central figure was obviously Callie, a small redhead with pink glasses holding on to a bright purple bicycle. Her smile was huge. Flanking her were two taller figures, one with dark hair, one with red-gold hair the same

color as the little girl's. Annie's throat closed. Annie and Hollis and
Callie. She wet her lips, willed her hands not to shake as she slowly
lowered the paper. "This is great, Callie. I guess you told everyone
about your bicycle, right?"

Callie nodded vigorously. "I'm going to ride it when I get home,
okay?"

"Absolutely."

"Is Hollis coming over to ride with me?"

"I don't think so, baby." Annie held out her hand. "Come on. Let's
head home. I think we've got enough time for Mommy to go to the bike
store and pick out a bicycle so I can ride with you."

Callie's eyes brightened, dispelling the shadow of disappointment
that had settled there when she'd heard that Hollis wasn't coming. Just
seeing how much Hollis's absence affected Callie after so short a time
made Annie even more certain she'd made the right decision. Even if
she was willing to risk her own heartbreak, she wouldn't risk Callie's.
"Want to walk home through the park?"

"Yes. Did you remember the duck food?"

"Always."

The park was unusually crowded, everyone trying to escape the
sultry early summer heat for a few minutes in the shade of the big oaks.
Annie made her way around the edge of the pond, searching for a bench
or a grassy area where she could sit and watch Callie. She'd never
noticed how many couples came to the park—everyone seemed to be
holding someone else's hand, exuberant teenagers in the first throes of
new love, lovers strolling with heads bent close, elderly couples reading
newspapers side by side, passing pages wordlessly back and forth in a
well-choreographed duet.

Annie had never felt alone before, but she did today.

The benches were all occupied, but she found a thick grassy spot
under a tree and settled down with her back against the wide trunk. The
walking path was just a few feet in front of her, and on the far side of
that, the pond. She opened her bag and handed Callie the duck food.
"Go ahead. I can see you from here. Feed them right from the edge and
try not to get your shoes in the water."

Callie laughed. "I'll try, but sometimes the water just comes up."

Laughing, Annie said, "Do your best. I'll be right here."

As Callie raced to the water and squatted a safe distance from the edge, Annie allowed herself a minute to close her eyes, tired from two nights of restless sleep. The sky darkened through her closed lids, probably the sun dropping behind clouds. She couldn't remember if rain was expected, and she opened her eyes to scan the sky. Not rain clouds. Hollis stood over her, blocking the sunlight. She was in scrubs, had probably just run out between cases. It was too early in the day for her to be done.

Annie's pulse thundered in her ears.

"Mind if I sit down?" Hollis said.

"No, please," Annie said, gesturing to the grass beside her.

Hollis sat cross-legged, far enough away that no part of their bodies touched. She faced the pond, her gaze distant. "Why did you quit the exploratory committee, and don't tell me it's because you're too busy. You've been too busy since the beginning."

Annie caught her breath. She'd never heard the flat, hard tone in Hollis's voice before. Her face in profile was just as hard, etched in stone. "You're angry."

Hollis's head whipped around. "Damn right I'm angry. You couldn't have talked to me about it?"

Annie thought of a thousand rationalizations, none of them anything but flimsy excuses. "I couldn't."

"Why the hell not? Why all of a sudden won't you talk to me? You talked to me before—you told me things that mattered. Now all of a sudden nothing matters?"

Annie drew away from the pain and fury in Hollis's voice. "Please, can we not do this?"

"I never took you for a coward."

"But I am," Annie said softly. "I am, I just hide it well."

"Bullshit. Look at what you've done with your life. Look at her—" Hollis swept her hand toward Callie crouched by the pond. "You didn't give up. You made a life for yourself and for her. You fought for her." Hollis ran her hand through her hair. "You don't know how many don't."

"Hollis," Annie whispered, resting her hand on Hollis's thigh. Hollis's eyes were filled with so much pain. "I don't want to hurt you."

"What do you want?"

"I want us—" *to be friends*. Annie stopped, ready to give the answer she knew so well, the answer that protected her, guarded her, kept her safe at night. Safe. Her parents had professed they'd only wanted to keep her safe even as they'd turned away from her. They knew what was best for her, and all she had to do to have a safe, happy life was listen to them. Give up her dreams, give up her daughter, and everything would be fine. She'd walked away from a life without choices, and now, it seemed she'd stopped making choices all on her own.

"I'm so afraid," Annie whispered.

Beside her, Hollis's stiff body relaxed and she let out a long breath. "Of what?"

"Of feeling, of needing." She glanced at Hollis, saw the strength in her face, the gentleness in her eyes. "Of needing you."

Hollis sucked in a shaky breath. "You think I'll hurt you."

"No," Annie said, "I'm just afraid you will. I told you I was a coward."

"Everyone is afraid." Hollis watched Callie throw seeds onto the water. "Rob's daughter would have been about twice Callie's age by now. Sometimes when I look at Callie, I imagine what it would've been like to be part of her life. To watch her grow up." She laughed shortly. "Everyone else in the family has boys, but Rob was going to have a daughter. He was beyond excited. He said she'd probably turn out to be just like me, and I was secretly so happy about that."

Annie carefully took Hollis's hand, afraid she might pull away but needing to touch her so much. "What happened?"

Hollis turned from watching Callie and gazed at Annie. "His wife—Nancy—couldn't stand to be anywhere near the city after he was killed. Said the place terrified her. So she joined her best friend on a commune in West Virginia. She just up and left."

"God, that must have been awful," Annie murmured. "So many lives destroyed that day."

"I know, and I think I understand why she left. We all reminded her of Rob, and when he died, we pulled closer together. Maybe she felt left out. But what she did…" Hollis clenched her jaw. So much pain.

"What," Annie asked, rubbing Hollis's suddenly cold hand between hers. "What did she do, sweetheart?"

"She didn't just move away, she cut off all contact." Hollis grimaced. "I tried to trace her, but the group she joined lived off the grid—growing their own food, making their own clothes, living a life completely different from what she'd had with Rob. She had a right to her own life, and when I couldn't find any contact information, I gave up. Just hoped she'd reach out to us when the baby was born. Another mistake, probably."

"She made the choice, and you respected that," Annie said, thinking of all those who had never given her as much consideration, even when her choices had hurt no one. Hollis had been devastated by loss upon loss and still she'd accepted Nancy's decision. Imagining Hollis's pain sliced at her heart. She squeezed Hollis's hand. "What happened?"

"Nancy decided to have the baby at the commune. They were fifty miles up a goddamned mountain with no medical backup. No midwife—at least not one with any kind of training—nothing."

Annie's stomach tightened. A home birth—no wonder Hollis had resented the idea. "She had problems?"

"We don't know for sure what the hell happened. What she remembers—or is willing to tell us—is sketchy. My best guess is the cord prolapsed and they didn't detect it until it was too late. The baby was born dead."

"Oh, Hollis," Annie murmured, her heart bleeding. "I am so, so sorry."

"I don't know why I'm telling you this. You're nothing like her. I'm sorry."

Hollis trembled, and that moved Annie more than Hollis's anger or her own fears. Scooting closer, she wrapped both arms around Hollis's waist. "You have nothing to apologize for. It's all right now."

"Is it?" Hollis shuddered. "I don't think so. If only Rob hadn't been at the station that day."

"Shh." Annie stroked Hollis's hair, her cheek, her neck. "That's not your fault. You need to forgive yourself, Hollis."

"I don't know if I can."

"You're not alone anymore," Annie whispered, and she felt the words in her soul. She wasn't alone either.

After a long moment, Hollis drew away, rubbing her face as she sat upright. "Sorry. I thought I was past all of that."

"I'm glad you told me."

Hollis stood, hollow-eyed. "Come back to the clinic, Annie. It's where you belong. I'm not going to bother you anymore."

"Hollis," Annie said, rising quickly. "Don't—"

What was she going to say. Don't go? She'd told Hollis to go and she was still afraid. But the answers didn't really matter. Hollis was already gone.

CHAPTER TWENTY-SEVEN

The buzz of her cell phone pulled Hollis from an uneasy sleep. The early-July night air hung heavily in the room, and she shook her head to clear away the haze. "Monroe."

"Hollis? It's Annie."

"Annie?" Hollis jolted upright, the tendrils of sleep fractured by sudden alarm. She hadn't seen Annie or heard her voice in nearly a month, but she recognized the tightly controlled tension in her words. Her stomach twisted. "What is it?"

"I've got a patient with a breech. External version hasn't worked, and I'm concerned we've got a footling presentation. We've waited long enough."

"Where are you?"

"We're fifteen minutes from the medical center. I've already called for transport…wait a minute. The ambulance is just pulling up. I don't know if you're on call—"

"I'll be right there."

"You have my number. If you could call me after you see—"

"No, you stay with her. She'll want you there." Hollis took a breath. "So do I."

A fraction of silence. "Of course. Thank you. The paramedics are here. Do you want to talk to them?"

"No. You know what to do. I'll meet you in the ER." Hollis disconnected, stripped off the shorts and T-shirt she'd fallen asleep in, and pulled on jeans and button-up shirt she didn't bother to tuck in. She glanced at the clock on her way out. Eleven forty. Of course. She swiped her keys from the table inside the door and hurried down the sidewalk. Annie would have already talked to the ER docs. The EMTs would take care of stabilizing the patient en route, and Annie would prepare the patient for what would happen at the hospital. Annie could handle things.

God, Annie. She'd been trying not to think of her and now she didn't even pretend she didn't want to. Hollis drove the route to PMC automatically and replayed the last few rotten weeks. Annie had not come back to the clinic. Suzanne had rotated through for a week, then a guy named Chris—apparently the only male midwife in the region— then Allison. Each Monday Hollis had looked for Annie, but Annie had not come. She'd told Annie she wouldn't bother her anymore, and she'd kept her word. She hadn't called her. Pride maybe, or fear. Fear if she called, Annie would send her away and truly be gone. That would cut in ways she hadn't thought she could hurt any longer.

Avoidance wasn't in her nature, and every morning when she woke, her first conscious thought was of Annie. The surge of happiness when Annie's face flashed into her mind quickly dissolved into pain when she realized Annie was gone. She missed her. She missed the challenge of her, the tenderness of her, the desire that swelled each time she saw her. She missed Callie too, and the unadulterated pleasure of watching her embrace the world with unbridled enthusiasm. Joy, desire, longing, and wonder. She hadn't felt any of those things since the day Rob died. She hadn't realized until now that she missed them. She'd decided long ago that the pleasure was not worth the chance of pain, but maybe she had been wrong.

She pulled into the nearly empty physicians' lot at PMC and focused on the job ahead. Her pulse steadied, her mind cleared. When she walked into the emergency room, the first person she saw was Linda. "Are they here yet?"

"ETA two minutes. We've got twelve set up for her. The ultrasound is in there already."

"Good. The OR on standby?"

Linda nodded. "I thought Moorehouse was on call for you guys."

"Special patient. How are you doing?"

Linda looked the way pregnant women did when they were approaching the last stages. The full mound of her abdomen dominated her small frame, her skin glowed with a rosy hue, her eyes shone with secret expectation. She was beautiful.

"I've been doing fine." Linda held up crossed fingers. "Not a twinge. Annie says the baby is right on schedule. Twelve weeks and counting."

The mention of Annie's name sent a pang through Hollis's belly, but she kept her smile in place. "Excellent."

"I haven't seen you much this summer," Linda said, a probing tone in her voice. "You missed a couple of spectacular barbecues."

"Been busy."

"Uh-huh. I heard you and Quinn are training together."

"We're putting in some miles. Arly is tireless. Been keeping me jumping."

"Uh-huh," Linda said again, eyeing her with a look that said she knew there was more to the story.

Behind her, the ER doors whooshed open, and Hollis turned, grateful for the interruption. The paramedics pushed in a stretcher bearing a pregnant woman covered to her shoulders by a thin white sheet and surrounded by equipment. A balding man in a rumpled shirt, camo shorts, and flip-flops hurried alongside, his hand gripping hers. Annie, in a plain blue scrub top and tan pants, held on to the side rail, her head bent to the patient. The sight of her was a kick to Hollis's chest. Annie looked tired, but more beautiful than ever. Her hair was loose around her shoulders, her expression calm and steady. When she looked up and saw Hollis, color rose to her cheeks.

"Take her in twelve," Hollis told the EMT.

"You got it," he said in passing.

Annie stepped away and Hollis said, "Hi."

"Thank you for being here." Annie followed the stretcher as it turned around the corner and disappeared. She looked at Hollis, her gaze searching. "I didn't know who was on call, but I wanted you."

"Anytime." Hollis wanted to say more. Wanted to say *I've missed you, I wanted to call. I should have called. I was an idiot to walk away.* Later, maybe later. Now they had another battle to wage. "Tell me what's going on."

"She's thirty-six weeks and went into labor about seven hours ago. It's her second child, the first was an uncomplicated vaginal delivery." Annie's gaze followed the stretcher down the hall. "We knew the baby was breech, but she really wanted to try at home. Suzanne was with me. She's delivered a lot of breeches, and we've been watching her carefully. External version seemed to work, but the baby flipped again and I think a foot is down. She's stalled and I'm not comfortable with the whole situation."

"Any prenatal problems?"

"Some edema that started at about seven months, but nothing else." Annie shook her head. "I've been concerned about the presentation all along, and I told her we might need to change plans. She's prepared."

"All right. Let's have a look."

The ultrasound confirmed Annie's impression. The baby was facing the right side, head up, and one leg down.

"The cord is low lying," Hollis said to Annie as they reviewed the scan. "If we try for a vaginal delivery we risk cord compression, especially if we need to go to forceps."

Annie sighed. "I'll talk to her, unless you—"

"No," Hollis said. "You have the relationship with her. Let's go."

"Dr. Monroe and I agree," Annie said, taking Kathy's hand. "The safest thing for the baby is to go with a C-section."

"When?" Kathy's gaze flicked to her husband, who nodded.

"It's time," Annie said. "Dr. Monroe will do the surgery as soon as the OR is ready."

"Can you keep me awake?" Kathy looked at Hollis.

"That's up to anesthesia," Hollis said, "but we'll try. You'll need an epidural, and depending on how things go upstairs, you may need to be sedated or even given general anesthesia. But we'll try."

Kathy gripped her husband's hand. "Can Frank—"

"Yes." Hollis turned to Kathy's husband. "You can stay at the head of the table with anesthesia while we do the delivery. Both of you will be able to see your baby as soon as we get her out."

Annie squeezed Kathy's arm. "This is the best thing. You can trust Hollis on this."

"If it were you—" Kathy said, looking at Annie.

"I'd do whatever Dr. Monroe advised. I trust her."

The words settled in Hollis's heart like a soothing caress. Annie's trust was the one thing in the world she wanted. At least here in the hospital, she had it. "We've got a plan, then."

Annie smiled at Hollis. "Can you get me in too?"

"Yes." Hollis nodded. "Come with me."

❖

"Here you go," Hollis said, handing Annie a pair of faded green scrubs.

"Thank you." Annie took the scrubs and put her bag in the bench. The locker room was empty and their voices echoed hollowly. Now that they were alone, she was hyperaware of Hollis's every move. Hollis looked so damn good. Her hair was a little longer and wilder, her body a bit leaner. Her face was sharper, more austerely handsome. Annie ached to touch her. She gripped the scrubs to her chest.

Hollis opened a narrow metal locker. "You can put your clothes in here with mine."

Annie hesitated to take off her shirt, then realized she was being foolish. Hollis, as if knowing undressing in front of her would make Annie uncomfortable, turned away to give her privacy. Hollis always seem to know what she needed. Annie quickly changed into the fresh scrubs and hung her clothes next to Hollis's in the locker, a strangely intimate thing. "All set."

"I don't expect any problems," Hollis said as they walked through the silent corridor to the OR, "but should there be a complication, the nurses will ask the husband to leave the room. You can stay if you feel that you want to."

"All right. I appreciate you doing this."

Hollis cut her a sharp glance. "Annie, she's your patient too. Besides, the more all of us know about every aspect of our treatments, the better we're going to be able to take care of our patients together."

Annie smiled. "I think you've mellowed."

Hollis laughed and some of the shadows disappeared from her eyes. "If I have, it's your fault."

"I'm not going to apologize for that," Annie said, thinking of all the things she *did* want to apologize for. When she'd realized Kathy was going to need to deliver in the hospital, the only person she'd thought of was Hollis. She'd thought of Hollis every day since the last time she'd seen her. She'd wanted to call her, every single day, and in the last few days she'd gotten as far as scrolling to Hollis's number. The only thing that kept her from completing the call was the fear of discovering she'd lost her chance to have what she hadn't realized she'd wanted. She wanted more than friendship, and she wanted Hollis.

Hollis stopped in front of a line of stainless steel sinks with high curved faucets operated by foot pedals. "I'm going to scrub while they get her prepped. The nurses will show you where to stand."

"Thanks."

A nurse came out, nodded to Annie, and said to Hollis, "We're ready, Hollis."

"Be right there. Nora, this is Annie. She's a midwife. Can you show her where to go?"

"Sure. Come on in with me."

Annie took her place by Kathy's right shoulder while the nurses prepped her abdomen with Betadine and draped everything with sterile sheets and towels. They stretched a drape across Kathy's chest and attached it to IV poles, creating a barrier between the nonsterile and sterile areas. Past the sheet, the mound of Kathy's belly was highlighted by the brilliant OR lights. Kathy was sedated, but aware. Her pupils were large, her expression lax. Frank stood on the opposite side of the narrow OR table, his hand on Kathy's shoulder. His eyes above the surgical mask were calm. Annie smiled at him, even though she knew he couldn't see most of her face. His eyes smiled back.

Hollis came through the swinging door, her hands held up in front of her. One of the nurses walked to her with an open gown, and Hollis slid her arms through the sleeves. The nurse helped her into gloves, and Hollis stepped up to the table.

"Ready, Andrea?" Hollis said.

"Go ahead." The anesthesiologist bent down and murmured to Kathy. "We're going to get your beautiful baby now."

"Okay," Kathy said slowly. "Sooner the better."

Annie couldn't take her eyes off Hollis. She didn't need to see Hollis's face to know she was completely focused on what she was doing. Her eyes above her mask were intense and strong. When she held out her left hand, the nurse slapped a scalpel into it without being asked and passed Hollis a snowy surgical sponge. Hollis made the incision and a bright, thin scarlet line blossomed on the mound of Kathy's abdomen. Annie held her breath as everything surged into kaleidoscopic motion—Hollis's fingers flowing over the incision, gleaming clamps passed from hand to hand, brilliant colors blooming. Tissues parted and the deep maroon uterus, lush with blood, rose into the wound bearing its astonishing contents.

"Get the suction ready," Hollis said.

The neonatologist, who had come into the room five minutes earlier, moved closer. Hollis made a small incision in the uterus and the nurse handed her a large pair of scissors. The cut was rapid, and a gush of golden fluid flowed out of the uterus. Hollis slid her hand inside. A head appeared in the palm of Hollis's hand, then shoulders, and then the entire body slid out into her waiting hands, the cord a white-blue coil as thick as Annie's thumb still tethering the baby to her mother. Hollis cradled the baby in her hands while the nurse suctioned her mouth. The tiny chest expanded. The baby's blue color blushed pink and she emitted a sharp cry of protest. Hollis laughed, a deep sound of pure pleasure, and Annie's heart swelled.

Hollis rapidly clamped the cord and passed the baby to the waiting neonatologist. He quickly wrapped the baby in a sterile towel and moved to the head of the table.

"Here's your daughter," he said, holding her up so Kathy and Frank could see her.

Annie gazed at the baby and then at Hollis, who looked directly at her with a question in her eyes.

"She's beautiful," Annie said.

"Yes," Hollis said, still holding Annie's gaze.

Annie's breath stopped and didn't resume until Hollis turned back to the incision. She had been in Kathy's place once, and how lucky she had been to have Hollis caring for her. Hollis, whose heart—generous and unwavering—matched her skill. How could she ever have doubted her? God, how could she ever have let her go?

After Hollis finished the surgery, Annie followed her out into the hall. "That was amazing. They're both doing so well."

Hollis stripped off her mask. "It was a good call on your part. I don't think that baby would have come out without trouble otherwise."

"Thanks. I liked watching you work."

Hollis blushed. "Likewise."

"Well." Annie, suddenly at a loss for words, took a breath. "I'm glad I could see that. I'm glad I could see the baby." She laughed. "It wasn't hard to imagine that Callie looked like that."

"She did, only like I said, more hair." Hollis laughed.

Annie plunged on, heedless of the risk. She was more afraid of what she'd lose if she didn't try. "I'm glad you were there back then—

not just because you took such good care of us, Hollis, but because you were the one to see her first."

Hollis swallowed. "I have to check Kathy in the recovery room."

Too late. She was too late. Annie's vision blurred and she turned away. There, at the end of the hall—an exit sign. "Of course. I can find my way out."

"No! Annie wait." Hollis grasped Annie's forearm, turned her. "I mean, if you don't mind waiting a few minutes, I'll drive you home. You can wait in the lounge."

Hollis's eyes held uncharacteristic uncertainty.

"I'll wait," Annie said softly. "Don't worry. I'll wait."

CHAPTER TWENTY-EIGHT

Hollis pulled to the curb in front of Annie's house, but she didn't turn off the engine. She gripped the wheel and stared straight ahead. Annie waited for Hollis to say something and, after a moment, realized it was her turn to take a chance. Hollis had been the one to drop her shields and reach out at every step, and now she was hurting.

"Remember I told you I was a coward?" Annie said.

Hollis glanced at her, still gripping the wheel. At close to three a.m., the only light in the car was a slanting sliver of moonlight. Annie couldn't see Hollis's eyes, and they always spoke the truth. Not knowing if Hollis was angry or hurt, or worse, beyond caring, Annie pushed on, trembling at the feeling of vulnerability she'd thought she would never experience again. Perhaps that was the price of happiness—risking the pain.

"I'm still afraid," Annie said. When Hollis made a low grumble in her throat, Annie pulled her hand from the wheel and held it tightly, hoping Hollis wouldn't disappear before she said what really mattered. "I *am* still afraid, and I hope that one day I won't be. But what I'm afraid of now isn't what has made me shut away parts of myself since before Callie was born."

"Annie," Hollis murmured, her voice tender. "You don't need to—"

"I do." Annie shook her head. Maybe all was not lost. Not yet. "I need to get this out. I need to say this to you."

Hollis nodded. "All right."

"I thought if I made it so I never needed anyone ever again, I would never be helpless again. I would never be lost or deserted or devastated by betrayal." Annie cradled Hollis's hand in her lap, needing some small part of Hollis closer, drawing courage from Hollis's solid presence. "I don't think I was completely wrong. I don't think I'll ever be dependent on anyone again—not the way I was. But needing is not the same as being hopelessly dependent."

"I wouldn't abandon you," Hollis said gruffly. "I can't promise I won't hurt you by mistake, but never intentionally. I swear that."

"I know that. I do. I've always known that, I just didn't trust myself to be strong enough not to lose myself." Annie laughed shakily. "And I didn't realize how crazy falling in love was going to make me."

"Is that what you did?" Hollis murmured. She shut off the ignition and slid her arm around Annie's shoulder, tugging Annie closer until Annie's breast pressed to Hollis's side. "Is it, Annie?"

Annie braced her palm in the center of Hollis's chest, leaning on her, steadying herself, connecting them. "Yes. That's exactly what I've done." Annie kissed her, slowly, softly, and finally drew back just enough to whisper, "I love you. I love you so very much."

Hollis shuddered and closed her eyes. The arm around Annie's shoulders quivered. "If I let you in," Hollis said, her voice a hoarse groan, "I'll need you more than you could know."

Annie stroked Hollis's face. "Then we'll be even, won't we? Because I'll need you too. So much. And trust you, Hollis. I'll trust you every day for the rest of my life."

Hollis framed Annie's face, her surgeon's hands strong and sure. Hollis kissed her, tenderly at first, then harder and deeper. A possessive kiss, one that took Annie beyond fear to joy. Annie fisted her hands in Hollis's shirt and kissed Hollis just as fiercely as Hollis did her, devouring her mouth with a hunger she hadn't known she harbored. When the coiling tension in her belly grew so huge she couldn't breathe, she broke away.

"Will you come inside?" Annie gasped. "Will you come inside and be with me?"

"Where's Callie?"

"With Suzanne. They don't expect me to come for her until the morning." Annie shivered, desire a living beast inside her. "Please, Hollis. I need you."

I need you. The words sliced through Hollis, severing her from the pain that anchored her to the past, freeing her to risk living. "Yes. Yes, Annie."

Hollis met Annie on the sidewalk and grasped her hand, threading their fingers together. She followed Annie up the sidewalk and across the porch, her heart thundering, her blood roaring. Annie fumbled her keys and almost dropped them at the door. Hollis cradled Annie's wrist, one arm around her waist, unwilling to break their connection. "It's okay, we've got plenty of time."

"No we don't." Annie's voice shook. "If we don't get inside where you can touch me in the next thirty seconds, I'm pretty sure I'm going to die."

Hollis laughed, wild exhilaration racing through her. "I only need ten seconds."

"Maybe," Annie muttered. "But I want more."

Hollis kissed her neck. "Anything you want."

When Annie got the door open, Hollis followed her in, slammed the door, and braced her back against it. She dragged Annie into her arms. "I love the way you fit."

"Me too." Annie's arms came around her neck, their legs entwined, their mouths met.

Hollis cupped Annie's ass and guided Annie against her thigh, sliding her tongue deep inside her mouth, aching to be inside her everywhere. Annie jerked the tail of Hollis's shirt out of her jeans and slid her hand onto Hollis's belly. The first touch of flesh on flesh had Hollis's head slamming back against the door.

"Christ," Hollis groaned. "I need you."

"Yes." Annie grabbed Hollis's hands and pulled her across the living room toward a hallway leading past the kitchen. Hollis stumbled after her, the triumphant light in Annie's eyes guiding her. At the bedroom threshold Annie released her hands, backed a few steps away, and grasped the bottom of her shirt. Watching Hollis, Annie pulled her shirt off over her head and dropped it. Hollis stumbled to a halt, paralyzed by the unexpected beauty of Annie, naked in a shaft of silvery light. Her mouth went dry, her legs shook, and every thought except one fled her mind. Annie. She didn't take her eyes off Annie as she shed her own shirt and pushed her jeans down, needing to get out of her clothes so she could feel Annie against her everywhere.

Annie paused as she pushed her trousers over her hips. "Hollis, you're the first."

"What?" All Hollis could see were Annie's breasts rising tight nippled and full, mesmerizing in their exquisiteness. Annie's belly was long and sloped, the incision Hollis had made in it hidden by the golden curls between her thighs. Annie was young and lovely and gloriously female. Hollis ached to drop to her knees and bury her face against Annie's belly. She took one step forward until only inches separated them. "The first what?"

"The first woman, the only woman," Annie said.

"You're...I'm..." Hollis drew Annie close and kissed her forehead, her eyes, her mouth. "Annie. I love you."

"Then teach me to love you."

"You already know how." Hollis undressed Annie the rest of the way and knelt, cradling Annie's hips. She kissed her thighs and her belly, then pressed her cheek where her mouth had been. Annie's hands came into her hair, fitful and restless. She kissed Annie's belly, open-mouthed, tasting her. "I want you everywhere, so much. If there's anything you need, anything—"

"You," Annie said, her fingers tightening in Hollis's hair. "I need you. Just you, Hollis."

Hollis rose and guided Annie to the bed, pushing the covers down with one hand so Annie could stretch out on the sheets. Hollis followed, leaning over her to kiss her again and again. She slicked her tongue over Annie's lips, between them and into her mouth, soft kisses, exploring kisses, teasing and tasting. She stroked Annie's breasts, her belly, the soft creamy skin of her inner thighs. She skated teeth down the column of Annie's throat to the hollow between her collarbones and rubbed her cheek over Annie's breasts. When Annie gasped and arched upward, she took a nipple into her mouth and tugged it gently with her lips. Then her teeth.

"Oh God!" Annie gripped the back of Hollis's neck. "Hollis, I need you to...more, I need you more."

Hollis shuddered, caging her restraint with every ounce of willpower she possessed. She wanted more too. She wanted more of Annie in her mouth, under her hands, beneath her body. She wanted Annie everywhere against her and inside her. Everything. She wanted everything.

"Annie." Hollis slid onto Annie, pushing her thighs apart so she could settle between her legs—against the heart of her. Her breasts brushed over Annie's center and Annie cried out in shocked surprise. Hollis kissed the junction of her thighs, pressed her forehead to Annie's stomach. "I need to make you come."

"Oh God, yes," Annie whispered.

Hollis glanced up, saw Annie watching, and slowly lowered her head. She licked her, drew her in, sucked and stroked until Annie was hard and pulsating against her tongue. When Annie's hips bucked, she filled her, driving her up and over. Annie came around her fingers, in her mouth, in long hard bursts. Annie's cries of pleasure made Hollis's heart pound between her legs, an exquisite pressure driving her mad. Still inside her, Hollis rose up and kissed Annie again, hard and deep, taking her, claiming her.

Annie's nails raked Hollis's back and dug into her ass. Annie's thigh rose hard between Hollis's legs, crushing her clit against satin skin.

"You're going to make me come," Hollis groaned.

Annie laughed, wild and joyful. "Oh yes. Yes."

Hollis rode the length of Annie's leg, still stroking inside her. When Annie cried out and came, Hollis followed, alive at last.

❖

Annie traced aimless circles over the sculpted muscles of Hollis's chest, caressing the exquisite rise of her breast and the tantalizing peak of her nipple. She could touch her forever and never satisfy the newfound hunger that lashed through her every time she looked at her. "I want you again."

"I'm not sure I can go again," Hollis said in a thick, lazy murmur.

"Really?" Annie nibbled at Hollis's throat, rewarded by a deep shudder that rolled through Hollis's gorgeous body. "I think you should've warned me earlier about your stamina problem."

Hollis raised her head and managed to open one eye. "Problem? Really? Is that so?"

"Mmm." Annie grinned.

"Is that so." Hollis flipped Annie onto her back.

"Hey!" Annie squirmed and found herself pinned. Her pulse jumped and she was instantly wet. "Hollis. You make me crazy."

"Good."

"Don't tease," Annie whispered. Hollis rose over her, her face looming inches away, her body wonderfully heavy on top of her. Annie arched, her super-sensitive clit trapped against Hollis's hard thigh. Her heart raced. She loved the feeling of power she got from driving Hollis beyond her remarkable control. "I have needs, remember?"

Hollis, her eyes glinting darkly, nipped her lip. "Do you, now?"

Annie gasped. "I do."

Hollis's hips pushed down harder between her legs, and the blood surged in her clit. Annie wrapped her legs around Hollis's ass, felt Hollis's muscles clench, felt herself start to climb again.

"What you do to me," Annie sighed.

"You make me feel so much. More than I thought possible." Hollis pressed her face to Annie's neck. She kissed Annie's throat, the curve of her ear, her mouth again. "I want to make you mine. I've never wanted anything so much in my life."

Annie gripped Hollis's shoulders and cleaved to her, feeling her orgasm surge closer. She held on as long as she could, the flood of pleasure threatening to drown her. She kept her eyes open as she came, letting Hollis see the truth for herself. "I'm yours."

Hollis's heart threatened to explode. Annie was so beautiful, so giving. She whispered, "I will always love you."

Eyes glazed with pleasure, Annie's neck arched as the last tremors shook her. Her body softened beneath Hollis, warm and languid. "See? I knew you had that in you."

Laughing, Hollis rolled onto her back and cradled Annie's head on her shoulder. "Couldn't let my reputation be tarnished."

Annie drew her thigh over Hollis's and stroked her stomach. "No worries there."

Hollis sucked in a breath. Her clit swelled and pumped. "Annie..."

"Hmm?" Annie stroked lower, gently took Hollis's clit between her fingers. "Here?"

"Yes." Hollis clenched her jaws. She was so close, so close already. A whimper escaped her.

"Oh yes," Annie breathed, her mouth moving over Hollis's breast. "You are so ready for me."

"Please," Hollis gasped.

Annie's fingers moved faster. "I want you to be mine too."

"I am." Hollis kissed her, a white-hot blaze burning through her. "Always yours."

Chapter Twenty-nine

Hollis halted on the sidewalk in front of Annie's car. "Are you sure you want me to come with you?"

"Very sure." Annie smiled. They'd been out of bed exactly twenty minutes, just enough time to shower and grab coffee and toast before Annie needed to leave to pick up Callie. Thank God it was Saturday and neither of them had rounds scheduled. She wasn't sure her brain was functioning—only her body seemed to be working, and that was in overdrive. She couldn't get within two feet of Hollis without wanting her again. "If it was up to me, I wouldn't let you out of my sight for the rest of the weekend."

Hollis grinned. "That works for me—except I promised to go riding with Quinn and Arly at least once."

"Well," Annie said slowly, running her finger down the center of Hollis's stomach and hooking the tip inside her waistband, "I suppose I could do without you for a little while."

Hollis grabbed her, pulled her close, and kissed her. She leaned back, her arms still looped around Annie's waist. "I hope not for too long."

Annie still wasn't used to the flood of love and desire that crashed through her every time she looked at Hollis. She'd scarcely dared move when she'd awakened in Hollis's arms, afraid she might break the spell. And then she'd stirred and Hollis had kissed her and she'd realized the dream was real. Every moment they shared was magic, and the magic didn't have to end. She threaded her arms around Hollis's neck and kissed her back. "Not very long at all."

"Good." Hollis didn't move as an elderly man walking an ancient poodle turned the corner and headed their way. Annie held her tighter.

Hollis grinned as the man gave her a cheery wave. Rubbing her cheek against Annie's hair, she murmured, "You smell so good. So sweet."

"Hollis," Annie breathed. "We have to go. I can't think with you touching me."

"Okay. I'll let go for now." Hollis quickly stepped away and slid her hands into her back pockets. If she didn't keep her hands occupied, she'd have them on Annie again. "Maybe we can take Callie out for a bike ride later."

"She'd love that." Annie started around the car, stopped. She walked back to Hollis and kissed her. "I love you so much."

Hollis's heart skittered in her chest. "I love you like crazy. Someday, I want…"

Annie searched Hollis's face. She so rarely sounded uncertain. Now, her eyes were filled with questions. "What, sweetheart. What is it you want?"

"I want us—the three of us, you, me, and Callie—to be a family."

"Oh," Annie gasped. "You take my breath away."

Hollis laughed, forgetting she said she wouldn't touch. She leaned against the car and snugged Annie against her front. "Is that a yes?"

Annie pressed her face to Hollis's neck, fighting tears. She'd never really believed that people cried out of happiness, but now she realized they did. "Yes. That is very definitely a yes."

"Well then, let's go get the kid so I can get working on that family thing."

"Believe me," Annie said, "you don't have far to go."

❖

Mid-afternoon on race day, Callie jumped from foot to foot in front of Annie, peering up the long stretch of highway leading into Atlantic City that had been cordoned off for the riders. "Mommy, when will Hollis get here?"

"Soon, baby." Annie shielded her eyes and searched in the same direction.

Beside her, Honor said, "The last announcement said the first riders were only two miles away. Any minute now."

A wave of colored jerseys appeared around the bend, and the

fastest cyclists streamed past them toward the finish line a block from the Atlantic shore. More riders appeared and the street filled up.

Jack stood on an ice chest, Honor steadying him with a hand on the back of his T-shirt. He pointed and shouted, "Arly! Arly!"

"She'll be here soon, honey," Honor said, readjusting his red Phillies cap.

"Mommy," Callie said, "can I ride with Hollis and Arly and Quinn next year?"

Annie stroked Callie's hair. "Maybe not next year, baby. This is a really long race. But there will be other ones you'll be able to do soon."

"You too?"

Annie laughed and glanced at Honor, who grinned and rolled her eyes. "We'll see."

Callie edged closer to Jack, her attention on the steady stream of riders passing a few feet away.

Honor said quietly, "Rumor has it you and Hollis are moving in together."

"Let me guess—Linda?"

"I never reveal my sources. However, now that a certain flight nurse is sidelined until the baby comes next month, she's taken a serious interest in all the hospital news."

"Uh-huh. Like I said." Annie smiled. "Callie and I are moving into Hollis's at the end of the month. As soon as Hollis and I—well, Hollis really…I just hold tools and things—finish Callie's room."

"That's great. She looks happy—you both do."

"Oh, I am. She's…amazing." Annie blushed.

"Mmm-hmm." Honor laughed. "Rumor also has it the high-risk OB clinic is opening next month with joint staffing from PMC and GWWC."

"Also true. We're just working out the schedule now." Annie caught her breath as she recognized Hollis's red jersey and dark blue shorts. Then she spotted Quinn and Arly. "Here they come."

"They made it—they all look good too," Honor said. "Come on, let's meet them over by the finish line."

Annie took Callie's hand and followed Honor and Jack through the crowd. By the time they reached the finish line, Quinn, Arly, and Hollis had parked their bikes in the shade of a stand of pine trees and

were pulling off their gloves and helmets. The breeze wafting in from
the ocean ruffled Hollis's dark hair and Annie's throat tightened. Hers.
That beautiful woman was hers.

Callie raced away. "Hollis!"

Hollis saw Callie and grinned. "Hey, Cal!"

"I saw you coming from way far away," Callie cried, spreading
her arms wide.

Hollis bent down, scooped her up, and spun around. "Did you?
Where's Mommy?"

"Right here." Annie slipped her arm around Hollis's waist and
kissed her cheek. "Congratulations, baby. You looked awesome."

"Hi." Hollis slung Callie onto her hip and kissed Annie softly on
the mouth. "You're all I could see for the last hundred yards. Thanks
for being here."

Annie ran her fingers through Hollis's hair. "I'll always be here. I
can't imagine being anywhere else."

"I love you," Hollis said.

"I love you too."

Callie tugged on Hollis's jersey. "Can we get ice cream before we
go home?"

Hollis raised an eyebrow at Annie. "What do you say?"

"Sounds good to me." Heart full, Annie rested her head on Hollis's
shoulder. "Especially the part where we go home."

About the Author

Radclyffe has written over forty romance and romantic intrigue novels, dozens of short stories, and, writing as L.L. Raand, has authored a paranormal romance series, The Midnight Hunters.

She is an eight-time Lambda Literary Award finalist in romance, mystery and erotica--winning in both romance (*Distant Shores, Silent Thunder*) and erotica (*Erotic Interludes 2: Stolen Moments* edited with Stacia Seaman and *In Deep Waters 2: Cruising the Strip* written with Karin Kallmaker). A member of the Saints and Sinners Literary Hall of Fame, she is also a RWA/FF&P Prism award winner for *Secrets in the Stone*. Her title *Firestorm* is a 2012 Lories winner in the Mainstream Fiction category.

Books Available From Bold Strokes Books

Crossroads by Radclyffe. Dr. Hollis Monroe specializes in short-term relationships but when she meets pregnant mother-to-be Annie Colfax, fate brings them together at a crossroads that will change their lives forever. (978-1-60282-756-1)

Beyond Innocence by Carsen Taite. When a life is on the line, love has to wait. Doesn't it? (978-1-60282-757-8)

Heart Block by Melissa Brayden. Socialite Emory Owen and struggling single mom Sarah Matamoros are perfectly suited for each other but face a difficult time when trying to merge their contrasting worlds and the people in them. If love truly exists, can it find a way? (978-1-60282-758-5)

Pride and Joy by M.L. Rice. Perfect Bryce Montgomery is her parents' pride and joy, but when they discover that their daughter is a lesbian, her world changes forever. (978-1-60282-759-2)

Timothy by Greg Herren. Timothy is a romantic suspense thriller from award-winning mystery writer Greg Herren set in the fabulous Hamptons. (978-1-60282-760-8)

In Stone by Jeremy Jordan King. A young New Yorker is rescued from a hate crime by a mysterious someone who turns out to be more of a something. (978-1-60282-761-5)

The Jesus Injection by Eric Andrews-Katz. Murderous statues, demented drag queens, political bombings, ex-gay ministries, espionage, and romance are all in a day's work for a top secret agent. But the gloves are off when Agent Buck 98 comes up against the Jesus Injection. (978-1-60282-762-2)

Combustion by Daniel W. Kelly. Bearish detective Deck Waxer comes to the city of Kremfort Cove to investigate why the hottest men in town are bursting into flames in broad daylight. (978-1-60282-763-9)

Ladyfish by Andrea Bramhill. Finn's escape to the Florida Keys leads her straight into the arms of scuba diving instructor Oz as she fights for her freedom, their blossoming love…and her life! (978-1-60282-747-9)

Spanish Heart by Rachel Spangler. While on a mission to find herself in Spain, Ren Molson runs the risk of losing her heart to her tour guide, Lina Montero. (978-1-60282-748-6)

Love Match by Ali Vali. When Parker "Kong" King, the number one tennis player in the world, meets commercial pilot Captain Sydney Parish, sparks fly—but not from attraction. They have the summer to see if they have a love match. (978-1-60282-749-3)

One Touch by L.T. Marie. A romance writer and a travel agent come together at their high school reunion, only to find out that the memory of that one touch never fades. (978-1-60282-750-9)

Night Shadows: Queer Horror edited by Greg Herren and J.M. Redmann. *Night Shadows* features delightfully wicked stories by some of the biggest names in queer publishing. (978-1-60282-751-6)

Secret Societies by William Holden. An outcast hustler, his unlikely "mother," his faithless lovers, and his religious persecutors—all in 1726. (978-1-60282-752-3)

The Raid by Lee Lynch. Before Stonewall, having a drink with friends or your girl could mean jail. Would these women and men still have family, a job, a place to live after…The Raid? (978-1-60282-753-0)

The You Know Who Girls by Annameekee Hesik. As they begin freshman year, Abbey Brooks and her best friend, Kate, pinkie swear they'll keep away from the lesbians in Gila High, but Abbey already suspects she's one of those you-know-who girls herself and slowly learns who her true friends really are. (978-1-60282-754-7)

Wyatt: Doc Holliday's Account of an Intimate Friendship by Dale Chase. Erotica writer Dale Chase takes the remarkable friendship between Wyatt Earp, upright lawman, and Doc Holliday, Southern gentlemen turned gambler and killer, to an entirely new level: hot! (978-1-60282-755-4)